M

I

HOUSE

An addictive crime mystery full of twists

ROY LEWIS

Arnold Landon Mysteries Book 6

Originally published as
A Wisp of Smoke

JOFFE BOOKS

Revised edition 2021
Joffe Books, London
www.joffebooks.com

First published in Great Britain in 1991
as *A Wisp of Smoke*

ISBN: 978-1-78931-894-4

NOTE TO THE READER

Please note this book is set in the 1980s in England, a time before mobile phones and ubiquitous CCTV, and when social attitudes were very different.

CHAPTER ONE

1

Down among the trees that thronged the gully, thick and tangled where the stream struggled over limestone slabs as it made its way eastwards to the sea, a woodpecker drummed insistently on decayed, grub-laden timber. The sound dragged him from his slumber and he reluctantly twitched open his encrusted eyelids, mouthing unspoken obscenities.

Vague shapes danced across his blurred vision: sunlight filtering through the tall trees, dappled shade and light, a movement across to his left as some animal, disturbed by his awakening, sought cover in the undergrowth beyond the crude hide where he spent his nights.

It could have been a rabbit. He liked rabbit, but the skills necessary to catch them eluded him still. He had lived for twenty years away from his fellows and the gully was his home but he would never become a countryman. He was too old now, anyway.

He pushed aside the old sacking that had covered him while he slept and clambered stiffly to his feet. A bottle clinked against his foot; with interest, he picked it up and sniffed at it. The bottle was empty and disconsolately he tossed it aside into the undergrowth outside the hide, where it joined other discarded rubbish. He peered around him at the filtering sunlight but it was the old problem: encrustations on his rheumy old eyes made it impossible to see anything other than blurs.

He shambled his way down the slope to the stream, the path familiar, a worn track from the hide to the water, one he had tramped for years and could walk blindfolded.

Clutching the torn, long-skirted overcoat around him, he knelt down beside the stream, running cold and sharp at his feet. Stones cut into his knees but he ignored them as he dipped his fingers in the water, careless whether the fingerless woollen gloves remained dry. Gently he massaged his eyes with the cold water until the encrustations softened and were wiped away and then he could see the dark, wide pool in front of him, rippling gently before it dropped fifteen feet over a rushing waterfall.

He could see his face in the water now, dimly. Foxy Fernlea they called him at school, and ever since. He could only vaguely remember why the nickname had been given to him. It had been something to do with that day in the chicken run at the farm near the school. The older boys had found him there, and the chicken was dead. He could not recall why it had died . . . and yet there was always that distant stirring of his loins to be recalled, the warmth of the chicken in his hands, the movement of its breast, warm and exciting. It had all been so long ago.

And the face that stared back at him was hollow-cheeked and constantly unfamiliar. The skin was grubby, with two white patches around the eyes, the result of morning ablutions that extended only to a removal of encrustations. His dirty beard was sparse: he had never been a particularly hirsute man, and more seemed to fall out than was retained, so that it presented a patchy bare lawn appearance above the blackened teeth that were exposed when he muttered to himself. There were only the birds above his head to strain to listen to his words.

It was almost an hour later when Foxy came out of the gully and crossed the field that took him down towards the

Country Manor Hotel. The sun was high, and warm on his back as he shambled his way along the edge of the field, clutching the worn sack that he used to collect edible garbage from the bins at the back of the hotel. From the top of the field he could see Durham Cathedral and the castle, high on the spur above the river, but he gave it no more than a passing, blurred glance. He was worried and uncertain: there were too many cars parked in front of the hotel. In his experience, if there had been some sort of party or dance at the hotel there were too many people around to make his grubbing at the back rewarding. The porters didn't like to see him and didn't like the guests to see him. On the hill he hesitated, watching for a while, then he turned away and took the track down towards the burn, crossing to the other side and walking in the grass verge of the road that led to the converted barn behind the spinney.

The pickings had never been as good there as at the hotel, of course. But if the hotel was dangerous, there was only Bodicote Barn House, or Durham City itself. It was a long trudge down to the town and a longer one back, and Foxy's mouth had a sour taste, his tongue thick and swollen from whatever he had drunk last night. He'd had a windfall of some kind, that was certain, but the memory of it was vague.

The bottle, this morning . . . it had been different.

It was only when he made his way up the lane towards Bodicote Barn House that images came back to him, like photographs streaked with diffused light. There had been something at the back of the house, before the cars rasped over the gravel in the lane and he had struggled to hide in the orchard before he was seen.

There had been noise in the house, shouting, angry and violent. The car had gone for at least twenty minutes before Foxy had come out of the orchard. The owner of Bodicote Barn House was still inside, he recalled now, because his car was still there, but Foxy had been forced to hide a second time when the man had come walking up the lane.

But what had been in the bottle?

Foxy shook his head in befuddlement as the black clouds descended again on his brain. He looked at his hands: they were powerful hands and calloused, but he seemed to remember a time when they had been soft. Long ago.

The warm sandstone of the converted barn seemed to glow in the morning sunlight as Foxy made his cautious away along the lane verge until he could step through the trees and shuffle around to the kitchen at the back of the house. The bins were located in a small lean-to, and in Foxy's experience the owner of Bodicote Barn House was profligate with his garbage. But now as he turned the corner he saw what was standing on the kitchen doorstep and he remembered what had been in the bottle.

Brandy.

The case stood on the back doorstep, a delivery of wines and spirits. It had been there yesterday, one side of the case gaping open as it had been delivered. Foxy remembered now. He had been unable to resist the temptation. He had extracted a bottle; it now lay, empty in the undergrowth near his hide.

He was scared. His heart began to pump unpleasantly.

The lure of the broken case beckoned, but he was not sure he dared take a second bottle. He licked his dry lips, and cast his blurred glance around towards the kitchen windows, and above, to the bedrooms.

There was no sign of life.

Foxy shuffled forward, his gait quickening. He hovered over the broken case, touching one of the bottles, half drawing it out. He had a brief glimpse of better days suddenly, the flash of cut glass winking under the bright lights of a chandelier, and it disturbed him. He dropped the bottle back into the case and looked around nervously.

The back yard of the house was still. There was no sound from inside the house itself. Foxy was puzzled, and vaguely uneasy: it was many years since he had indulged in logical thought, for first whisky had blurred his brain and in later years the deterioration had gathered apace as he had turned to cheaper routes towards alcoholic dependence. But the case in the yard of Bodicote Barn House had been there at least twenty-four hours, untouched, his depredations seemingly unnoticed.

Nervously Foxy approached the back door. He put out his hand to the doorknob. It twisted in his grip. The back door was open.

Foxy almost ran away. His heart was pumping. He could not remember whether he had ever been a brave man or a cowardly one, but he certainly could not recall ever having raided a house before. Is that what this was . . . a raid?

The kitchen was large, furnished with dark oak table and chairs, and lined with oak-fronted cupboards. A heavy Aga cooker stood blackly against the far wall: it gave out a steady heat and Foxy stood beside it for a little while, waiting for the pumping of his heart to slow.

There was a plate on the table. Foxy eyed the leg of cold chicken on the plate for a little while, then reached out and put the chicken in the capacious pocket of his overcoat. He was emboldened by this small, determined success. The bottle of white wine on the kitchen worktop had been uncorked and the glass beside it was empty. Foxy tipped a little of the wine into the glass and for reasons he could not remember, sniffed at the wine. When he drank it he found it was warm, and dry on his palate.

Palate. The word trembled uncertainly on his tongue.

His heart began to pump again with fear and excitement.

The door leading from the kitchen into the corridor beyond had an old iron latch. Foxy's hand trembled over it for a few seconds before he lifted the latch. The corridor seemed dark after the sunlit kitchen and he could hear the slow ticking of a clock. He hesitated, and then with nervous steps entered the corridor, the blood pounding in his head, confusing him.

He was aware of a vague buzzing sound and he shook his head, thinking it was inside his liquor-befuddled skull. It persisted, a droning noise that irritated him and his irritation gave him a surge of confident anger. He shuffled down the corridor, angry in an indeterminate way, forgetting who he was or what he was but dredging up an arrogance that had once been his, a long time ago.

The door to the sitting room was slightly ajar. Foxy pushed at it, and the door swung open silently, well-oiled. The room was large, with a window that looked out to the spinney and the rising hills beyond. Up there was Foxy's gully, and he stared vacantly for a few seconds at the blurred green hill.

The buzzing seemed to have increased. There was also a sweetness in the air. There was something familiar about that odour, but he had forgotten it lay in his past.

As did the buzzing.

A shadow crossed his mind, the whirring of wings, thunder in the morning, sweetness and wetness, the buzzing of flies.

He dragged his glance from the window. It was several seconds before his crusted eyes became accustomed to the light in the room. He saw the brocaded settee, the chairs, the drinks cabinet and he stepped forward uncertainly.

The man was lying on the floor beside the settee. There was blood over the wall and the wall itself seemed to move. So did the man's head — or what was left of it. Half of it seemed to have disappeared, but the red-black part that was left seemed to move and buzz and waver.

The wings and the thunder were in Foxy's head again, violent and disturbing, and panic took him by the throat.

He blundered back into the corridor, and out into the kitchen. The door was left swinging open behind him when he left. He hurried past the broken case of bottles, aware of what they contained but now too panicked to take advantage of their availability and slunk down the lane, hugging the grass verge as usual.

It would have to be the hotel, he thought, and already the image in his mind was fading, the blood retreating, the thunder again a lost memory.

Behind him, in the sitting room of Bodicote Barn House, he left the flies to continue with their labour, patiently cleaning the skull of the dead man.

2

'Of all the castles built by Edward I to contain the rebellious Welsh,' the young woman said primly to the group, 'Harlech is perhaps the most impressive, designed as it was to withstand any assault weapon which the ingenuity of mediaeval man could devise.'

They stood on the gated, once heavily fortified stairway, a small group of tourists, one with a loud shirt proclaiming an American origin, and addressed by a guide who had some superficial knowledge of the site, Arnold Landon conceded to himself. Her voice was thin and reedy but it carried on the light breeze and Arnold had little choice but to listen.

'Rising some two hundred feet on this rocky promontory, which was once skirted by a tidal creek, the castle remains largely intact. Its stone towers are still capable of overawing visitors by their enormous bulk and strength.'

'That phrase was something she got out of a book,' a voice murmured at Arnold's elbow.

He was standing near the massive gateway, looking out seawards. The broad sweep of the sands and the golf course below him glittered in the late afternoon sunshine as dark clouds gathered above the Llyn peninsula. The houses seemed to huddle together for protection on the steep slope below the castle, as he himself had sought protection from the tourist-thronged narrow streets of the village. The guide's insistent tones irritated him, as he sought the peace of the sea and the mountains; he was further irritated now as he was spoken to by a stranger.

'I beg your pardon?' he said and looked at the woman who had spoken to him.

She was of average height, brown-haired and snub-nosed.

Her face was round, her eyes brown and wide-set but she gave an overall impression of plainness. He judged her to be about thirty years of age, dressed in jeans and a windcheater, open-throated in the warm sunshine. She was smiling, and would always be quick to smile, he guessed. It made his mood no more pleasant.

'I would reckon,' the woman continued, 'that she's a student doing a holiday job. She'll have boned up on the castles of North Wales and will expect a hefty tip from the ignorant bus trippers at the end of the day who will all be amazed by her erudition.'

Arnold turned his head to listen to the guide. '. . . designed to be victualled from the sea. The chief threat of attack was from the eastern landward side. So this was protected first by a great ditch, then by a curtain wall, and finally by the massive four-towered gatehouse, which housed the main private accommodation . . .'

'She seems to have done her homework and is doing well enough,' Arnold suggested.

The woman shook her head emphatically. 'I don't think so. It's such a shame. She's got her knowledge of the mechanics all right, but she's losing all the romance of the place. I mean, look at it, raised there on the promontory! She should be emphasizing its history, the sweep of events, the people who built it, and the people who died because of it. The story of Harlech isn't just about stone and wood.'

Arnold's irritation increased. 'The stone survives; people don't.'

'How philistine,' the woman responded, staring at him with wide eyes. 'Don't you feel any of the romance of Harlech?'

'I'm sorry,' Arnold said shortly. 'I've no idea what you're talking about.'

'You mean you've never heard of the Arthurian connection with Edward I and Harlech castle?'

'The story is rubbish,' Arnold said and walked away abruptly.

* * *

It had been a bad day.

One of the good things about his job was that as a planning officer he was obliged to travel, to visit sites within his authority, and to get out and about Northumberland. The distaff side was the paperwork — which tended to mass on his desk during the summer months when the Senior Planning Officer paid rather more attention to his golf handicap than to his work schedules. The conference in Cardiff had been a welcome break for Arnold: the Senior Planning Officer had intended to go, but at the last moment the prospect of a tournament in Morpeth had led him to suggest that Arnold should take his place.

Arnold had decided it would be a good opportunity to take some leave. He had never visited the castles and old manor houses in Wales; he had enjoyed his stay in Cardiff and found the odd couple of hours to slip away into the hinterland, to visit some of the old, abandoned mines in the valleys and look at sites of industrial archaeological interest. But the conference itself had been boring, and he'd been looking forward to the three days' leave he'd planned.

Dutifully, he'd left his itinerary with the office. It had been a mistake. The Senior Planning Officer had that morning contacted him at his hotel in Llandrindod Wells and told him he was required back in the office.

A crisis.

The nature of the crisis had not been explained. It would be either a matter the Senior Planning Officer was not capable of handling, or it would be one he would find it politically embarrassing to conduct personally. Arnold was always available as a convenient scapegoat.

The recall meant Arnold would have only one day's wandering in North Wales. To cap it all, the hotel he'd been forced to book into was a disaster. The bedroom was cramped and he had unfortunately booked dinner before he had seen the dining room. A quick glance before he went up to walk around the town and the castle convinced him that the meal that evening was unlikely to be a gastronomic event, served as it would be in a drab, basically furnished and green-painted room that showed all the signs of advancing decrepitude.

Even so, while he had an excuse for his shortness and rudeness to the stranger who had spoken to him at the castle wall, it had not been a good excuse, and he regretted the way he had spoken. It was with a certain degree of embarrassment, therefore, that he caught sight of her when he entered the dining room that evening.

She had made the same mistakes as he: staying at the hotel, and deciding to dine there. She was seated alone, near the window which offered a curtailed view of the golf course: As Arnold entered, she looked up and their eyes met briefly. There was a certain frostiness in her glance; she looked away, back to the book she was reading while she waited for service.

'Just one?' the waitress asked.

Arnold hesitated, looking uncertainly at the woman sitting alone. He sighed. 'Just a moment,' he said to the waitress, and walked across to the table near the window.

She looked up as he approached. Her expression did not change: polite but cool.

'I . . . er . . . I see you're dining alone,' Arnold said, flustered.

'I prefer it that way,' she replied.

'Oh.'

She had lowered her head again, to her book. Arnold stood helplessly beside her table for a moment, then looked to the waitress for help. She gestured towards a table at the other side of the room. Arnold walked across the room with his head down. He was aware that his cheeks were flushed under the curious gaze of three families already eating, and observing his embarrassment.

The meal was all he dreaded. The menu was restricted, the food badly cooked, and the wine he asked for was not available. When he was asked if he wished to take his coffee in the lounge rather than the dining room he took the chance to flee, even if the raucous sounds of young locals in the pool room next to the lounge made it rather less than a haven of peace.

He sat there miserably, depressed, and wishing he'd never bothered even going to Cardiff. The Senior Planning Officer loomed large in his thoughts. The man still had it in for Arnold, and seemed determined — in so far as determination was any part of his character — to make life unpleasant for Arnold. He was not looking forward to going back to Morpeth.

'You were rude this afternoon.'

Arnold was startled. He had not noticed the woman approaching his chair.

'You were rude this afternoon,' she repeated, 'and I was rude this evening. I think that makes us quits.'

There was a hint of a smile back on her lips, the easy smile he had recognized earlier. 'I . . . er . . . I came across to apologize,' he said, and began to struggle to his feet.

'Yes. And I didn't allow it. Please don't rise.' She looked at him steadily for a moment. 'Perhaps I could join you for coffee? It would give us a chance to start again.'

Arnold sank back into his chair, surprised. He did not find it easy to talk to women. He had been a bachelor too long, and his interests in wood and stone caused him to lead a relatively unsociable life. He gestured vaguely with his left hand to the chair opposite him. 'Please . . .'

She sat down, and turned her head to signal to the waitress. 'Do you want some more coffee?' she asked Arnold. 'I thought I'd like a little chat, so I hope you're not going to rush away.'

'Chat?' Arnold swallowed nervously. 'About what?'

'Edward and Arthur.'

'Oh, that.'

'You said it was rubbish. You were so positive and direct in your judgement that it seemed to me you might know something about it.'

'Well . . .'

'I've always thought the tradition was strong.'

Arnold shrugged. 'Traditions can be . . . spurious.'

'You're suggesting that because Arthur is a legendary figure, there can be no truth in the Edwardian connection?'

Carefully, Arnold said, 'I haven't yet said anything—'

'Except that I was talking rubbish.' The smile took the sting out of her words. 'But there are facts that can be pointed to. Edward celebrated his conquest of Wales by holding a Round Table at Nefyn.'

'I believe that is so, but—'

'He held another at Falkirk in 1302. And at Acre, during the Crusade of 1285, scenes from Arthurian romances were acted out.'

Her chin was jutting at him challengingly. Arnold wriggled in his chair. This was not a discussion he had sought, and the irritations of the day were still with him. She was clearly very interested in the subject and it wasn't his field. Even so . . . He waited until a second cup of coffee had been placed in front of him before he replied. 'All right, that may be so, but if Edward was such a great enthusiast for the Arthurian past and saw himself as connected in some way to those mystic days, it's rather surprising that the great chivalric occasion of the knighting of his eldest son in 1306 appeared to have no Arthurian overtones.'

'You're throwing negative evidence at me,' she challenged, her eyes beginning to sparkle angrily. 'Edward and his queen visited Glastonbury and saw the opened tomb, the two coffins and the figures of Arthur and Guinevere—'

'Oh, come now, you must accept that was a con trick by Glastonbury monks trying to increase their revenues by tourism!'

'That's a cynical viewpoint,' she snapped. 'In any case, there's other evidence. What about the foundation of Caernarvon castle? It referred to *The Mabinogion* of Magnus Maximus, father of Constantine, and the dream of a beautiful maiden dwelling in a great castle with multi-coloured towers at the mouth of a river—'

Arnold held up a hand, disparagingly. 'And Edward made a reality of the legend by building the castle with dark-coloured bands in the masonry, and polygonal towers that echo Constantine's city of Constantinople? Really, the fact that Edward — like most Europeans of his time — was fascinated by the Arthurian legend, does not mean that there is a connection between Edward and Arthur.'

'Then what about *The Chronicle of Brabançon*?'

Arnold was surprised. He stared at her; his own interests were, he knew, esoteric, and his passion for wood and stone and the part they played in history was one shared by few. But she was clearly well read, in areas that had also interested him.

'Are you an academic historian?'

'No.'

He shook his head slowly. 'The chronicler of Brabançon describes an Edwardian feast in Arthurian terms. Complete with Round Table. But you surely have to admit that the chronicle is unreliable in the extreme. The description of Edward's conquest of Wales is totally fictional, culminating, for God's sake, with the King's descent into a cave containing Arthur's bones. It cannot be taken seriously.'

'Some historians have done so,' she said sharply.

'Then they can be described only as gullible and absurdly romantic. *The Chronicle* is best treated as evidence not of Edward's attitudes, but of the way in which foreigners viewed him.'

'Edward justified his actions in Scotland to the Pope by referring to Arthur—'

'That was merely one of a massive list of precedents cited by the clerks who drafted it. It shouldn't be made too much of. You know, I appreciate you're remarkably widely read on this subject, and it is clearly close to your heart. But the thesis you're pushing, it's just romantic nonsense. The realities of life lie around us and are far too interesting for us to waste time on legends and word of mouth. The stone tells you; ancient woods speak to you. That's where the truth lies. But Arthur and Judas Maccabeus and other such chivalric heroes, they were just part of the common currency of the knightly culture of the day. They don't reflect reality — they were an escape from reality to a better, mythical time, when chivalry could be described as a state to which one should struggle to aspire. Rather than the reality, which was blood, thunder, murder, rapine and treachery.'

There were spots of colour in the woman's cheeks. She stared at Arnold, cool and under control in spite of his outburst. 'You seem to discard culture very easily,' she said. 'Queen Eleanor had a book in her library of romances which was dedicated to her by its writer, Girard of Amiens. It was Arthurian—'

Exasperated, Arnold interrupted. 'Queen Eleanor's main activity was the production of children. I understand she gave Edward fifteen. Her numerous pregnancies would have given her time to read a great deal, I've no doubt. And when they have time on their hands, women traditionally read light romances with chivalrous heroes.'

'The facts—'

'The facts are there. They're all around us. But written interpretations from the mediaeval period must be taken with a pinch of salt. For that matter, so must modern works. People get carried away by their own wish fulfilment and prejudices. You seem well versed in this Arthurian nonsense. I read a book recently — someone called — what was it? Jane Wilson. It was a complete mish-mash of half-baked theory, potted history and romantic daydreaming. It was the kind of book that demanded quantum leaps of the human mind to reach a certain conclusion from uncertain premises. You may well have read it.'

She shook her head. She sipped her coffee daintily, then rose. 'No. I didn't read it.' She pushed back her chair. 'I wrote it.'

Arnold groaned to himself.

It really had been a bad day.

3

Storm clouds had gathered over the Durham hills and the wind had risen. Scattered spots of rain appeared on the windscreen of the police car parked alongside the dark blue Ford stationed in the driveway of Bodicote Barn House. Detective Inspector Greybrook shrugged and shook his head as he handed the radio microphone back to the driver. The constable, a fresh-faced young man with attitudes to match, raised interrogative eyebrows.

'The old man's coming out, then?'

'Chief Superintendent Redvers is on his way, yes.'

'And the scene-of-crime unit are to touch nothing till he gets here? That's a bit unusual isn't it?'

'How the hell would you know? You're still wet behind the ears.'

'It's why I was asking. Sir.'

Greybrook scowled. He was in no mood to indulge in unproductive chatter with the driver and he was certainly not prepared to discuss the reasons why the Chief Superintendent might wish to attend this one personally. It was unusual, certainly. Redvers was not a great attender of scene-of-crime investigations, preferring to come in when the television cameras arrived and statements were requested. But he certainly wanted in on this one, right at the start. He'd want to be filled in on the detail. It bothered Greybrook: it could cause problems when the Chief interfered. He would have liked to sew this one up personally. He certainly could do without the Chief coming up from police headquarters at Aykley Heads.

Greybrook squinted at his notes. The milkman, apparently, was an erratic visitor, accustomed to the owner of Bodicote Barn House — one Kenneth Andrews, ex-Army type — requiring a modicum of milk and that only every three days or so. When he had arrived this morning at eight o'clock he had gone around to the back as was customary and had been puzzled to find an opened crate of wine and spirits on the back step. The back door was also open.

He had called, ventured inside and then immediately dialled for the police. He was still shaking when they had arrived.

'How long we got to wait, then?' Detective Sergeant Eyre, in charge of the scene-of-crime unit, was standing beside the car. 'The fingerprint people have arrived. Can't they get stuck in?'

'Better wait. Redvers is on the way. He wants to take personal charge.'

'Is that guy in there important, then? I never heard of him. Why does Redvers want to take over?'

'I don't know.'

'Hell of a mess in there. You think it's suicide?'

'Would you expect me to commit myself before Redvers can sum up the position?' Greybrook replied sarcastically. 'Look out, I'm going inside. It's going to pour soon, and there's no reason why we should wait outside.'

Detective Sergeant Eyre backed away as Greybrook opened the car door and hurried to the porch that had been built at the front of the converted barn. The sergeant followed him, looking appreciatively at the old, warm stone. 'Bet this place cost a packet. What line was the deceased in?'

'The deceased?' Greybrook grunted. 'You're reading too many crime reports. You're beginning to sound like one. His line of business? I don't know. Ex-Army, that's all I know. But I have a feeling I've come across his name in some connection.'

'Bigwig?'

'Would Chief Superintendent Redvers come out for any other?'

'The lads are getting edgy, hanging around. And the smell in there, with the flies . . .'

'Tell them to have a smoke. But for God's sake, not in front of Redvers.'

They waited in the porch. The sky turned a darker shade of grey and the rain came, drizzling at first, then lashing itself into a fury as the wind rose, whipping frenziedly at the trees in the spinney and moaning under the eaves of the house. It was almost twenty minutes before the big car nosed its way into the drive, headlights blazing, and drew up near Greybrook's more modest vehicle. Redvers got out, head lowered against the driving wind, and hurried as fast as his ponderous bulk would allow to gain the shelter of the porch where Greybrook waited.

Redvers wasted no time in preliminaries. 'Where is he?' The heavy face and red-rimmed eyes glared into Greybrook's. Redvers was now in his mid-fifties, grizzled of disposition, somewhat soured by his failure to progress beyond his present rank. Below his military moustache, grey and bristling, he had a disappointed mouth which was quick to vent anger on subordinates and he had a reputation as a man who reacted swiftly to imagined slights. He was a political animal by nature, but one who had failed to obtain the desired rewards for his politicking: he was on good terms with local councillors and was occasionally a guest of the Lord Lieutenant, but if he had hoped to obtain preferment, it had never come. There had been the odd garden party at Buckingham Palace but nothing more. There was a whisper that he had pushed a local politician too hard on one occasion, and his importunity had led to a silent conspiracy, an agreement that he was 'unsafe'. His blacklisting had soured him. The contacts remained over the years; the rewards were denied.

Greybrook led the way into the sitting room. In the doorway, Redvers put thick fingers on his shoulder. 'Wait. I want to get the feel of this one for myself.'

Greybrook stood rigid, unhappy, as Redvers pushed past him. The Chief Superintendent marched into the room and stood near the settee, staring down at the destroyed head at his feet. Greybrook remained in the doorway. He could see Redvers wrinkling his red-veined nose in distaste. The Chief Superintendent scowled. 'Us coppers are always the ones who have to clear up the mess. The photographers been in yet?'

'They're half finished—'

'I thought I told you I wanted no one in here until I'd sussed the thing out!'

'They were already in and started before you came over on the radio. At the time I wasn't to know you wanted to look at this yourself, sir. Once I spoke to you I hauled them out until you could get here.'

Redvers stared suspiciously at Greybrook, as though unwilling to believe him. 'Mmm . . . I don't like clodhoppers trampling around a scene like this, not if I'm to be involved. I like to be first in . . . an experienced eye . . . before those idiots place their big feet everywhere.'

Greybrook hoped he wouldn't notice the smudged carpet where one of the photographers had actually stepped in a patch of blood and brains, blown away by the force of the blast.

'And that's the weapon?'

'Sawn-off shotgun.'

'Sawn-off, hey?' Redvers leaned over to inspect it more closely, where it lay near the curled fingers of the dead man's right hand. 'Unusual, in this kind of suicide.'

Greybrook was still. He said nothing, as Redvers began a slow perambulation of the blood-spattered room. He walked with his head jutting forward, the short grey skullcap of hair nodding as he walked, peering at the state of the room. He reached the drinks cabinet and looked it over as though expecting a solution to emerge. He swung around abruptly.

'Fingerprints here?'

'He's waiting outside. With the photographer.'

'Right. Get them. Get this bloody thing organized, and I don't want any press or television people in here at all. I'm going back to the office, once I've had a quick shufty at the rest of the house. If there's to be any statements issued in the next twenty-four hours I'll make them, and they'll come from Aykley Heads.'

'Who was this man, sir?'

'Who?' Redvers's eyes were glazed dully, as though he only half understood the question. 'Why do you ask?' Greybrook shrugged. 'All the milkman could tell us is that Andrews was ex-Army. The name's familiar, but—'

'Well enough known in Durham,' Redvers grunted. 'Now get those bloody layabouts in here.'

Greybrook turned and went back into the hall to call the men in to continue their interrupted work. As he returned, Redvers came bustling out of the sitting room. He seemed to be in a hurry, and his eyes were oddly angry. 'I'll see you back at Aykley Heads,' he grunted. 'I'll want a full report.'

Greybrook stayed in the sitting room as the photographer went to work. The flashing of the bulbs lent a harsh aspect to the scene, as though they highlighted the destruction that had occurred here, picking up the spattering of blood and grey matter on the walls and the settee. When the photographer had finished, one of the constables on duty at the front came in. 'Doc Evans is here, sir.'

Greybrook nodded and walked to the front door. Evans was just getting out of his car. The police surgeon was short, Welsh, and round-shouldered. His skin was dark and he always seemed unshaven. He squinted up at Greybrook, nodded a greeting and asked where the corpse was.

Greybrook was slow in answering. He was staring over Evans's shoulder. The Chief Superintendent had said he was going straight back to Aykley Heads after a quick look at the rest of the house, but his car was still in the drive. Greybrook frowned, and half turned.

'Hey!' Evans plucked at his sleeve. 'You still with us? I asked where the bloody corpse was!'

'I'm sorry.' Greybrook led the way into the sitting room and stood there uncertainly as the doctor began his brief examination. 'Well, he's dead, that's for sure,' Evans said with a macabre chuckle.

'I'll sort out the body bag,' Greybrook replied, and stepped back into the hallway.

The Chief Superintendent's car was still in the driveway.

Greybrook glanced uncertainly towards the stairway, wondering if Redvers had gone upstairs. If he followed, Redvers would be sure to lose his temper. Whatever Redvers was doing, he would want to do it alone. Greybrook walked into the kitchen; it was empty, except for a constable standing on guard at the back door. Back in the corridor leading to the front hall Greybrook hesitated outside the door to the dead man's study. He could not be sure, but he thought he detected sounds of movement within the room. He put his hand out to the door, hesitated, and then turned away. This was no time to cross Chief Superintendent Redvers.

In the sitting room Dr Evans was straightening, wiping his nose on his sleeve. 'Well then, Greybrook, that's about it. Can't really do much more here. Might as well get the body bag in and get this lot off to the pathology lab.'

'When can we expect a report?'

'Hell's flames — don't rush me, son! We got more than enough on at the lab at the moment. It'll take maybe three days before I can get a preliminary report out.'

'No first impressions?'

'He's dead.'

Patiently Greybrook ignored the old joke. 'And . . . ?'

'Time of death . . . well, at least forty-eight hours would be my guess. But don't hold me to that. I'll have to make the usual tests back at the lab. OK, I'll go and wash up now—'

'The Chief Super's here.'

'Redvers? What's he poking his nose in for?'

Greybrook paused, measuring his words. 'The Chief seems to think it might have been suicide.'

'Does he now?' Evans looked at Greybrook for a moment, then turned to gaze again at the corpse. He shrugged, and lifted his hands in doubt. 'Could be, I suppose. With a sawn-off shotgun like that, he could have placed it just under the chin and pulled the trigger easily enough. They usually shove it in their mouths, you know.' He snickered to himself. 'Maybe he didn't want to damage his dentures.'

'So you think it could have been suicide?' Greybrook persisted.

'What the hell do you mean by asking me that?' Evans demanded, opening his eyes wide. 'I thought you were an experienced police officer. You've been around a while, I understand — other forces, Bristol and the like. Didn't they teach you anything there? I can't be expected to come up with a theory like that, especially at this stage. I deal in facts. It's up to you buggers to theorize. How the hell do I know whether he committed suicide, or whether someone else shoved that muzzle under his chin?'

Greybrook stepped aside as Evans bustled past him. He remained in the sitting room for a little while, looking around. He had a vague sense of disquiet but could discover no reason for it. Something was missing, in the room or in his thoughts — there was a jigsaw piece lost, or misplaced. The thought irritated him. He was a man with a logical, tidy mind, who worked along precise, pre-ordained lines. All his life he had planned, researched, clearly delineated his objectives, and police work suited him and his targets in life. He knew some people thought him boring, pedantic, and over-concerned with detail. He couldn't help that.

When things got out of phase, or issues did not reach expected conclusions, he became irritable. Care and precision were part of his make-up: planning was all. There was no passion in his life — just determination to do the job.

And something here was out of place. He could not put his finger on it, but something was wrong.

He walked back into the corridor. Chief Superintendent Redvers was coming out of the room that had served as the dead man's study. He did not look at Greybrook. His face was stony as he pushed past Greybrook and headed for the front door. Greybrook followed and watched his superior officer clamber awkwardly into the big black car. It roared into life and swung importantly down the driveway, rasping gravel as it went. The constable on the door looked at Greybrook inquiringly. Greybrook said nothing.

He went back inside and entered the study that Redvers had left.

It was untidy.

He had no way of knowing at this stage whether the untidy litter of papers on the desk beside the typewriter was the normal situation for Andrews, or not. He had no idea whether Redvers had disturbed anything. Papers on the desk had been scattered, nevertheless.

Greybrook walked over to the desk and looked at some of the sheets. They formed part of a narrative, certainly. But it wasn't fiction — more like a research project of some kind, or a book on mediaeval history.

He wandered around the room uncertainly, not clear what he was looking for. Redvers had stayed in the room for at least twenty minutes, and it puzzled Greybrook that the Chief Superintendent should have devoted so much time to this room. It was as though he might have been looking for something.

Thoughtfully, Greybrook did his own inspection of the room, touching nothing, but looking for anything that might seem out of place or out of the ordinary. At last he walked back to the hallway and told the others to get to work, searching the house for a suicide note or anything else of significance.

'The crate of bottles outside, sir.'

'Yes?'

'I brought them in. The crate had been opened, and there's a bottle missing.'

'There's a bottle in the kitchen, on the worktop,' Greybrook said.

'Don't think it's from the crate, sir. But we can check.'

'Check for fingerprints . . . bottle, glass, the crate also . . .' Greybrook hesitated. 'After that I want the study dusted too. Carefully.'

He himself had touched nothing in the study, but Greybrook wondered whether, when the room had been dusted for fingerprints, Chief Superintendent Redvers's prints might show up anywhere.

4

The gardens outside police headquarters in Morpeth were bathed in sunshine. Arnold Landon occasionally went up into the municipal park to eat his lunchtime sandwiches; it gave him an opportunity to escape the Senior Planning Officer and the drudgery of his desk.

That was the only way to describe Arnold's desk at the moment: drudgery. There had been no real crisis, as Arnold had suspected. Rather, it was a panicked Senior Planning Officer who had decided that his own desk was too overburdened — so overburdened, in fact, that he might be forced to make some decisions. Consequently, he had ploughed through the files, initialled them, and called for a report on them from Arnold.

It was the usual range of stuff.

There was an application from two members of the Ramblers Association, claiming to be 'persons aggrieved' by an order made under the Wildlife and Countryside Act concerning a woodland footpath near the Cheviot; a local business consortium was arguing about the construction of a business park in an area Arnold, at least, considered most unsuitable; a local artist was asking for permission to construct a studio in an area that was primarily residential; and there were several other thick files with which Arnold was basically familiar but which now would have to be ploughed through again to deal with the Senior Planning Officer's niggling little queries.

Arnold had been dealing with them when, to his surprise, the Senior Planning Officer had called him to his office. It was an unusual request because the Senior Planning Officer indulged in a management style that ensured he hardly ever saw his managers; while it demanded levels of efficiency designed to cover up the senior officer's mistakes, as far as Arnold was concerned it wasn't a bad system. The less he saw of the Senior Planning Officer the better he was pleased.

When he had reached the Senior Planning Officer's room, he had realized just why his presence had been requested. The Senior Planning Officer was not alone: seated with him was Councillor Sandy Bryman.

* * *

As he sat in the sunshine in the municipal gardens, Arnold thought over the meeting. He had come across Councillor Bryman often enough because the man was a member of the Planning Committee of the council. He was a thickset, dark-browed man in his early forties who possessed a belligerent manner and a sharp tongue. He was not a north-easterner — he came originally from Yorkshire, as Arnold did, but it was the building trade and the opportunities in the Newcastle area that had brought him north fifteen years ago. Arnold always considered it somewhat unethical that owners of construction firms, like Bryman, should take seats on the Planning Committee, but the rules simply said that as long as they declared their interests it was acceptable. The problem was, as Arnold saw it, there was the matter of inside information — particularly where tenders were concerned.

The meeting had not developed into a confrontation, but it had not been far from it.

'Ah, Mr Landon, I think you know Councillor Bryman,' the Senior Planning Officer had begun, waving Arnold to a seat. 'He's come in with a small query, and I thought you would be the best person to deal with it.'

In the presence of the Senior Planning Officer, of course. 'What's the problem, Councillor?' Arnold asked.

'Simple enough, really. I was interested to find out how the Orion business is going on.'

Arnold stared at him. 'It's due to come before the committee at its next meeting.'

'Not due for another month. I just wondered . . .' Bryman smiled a fleshy smile, his eyes slitting. The coldness of his smile made Arnold think of a snake. 'Just how far is it likely to go, do you think?'

'I think it's a matter for the committee.'

'But you will be preparing the case,' Bryman insisted. 'What will you be recommending?'

A brittle impatience was creeping into Bryman's voice.

Arnold hesitated; he had no desire to make an enemy of Bryman, and there was nothing inherently wrong in discussing the Orion application with a member of the Planning Committee. Nevertheless, Bryman was in a rival business and while Arnold was not aware of any counter proposals from Bryman Construction, he was left with the uneasy feeling that Bryman might be seeking some advantage Arnold was not yet aware of. 'I . . . I think it's a little early to be reaching conclusions—'

'Rubbish,' the Senior Planning Officer responded with an uncharacteristic geniality, a veneer glued to his voice by an eagerness to please Councillor Bryman. 'You've already annotated the file: I've seen your notes.'

'The report isn't written.'

'But the gist . . . ?' the Senior Planning Officer said, putting the tips of his fingers together and staring at them.

Arnold gave up. 'Well,' he said reluctantly, 'you'll be aware the Orion organization applied for planning permission for a road service area including a restaurant and filling station—'

'Yes, yes, I know the background,' Bryman snapped. 'The site is bordered by arable land and mixed woodland.

The site itself falls within the AONB designation — an area of outstanding natural beauty.'

'Orion is arguing the case on the basis of need,' the Senior Planning Officer intervened. 'Is that not the issue?'

Arnold nodded. 'The evidence produced points to a proliferation of undesirable makeshift services in lay-bys. There are, it must be agreed, no catering services and only one fuel service along the fifteen-mile length of the road in question.'

Bryman fished in his jacket pocket and brought out a pack of cigarettes. He asked no permission from the Senior Planning Officer before he lit a cigarette. He blew smoke in Arnold's direction. 'What counter arguments will you be raising? I presume you will be stating a case?'

Arnold nodded reluctantly. 'I think we're in a position where we would have to point to serious effects on the amenities. *If* the proposal were to receive planning permission. I would argue we could agree it only if the location in question could demonstrate a special need. Otherwise, I suggest we turn it down.'

'With no other, more positive suggestions?'

Arnold shrugged. 'I would recommend adequate screening if the committee did agree the proposal, and an assurance that the project was demonstrably a permitted exception to the normal policy restrictions.'

'Hmmm. I see. Well, we'll have to leave it up to the committee, won't we, Mr Landon?' Bryman regarded him carefully through a blue vein of smoke. 'I gather, by the way, that you're on an external working party established by the government to look again at planning criteria in road development schemes.'

Arnold nodded and avoided looking in the direction of the Senior Planning Officer. He was not quite sure how he had been selected. The Senior Planning Officer had been somewhat miffed when the request had come through from Whitehall that Arnold Landon be seconded to the working party to produce recommendations to the government, but he had had little choice but to accede. Arnold had to admit he did not find the work particularly interesting or exciting, and he disliked travelling to London for the working party meetings. There was also the suspicion that he had come to the attention of civil servants because of his external activities rather than the work he did for Northumberland. That was certainly the Senior Planning Officer's view of the situation.

'I just wondered,' Bryman considered, 'how far that work has gone. Where road building is concerned, that is.'

'I don't understand,' Arnold said, genuinely puzzled.

'Well—' Bryman hesitated, as though choosing his word with care — 'it occurs to me they might be considering certain yardsticks that could be laid down. For development purposes. On major roads.'

Arnold frowned. 'I'm not sure it would be useful . . . or ethical . . . for me to divulge the thinking of the working party.'

'You're a servant of this council, Landon,' Councillor Bryman warned coldly. 'If there's anything that might affect—'

'I'm sorry to disagree,' Arnold cut in. 'While I'm working for the Government Working Party I understand it's on the basis of a secondment, and each day's work I do is paid for by Whitehall, not the county. So in that sense, I'm not a servant of the council . . . not in this matter.'

'You're splitting hairs,' Bryman snapped angrily. 'All I did was ask a perfectly innocent question—'

But Arnold had doubted whether it was perfectly innocent.

* * *

And now, sitting in the sunshine, looking at the map on his knees, he became even more convinced that the question had not been innocent. Arnold had not been entirely truthful in explaining his reluctance to talk of the working party deliberations. There was one yardstick the group was discussing — they had in fact reached agreement on it. It was being proposed to the government that a circular be issued adopting a twelve-mile yardstick on busy major roads. If the yardstick were applied to the Orion application, Orion would certainly have a strong case.

But if there were service stations available within that twelve-mile yardstick, the case would fall to ground.

And why was Councillor Bryman interested? Arnold could hazard a guess, now he had had time to study the planning map. Over the fifteen-mile stretch of the road which lacked service facilities there was in fact one disused service station, closed down at least four years ago. It was derelict, and based just seven miles from the nearest active service area to the south.

But more interesting was the fact that the derelict station abutted on to land that was currently being developed by a construction company.

Bryman Construction Ltd.

Arnold was prepared to put money on the likelihood that Bryman had already purchased the derelict site. If Arnold had told him of the twelve-mile yardstick proposal, Bryman would have slapped in an application to the next Planning Committee meeting. That application could have effectively prevented the Orion proposal going forward — and Bryman's case, rebuilding a derelict site, would have been stronger than Orion's request to undertake new construction in an AONB area.

Arnold was pleased he had refused Bryman the information. These things had to be fought out cleanly, all above board. He was right in giving Bryman no advantage. It was also likely he had incurred Bryman's displeasure — and Arnold had already more than a few disgruntled enemies in the Morpeth corridors of power.

5

He arrived back at his office precisely at two o'clock. He worked at his desk for over an hour with three Tree Preservation Orders, one of which was a Monterey Cypress, claimed to have an incurable disease and to be dying. Arnold thought otherwise: he had visited the residential garden in question, and the real reason for its removal was a desire by the wealthy widow who owned the garden to improve her view of the town.

He was distracted from his work by a phone call from reception.

'Mr Landon? Call for you. A Mr Aspen.'

Before Arnold could ask who the caller might be, he was put through.

'Mr Landon? My name is Peter Aspen. I'm sorry to bother you at work, but I have a project I would like to discuss with you. Perhaps we could arrange a time and place to meet?'

* * *

Arnold usually enjoyed his visits to Newcastle. The city was going through a period of rapid development and change. The building of the shopping centre at Eldon Square had caused a storm of criticism — the removal of a delightful tree-lined square to make way for a shopping complex had dismayed many. Within two decades, immense competition had raised its head across the river in Gateshead, with the building of the huge Gateshead Metro Centre. But in other ways the city had retained its sense and appreciation of the past. Grey Street was still one of the finest streets of its kind in Europe and the Quayside retained the feel and vigour of a history that had seen the great sailing ships, and experienced the buzz of commerce among its narrow, steep-sided chares.

Peter Aspen had suggested meeting in a small Italian restaurant near Dog Leap Stairs and Arnold was sufficiently intrigued to agree to meet him. Besides, he had often enough eaten in the restaurant to know that it would be an enjoyable experience.

All Aspen had said was that he had heard of Arnold from friends — not least, from Ben Gibson, the squat little bookseller who lived and worked on the Quayside — and that he was a publisher. He had a project in which Arnold might be interested.

Aspen was already at the restaurant when Arnold arrived. He had booked a table: the proprietor, who knew Arnold, pointed him out and Arnold went across to join the tall, spare man who rose to greet him. Aspen was lean and hollow-cheeked, with thinning hair that he had grown white and long in the back as though to compensate for the sparsity of the crown. He was elegantly dressed in a pale grey suit and pink tie. He was aware of his sharp cuff and even sharper profile, which rather reminded Arnold of old movies of Franchot Tone. When he sat down he placed himself at a slight angle to the table, as though he wished to demonstrate, by distancing himself from it slightly, that he was not really terribly interested in food.

'I thought a simple Frascati would suffice, Mr Landon. Do you object?' Arnold did not.

'And some risotto to begin, and perhaps fettucine . . .' Arnold allowed him to order, since it was dearly something he enjoyed doing — though he was aware that Aspen, consciously or otherwise, avoided the more expensive items on the menu.

'I'm a publisher, as I told you,' Aspen said, as though that explained something. He poured Arnold a glass of Frascati and took a little himself. 'Now then, I'm told that although you work in the Planning Department at Morpeth, you have certain other interests which have brought you some . . . fame?'

Notoriety was more like it, Arnold thought glumly. When his father had taught him an appreciation of wood and stone, given him the sensitivity to feel the past, learn the ways and methods, the skills and touch, of the master masons and shown him how a three hundred-year-old past could come alive under his fingertips, he had never considered that it might one day lead him into embarrassments, difficulties and dangers. Or that it would lead to his senior officer threatening him with dismissal from his post.

'When Ben Gibson — with whom I've had many dealings in the past-heard about my little problem a few days ago, he suggested that I might get in touch with you.'

'Problem?'

'Mmmm. One of my authors has just died, poor chap. Such a dear man.' Aspen had pale eyes; they were lidded as he spoke, and there was something odd about his tone, as though he were in church, reiterating worn, insincere phrases about someone he'd never cared for.

'It was a sudden death?'

'You could say that.' The pale eyes flickered at Arnold. 'Did you not hear about it? Very sad. Suicide, they say, though there's been no inquest yet. Andrews. Kenneth Andrews.'

The name meant nothing to Arnold and it must have showed in his features. Aspen sighed, and went on, 'Mmmm. He lived in a converted barn — splendid place — near Durham, up on the fell. Retired ex-Army officer, I believe. He did a number of little books for me. Quite successful they were. I'm what you might call a specialist publisher — or two specialisms really. I've been told they don't sit well together in my list, but I make a living.'

'What are the specialisms?' Arnold asked.

'Military history . . . and the occult.'

'Oh.' Arnold twisted his mouth thoughtfully. He knew there was a large market in both areas. He knew also that in one of those areas there were a number of active charlatans, and worse. Nor had he forgotten his experiences of devil worship at St Michael's Church in Kentside.

Peter Aspen was watching him closely, perhaps aware of the distaste that had touched Arnold. 'It's in the field of military history that I first approached Kenneth Andrews. He seemed a good choice, with his background, and he turned out quite well, in fact. His ventures into the occult were not quite so successful . . . in fact, he's landed me with a few problems. But that's another matter and of no relevance to our meeting today. No, the fact is, he was working on a book for me which I'd like to see completed. Ben Gibson suggested to me you might be the right person to do it. Indeed, he even suggested I should have come to you in the first place, rather than poor Ken Andrews.'

'I've little experience of writing,' Arnold protested.

'Oh, my dear boy, it's the research that I want. I can always get some hack to put it into undying prose — at least, the kind of undying prose that Aspen readership demands.' He managed a faint, deprecatory smile. 'One has to write down to one's readership, I fear.'

Arnold waited until the first course had been cleared away and then he sipped his wine. 'What exactly is the project that Mr Andrews was working on?'

'I understand you recently visited Harlech . . . so Ben Gibson told me.'

'That's right.'

'Well, this should be right on your turret, so to speak, if you don't mind the pleasantry. I imagine you'll already know something about the subject. It's the Savoyards.'

'Under Edward I?'

'Precisely. And Master James of St Georges in particular. Ken Andrews was writing a book about the master mason and was trying to link in a theory about his work on the castles of Wales.'

Arnold nodded. He had heard of Master James, the great master mason to Edward I. When Edward married his Eleanor the marriage was negotiated by the Savoyard bishop of Hereford, and it was Peter of Savoy who became a frequent witness to many of Edward's charters. For three years or more, while Edward was asserting himself against his earlier tutelage, the Savoyards at court were a powerful faction. And from them had come the discovery of perhaps the greatest mason in Europe, for it was when Edward was renewing his family links with Savoy some fifteen years later that he visited St Georges. It was there he met Master James, the architect whose imaginative solutions to the problems of castle building were to place him among the ranks of the greatest of military architects.

'What was Andrews's theory?'

'That the prime reason for the castle building was political not military, and that Harlech and Criccieth were also part of the work of Master James.'

Arnold shook his head. 'Unlikely. Flint, Rhuddlan and Conwy had their value as military bases, but there's no evidence that Harlech and Criccieth served such a purpose, or that Master James was involved at those sites.'

'Ken Andrews suggests that Master James once wrote: "Welshmen are Welshmen, and you need to understand them properly."'

'So?'

'That is the key to the theory,' Aspen said blandly. 'Or so Andrews opined. Another bottle of wine?'

* * *

By the time the meal was over and Arnold had consumed the better part of a bottle of Frascati he was close to agreeing to accept the commission. He promised to let Aspen know in a day or two, and the publisher took his leave. Arnold stayed on for a little while, taking two espressos to attempt some counteraction to the wine. He had to drive back to Morpeth, and he was not sure he was in a fit state.

Rather, he was sure he was not in a fit state.

The theory that Andrews had propounded was light and unimportant enough. Arnold supposed it could be proved, or disproved, fairly easily. It did not attract him. On the other hand, he had always been interested in the work of the thirteenth-century master masons, and to complete the research would mean he'd have an opportunity — with expenses paid — to visit the castles, prowl around the masonry, consider the reasons for some of the more mysterious constructions devised by the ingenious Master James. The concentric drum towers at Flint, for instance, for which there had never been a convincing military explanation . . .

One thing he certainly had to do in any case: he ought to pay a call on Ben Gibson to thank him for mentioning his name. And to have another cup of coffee. The likelihood was, also, that Ben might offer him a bed for the night. He probably needed it, after the amount of wine he'd consumed.

Military history and the occult. Odd combination. Anyway, the agreement with Aspen was that if he decided to undertake the project, Aspen would let him have the notes compiled by Andrews. 'There is one small problem, dear boy,' Aspen had added. 'A little difficulty over some of the original material. You see, Ken Andrews seems to have shot himself — *felo de se,* that sort of thing — and the police haven't released his papers from custody, so to speak. But it should all be cleared up in a couple of days, and then you'll get the lot . . .' He had looked pensive for a moment. 'And then I'll get the other manuscript as well, I expect . . .'

It was almost nine in the evening when Arnold left the restaurant. Ben would have dosed up his shop, but he rarely went out so it was highly likely Arnold would find him upstairs at the house on the Quayside. He made his way down Dog Leap Stairs, one hand braced against the old stone walls. The waters of the Tyne glittered blackly below him. He had heard there was a great planning proposal in the wind for the redevelopment of the Quayside area. He hoped it would be handled sensitively.

He negotiated the steps safely, and made his way carefully along to Ben Gibson's house. As he had guessed, the shop window was in darkness. He rang the doorbell.

There was no answer. He rang the bell again.

There was a light in the flat upstairs, dim and shaded.

He heard the sounds of movement and stepped back. To his surprise an upstairs window was opened and he could see the dark shape of a head.

'Who's there? What do you want?'

'I want a word with Ben Gibson. Isn't he home?'

There was a short silence. 'You obviously haven't heard. Ben's ill. Who are you?'

Arnold's fuddled senses finally reached the realization it was a woman speaking to him. 'I'm Arnold Landon. Who are you? Ben's ill?'

'I'd better come down.'

Arnold waited, frowning. He had heard nothing of Ben's illness. It must have been recent . . . though he had to admit he hadn't been in touch with Ben Gibson for over a month. But Peter Aspen had said he'd spoken to Ben in the last few days . . .

He saw the light on the stairs, the shape of a woman moving through the shop. The door opened; the light was behind her.

'Mr Landon. I've heard of you — Ben's spoken of you. I'm sorry you hadn't heard—'

She stopped speaking suddenly. There was a short pause.

'It's you,' she said woodenly.

And he recognized her in the same instant.

'Jane Wilson,' he said in a strangled tone.

They stared at each other for several seconds in mutual, subdued hostility. Then she turned away, abruptly.

'You'd better come inside,' she said.

CHAPTER TWO

1

Arnold never managed to feel at ease in the company of matrons. Even if they were pleasant to him he still felt they exuded an aura of power which he found disconcerting in the strict, sanitized surroundings of a hospital. He had to admit that this particular matron was younger and prettier than some of the dragons of his acquaintance but she had the same brisk efficiency that inhibited him.

'I'd like to see Mr Gibson, if it's possible.'

'It's outside visiting hours.'

'I work in Morpeth, I'm afraid, and—'

'He's already got one visitor.'

'Ah.' Arnold tried a hangdog expression. It seemed to work. The young matron watched his mouth droop at the corners and softened. 'Well, all right, then, I suppose it won't do him any harm. And he'll only complain if he hears you've been turned away. Quite a complainer, our Mr Gibson.'

Arnold was glad to hear that Ben was keeping his end up. Matron led the way and he followed meekly behind. They passed through swing doors at the end of the corridor and turned into the last room on the left.

'Mr Gibson,' she said in a stern voice that nevertheless held a certain amount of self-mockery, 'I'm allowing you two illegal visitors. I expect you to behave this evening, as a result. That means you will eat your evening meal whether it's gruel or not. We serve gruel,' she explained ironically to Arnold, 'as a matter of course. At least, that's what he says.'

She turned back to her patient. 'As for your visitors, they have half an hour and no more.' She folded her arms across her starched bosom and frowned at him. 'No more, Mr Gibson.'

As she turned to brush past Arnold he was surprised to catch her closing one eye in a quick wink, even though her face was set sternly and her mouth stiff with austerity. 'Arnold!'

'Hello, Ben. How are you?'

'Better now the Phoenix has gone.'

'Phoenix?'

'I consume her with the fire of my tongue — but she rises from the ashes each time!' The little bookseller was lying in bed, propped up by pillows, and his face was pale. Arnold had always thought of him, affectionately, as a little frog of a man, with his hooded eyes and fleshy, squat face but now he seemed shrunken and older than Arnold remembered. Ben Gibson was past seventy, his small stature rendered even smaller by his crouching gait, a legacy of arthritic joints, but his illness had drained much of the vitality in his face that had always made Arnold forget his age. He had linked his gnarled fingers together on the counterpane, but as Arnold advanced he stretched out a hand. Arnold took it. The veins stood out starkly against the papery, freckled skin. His grip was weak.

'The old watchmaker-cum-bookseller laid low, hey? It's good of you to come, Arnold. Relatives, one expects. Friends . . . well, they aren't too numerous and they can be busy, anyway.' Some of the old mischief crept back into his welcoming smile.' I understand you've already met my niece, Jane.'

Oddly embarrassed, Arnold nodded, then managed a glance in her direction. She was seated on a chair beside the head of the bed. She was wearing a dark skirt with a white blouse this evening and she looked smart and businesslike.

She met his glance directly and nodded in return. 'That's right, Uncle, we've met before. Twice, in fact. The once I told you about — when he stayed at the house the other evening — and prior to that we met in Harlech. He was being a tourist, I believe. Of course, I didn't know he was the famous Arnold Landon then.'

Arnold's words came out in spite of himself, dictated by her own tartness. 'And I wasn't aware, Ben, that you had an authoress as a niece.'

Ben Gibson looked from one to the other, recognized the sharpness and giggled. 'I can see you two are going to get on famously. But what's this about staying at the house the other evening, Arnold? While Jane was under the same roof, unchaperoned?'

'He was drunk,' Jane Wilson replied. 'It was an act of charity on my part.'

'You should feel flattered, Arnold,' Ben Gibson stated soberly. 'My niece is an upright woman, but not noted for her charitable impulses. However, I haven't answered your first question. You should know better than to ask an invalid how he is. He's likely to tell you. At length. Unfortunately, I haven't the strength, so suffice it to say that I had a heart attack at the shop some five days ago, a second, less serious one shortly after I was admitted to hospital, but with care and good nursing — which I get here, a private patient in an NHS hospital, don't you know — I should be right as rain in a day or so, now. They think I can be discharged at the end of the week. Jane'll have her hands full then, but the Phoenix will have other patients to bully.'

'I'm pleased to hear you're recovering, Ben. I'm sorry I didn't come sooner—'

'How were you to know I'd been taken ill? I didn't trumpet the matter myself, and my heart attack was never an event likely to reach the newspapers. It was Jane who told you, I gather. Why had you come to the house, anyway? Haven't seen you in a while, but late evening's a funny time for you to call without warning.'

'I told you,' Jane intervened primly. 'He was drunk.' Hurriedly, Arnold said, 'I came to thank you for the introduction to Peter Aspen . . . and to have a chat about ways in which you could help.' He glanced quickly at Jane Wilson. 'And I wasn't really drunk. Peter Aspen had offered me the project over dinner, and maybe we'd had a little too much wine—'

'You were drunk and you were looking for a bed,' Jane Wilson retorted crisply. 'And has anyone ever told you that you snore?'

'Tush, girl, Arnold's a bachelor,' Ben Gibson announced with a slight smile. 'Who'd be around to tell him? Anyway, Arnold, you got your bed whether you were looking for one or not, and if you still want to thank me because of Peter Aspen, don't bother. He should have come to you in the first place.'

'I'm not so sure. I've written very little, and this fellow Andrews . . . well, I gather he'd written a few military histories—'

'Superficial stuff.'

'—and some books on the occult—'

'Particularly weird.' Ben Gibson waved his hand disparagingly. 'Besides, on that front he wrote second-hand, whereas you've got personal experience of that sort of stuff.'

'Which I'd like to forget,' Arnold said fervently. 'However, while we're speaking of this Aspen project I wanted to have a chat with you because there could be some difficulty. You'll be aware that Andrews's death has meant I can't get access to his papers.'

'Why not?' Ben Gibson demanded.

Arnold shrugged. 'I phoned Peter Aspen to tell him I'd take on the Andrews project and he seemed pleased, but then he told me the original papers, the ones Andrews was working on, are still with the police. There's some sort of investigation going on, and the papers are impounded for the moment. I've been in touch with police headquarters at Aykley Heads but they've not been particularly helpful so far.

I intend making another appointment: apparently it's a Chief Superintendent Redvers who's in charge. But if by chance I can't get hold of the original papers I thought I could do some browsing with you at the bookshop. I mean, I can get outlines from Aspen, and notes that Andrews passed to him from time to time, but otherwise . . .'

'I can't imagine the police will hang on to such boring stuff too long,' Ben Gibson suggested. 'And I'm afraid I can't help you too much. Rest is ordained by matron. She is formidable. She ignores my complaints. She has no pity for an old man. But I wouldn't wish to cross her. She's even told me I must curb my proclivities and cut down on my sexual activity.'

Arnold laughed, aware that the old man had been a bachelor all his life, far from priapic, and inherently suspicious of women.

'On the other hand,' the old bookseller continued, 'Jane has kindly offered to look after the shop for a few months, while she researches her new book, so I see no reason why she can't give you a hand. After all, she does regard herself as a bit of an expert in some areas of the period in question.'

Arnold protested. 'Oh, I'm sure that won't be necessary. I can manage—'

'Not a question of managing. What do you say, Jane? Won't be a problem, will it?'

* * *

For the first time since he'd met her, Arnold saw that she was flustered. 'Well, I don't know. I'm doing some research on Vegetius—'

'Fine.' Ben Gibson beamed. 'That fits in nicely. You can sit down together, side by side, and compare notes and all that sort of thing. That's settled then.'

Arnold glanced at Jane Wilson, trying to show her that as far as he was concerned it was far from settled. But she did not look at him. There was a tightness about her mouth that suggested she was not well pleased with her uncle's pressure. But Ben Gibson was off on another tack now.

'Funny, really, about Ken Andrews's death. I mean, he was an odd man in many ways, strange, I mean . . . and I never cared for him the few times he came into the shop, but with two books on the go, and a successful lifestyle, it's odd he should commit suicide. I mean, that's the gossip I understand. Shot himself.'

'So I've heard. But how do you mean . . . strange?' Arnold asked.

'Committing suicide, or his character?' Ben Gibson pulled a face: it made him look more like a decrepit frog than ever. 'Well, if you were in the middle of research, and writing two books to contract, would suicide be on your mind? Apart from that, I have to admit he was . . . odd. He was well in with the university crowd in Durham, you know, and he had some wealthy contacts in the North East. Glossy magazine stuff . . . you know, dinner-jacket group pictures in *Northern Life,* that sort of thing. But though he was ex-Army, he didn't mix in with the Durham Light Infantry crowd, which is a bit surprising. And in personal terms, there was something . . . cold and fishlike about him. He had strange eyes, I remember — the sort that could strip paper off walls. Satanic eyebrows, that was it. He used them to effect: shot them up like Bela Lugosi, if you know what I mean? He gave the impression he saw things . . . inside things . . . that you couldn't. Shuddery sort of guy.'

'That's rather fanciful, Ben,' Jane Wilson murmured. 'You can't have met him often.'

'Three times. Tallish feller, military bearing, cold hands, rather an effete way of speaking, but I got the impression that was an affectation. Could never quite pick up the accent that lay behind it, but there was the odd West Country touch crept in. Never married, it seems — one of the brigade with more sense, like you and me, Arnold, hey?'

'You said he was working on two books,' Jane said.

'Believe so. I have a feeling the other one was occultish, if you know what I mean. Don't really know exactly what it was all about.' Ben glanced wickedly at Arnold. 'Perhaps Peter Aspen will give you a contract on that one as well, Arnold. You could be a prolific author yet, just like Jane . . .'

* * *

Arnold stood awkwardly in the car park with Jane Wilson after leaving the ward. She seemed equally ill at ease, glancing up at the darkening sky, preparing to make a quick goodbye. Arnold swallowed hard.

'I seem to find myself apologizing to you every other time we meet.'

She looked at him, her brown eyes dark in the fading sunlight. 'Apologizing?'

'I think I should . . . about the other night. You were quite right. I *was* drunk. And . . . and I suppose I was hoping Ben would put me up to save the drive back to Morpeth. It was good of you to take me in. Anyway, I'm sorry.'

Her lashes were lowered as she pondered on his words.

She gave an awkward little shrug. 'Ah, that's all right . . . You were clearly shaken when I told you about Ben, and well . . .' She took a deep breath. 'At the same time, that was a cheap shot of mine, saying you snored. I wouldn't have heard you anyway, from the other side of the house.' She smiled slightly. '*Do* you snore?'

'I've never heard myself.'

She laughed. It lit up her face, and for a brief moment he was surprised he had ever thought her plain. She paused, and stared at him thoughtfully. 'So what are we going to do about this Savoyard business, then?'

Arnold was surprised. 'We? It's not necessary to listen to what Ben was saying! I've no intention of trespassing on your time and using—'

'You won't be using me. I must admit I wasn't pleased when Ben sort of thrust me into it, but I had time to think about it while the two of you were talking later, and I'm not averse to helping out with the research. After all, it is my period, and it'll help me sketch in some background on my Vegetius . . .'

'The only thing I know about him was that he wrote: "Every conceivable resort should be tried before incurring the inevitable risks of battle." Always seemed eminently sensible to me.'

'Maybe we should have followed his precept,' she said, smiling again. 'Still, I'm only interested in him because Queen Eleanor commissioned a translation of his work on the art of war while Edward was on Crusade.'

'You're very interested in Eleanor.'

'I have a streak of feminism in me,' she admitted, smiling. 'I think Eleanor has never had the press she deserved. Married at twelve, dead at forty-nine, fifteen children, and yet she found time to do a great deal — and fascinate Edward for nearly forty years.'

'She was land-hungry,' Arnold demurred.

'Who wasn't, in that century? After all, land was the one stable thing in their lives, life was short and brutish, and the prospect of death constantly hung in the air like a murderous wisp of smoke . . .'

'You should use that in a book.'

'Already have.' She cocked her head to one side quizzically. 'Well, then, Arnold Landon, Uncle Ben has suggested we work together. Do you think our separate personalities could stand it?'

'I'm not sure,' Arnold replied reluctantly.

'I'm prepared to help . . . if you're willing to ask for help.' Arnold felt almost trapped by her words. He had no real desire to work with Jane Wilson. There were moments when he found her likeable enough, and she had intellectual qualities that he had perhaps not recognized in her book, but he had always been a loner, a bachelor who needed neither men nor women. He enjoyed his own company, his own way of life, his own obsessions and prejudices. Sharing them meant giving something away, and the gift might not be measured favourably. But he might need help, and he would feel churlish if he refused. He compromised.

'I'll tell you what. Let's leave it like this. I'm going down to Aykley Heads this evening to see if I can get Andrews's papers. There might be enough there for me to work on. If not, I'll call in at the Quayside and maybe we can work together.'

'All right, if you wish.' There was a shade of disappointment in her voice, and he realized she felt she was being dismissed. 'Give me a call if you need to.' She paused, then looked up, staring at him squarely, and honestly. 'You could just have said 'No'. I don't hurt easily. You can still say it.'

'Let me try Aykley Heads first,' he begged.

When she walked away to her car he felt absurdly guilty.

2

Detective Inspector Greybrook left his office and walked along the corridor to the interview room. He carried the file on Ken Andrews with him: it contained the notes he had taken on the day Andrews had been found, together with the results of various other inquiries that he had carried out in the meanwhile.

When he reached the interview room Dr Evans was already there. He was sprawled in a chair, smoking a Sobranie cigarette. He waved it at Greybrook. 'I know, it'll kill me. I've been given medical advice. But I see death each day and I fear it not. Do you fear death, Greybrook?'

'Can't say I think about it.'

'You're a stolid, predictable, committed copper, Greybrook. I've always said so. Something about you I can't fix, even so. I'm a good judge of character, you know — oddly enough, when you see cadavers stretched out day after day, uncomplaining while you poke around their innards, you get to think you know the quick also; pride yourself on your perceptiveness with the living. It's a sort of occupational hazard, I find. I know so much about the dead. I have an urge to become completely au fait with the living, too. You know what I mean?'

'No.'

'I guess not,' Evans agreed, nodding sagely. 'In fact, I'd be disappointed if you did, because it would be outside the boundary walls of your character. At least the way I see your character.' He waved the Sobranie expansively. 'You're not like many of the people I come into contact with on the Durham Force. You have imagination, but I feel it's stifled; you have ability, yet it's curtailed; you are probably capable of passion and love, but I detect a lonely man; you have ambition, but you have sacrificed it. What a compound! What a conglomeration!'

'What nonsense!'

Evans grinned. 'Maybe, but good, though, innit? And if my vision of Leo Greybrook is right, what lies underneath it all? An unhappy childhood? A failed marriage? The madness that comes from lonely masturbation?'

He prodded the air with his cigarette. 'Or is it something else? Maybe it's the constraints of a job that makes you see only the seamy side of life-Saturday night drunks, bludgeoned wives, hooligans and whores and hazards. Maybe it's an obsession that drives you on. Maybe it's a combination of all these things. Or maybe it's just that you can't stand Fred Redvers. Why the hell are we meeting in here, anyway? What's wrong with the Chief Superintendent's office?'

'Maybe he doesn't like word-drunk Welshmen staining his air with hyperbole.'

'And Sobranie.' Evans sighed. 'Ah well, we are an unloved race. In England.'

Greybrook sat down impassively. He placed the file on the table in front of him. There was no tremor in his hand, but he was aware his mouth was dry. He wasn't sure whether it was Evans, or the impending arrival of Redvers that disturbed him. He wasn't sure whether it might be something else.

Redvers's voice boomed out in the corridor beyond the door: an admonition to some unfortunate constable who had crossed his path. Greybrook's lips tightened: Evans was right in that respect at least. He detested the man. Not that he would be working with him much longer. He was suddenly aware that Evans was watching him, smiling. He smiled back, thinly. 'His Master's Voice.'

The door crashed open as Redvers entered.

'Good, you're here, Dr Evans. Greybrook, you brought your file, I see. Good.'

The Chief Superintendent sat down next to Evans. He seemed to be in a good humour. Greybrook knew he had been out to lunch in the officers' mess at Catterick and had returned only a couple of hours ago: the hospitality would have been liberal. Greybrook did not drink. Redvers had remarked on it from time to time, implying that a man who refused alcohol could not be a balanced policeman.

Whereas Redvers, in Greybrook's experience, often lost his balance.

'Fine, gentlemen, let's to business.' Redvers leaned back in his chair and looked first at Greybrook, then at Evans. 'Now then, I thought we'd better have a short conference about the Andrews business. Greybrook is here because he's acting as my number two on this—'

Doing the work, Greybrook amended sourly to himself.

'—and you, Dr Evans, are here because I'm really rather puzzled about certain aspects of your report on the death of Ken Andrews.'

'And what aspects would those be, may I ask?'

Redvers eyed the curling blue smoke distastefully. 'You seemed somewhat . . . noncommittal in your summation.'

'I don't follow.'

'The official view . . . bearing in mind all the facts . . . looking at all the circumstances . . . my view, is that Andrews committed suicide. You seem to hold other views.'

'Do I?' Evans asked innocently, blue eyes widening. 'I'm not sure I've advanced any opinion on the matter.'

'That's the point, Dr Evans,' Redvers said, an edge creeping into his tone. 'You say nothing about suicide, and you imply—'

'Doubt, Chief Superintendent, honest doubt. That's all. As I say often enough, I deal in facts, not theories. You guardians of the public weal are the ones who pull rabbits out of magicians' hats. I see; I note; I tell. But facts only.'

'And the facts add up to suicide.'

'That's your opinion. It is not necessarily mine,' Evans retorted smugly.

Redvers's mouth turned ugly. He was becoming angry. Greybrook intervened. 'I think you're being unhelpful, Dr Evans.'

'And I, Leo, think I'm being railroaded.'

There was a short silence. Somewhere in the room a fly began to buzz. Greybrook's eyes sought it out, as he waited for the explosion. It did not come.

Chief Superintendent Redvers was making an effort to control himself but his tone was edged with steel. 'Railroaded? I don't think I understand what you're trying to say, Dr Evans.'

'Haven't I made myself clear?' Evans asked sweetly. 'I really am sorry. I'll try to spell it out more positively for you. I've told you: I deal in facts. You raise theories — but please, raise them from the facts, or I get edgy. And what are the facts?'

He flicked up a pudgy finger.

'First, Andrews's head was blown apart by a shotgun shell. The muzzle of the sawn-off shotgun was thrust under his chin. He could have reached the trigger, certainly. It doesn't necessarily follow he did reach, and pull the trigger. Facts.'

He flicked up a second finger, leered, and held both fingers towards Redvers, tauntingly.

'As far as I understand, there has been no suicide note discovered on the premises. No intimation as to why he killed himself — if that's what he did. The papers on the desk in his study related, I understand, to the literary work he was involved in, and was interested in. Odd, to commit suicide when he was active and enjoying life, from what one gathers from photographs in the quality journals. Didn't I see *you* in *Northern Life* recently, Chief Superintendent?'

Redvers's eyes were glittering angrily as Evans flicked up a third finger.

'Then there's the matter of the back door. A little bird on the Force tells me — and please, don't shout at me, there are always little mynahs who can't keep their beaks shut — a little bird tells me there were signs of entry at the back around about the time of the shooting. Facts?'

'If you're suggesting—'

'I'm suggesting nothing!' Evans protested. 'I'm dealing in facts. There are probably facts I'm unaware of. Such as fingerprint tests. I have heard that there are no prints on the shotgun — just blurred impressions, maybe even a gloved hand. But I've heard nothing about other prints in the house. So I'm not inclined to venture theories and suggestions. I'm just prepared to sign a report that points to what I've discovered about time of death, cause of death, and other matters within my competence. Fairy tales — they are within your purview, gentlemen, not mine. And I won't be bullied into a statement I can't support in front of the coroner.'

'You think Andrews was murdered?' Greybrook asked quietly.

'I don't think you hear me,' Evans said softly. 'I haven't the faintest idea. He may have committed suicide. He may have been murdered. You come up with some more items for forensic analysis and maybe I'll support a theory. But at this stage, my report says all it's going to say.'

Redvers took a deep breath. 'I think you've made your position clear, Evans.'

'I'm so pleased.'

Redvers stood up. 'I don't think we can gain anything by pursuing this discussion. There's no reason to detain you further.'

'Then I'll wish you good evening. It is after seven-thirty, isn't it? Ah, so much to do, so little time . . .'

He smiled cheerily at Greybrook, and left the room, whistling softly. Redvers stood with his back to the door, looking out of the window. A soft rain was falling, whispering along the dark tarmac of the wide driveway. A small group of cadets emerged from the training hall and ran across to the main building, pushing each other and laughing as they ran.

'Welsh bastard!' Redvers said bitterly.

Greybrook sat still, one hand on the file in front of him.

He had been expecting Redvers to rage at the little doctor; his failure to do so had had a draining effect on Greybrook. He was no longer certain which way Redvers would react.

The Chief Superintendent swung away from the window.

His face was grim. 'All right, you've been doing the leg work. What've we got?'

Greybrook hesitated, choosing his words, and their intonation, with care. 'You're discarding the suicide theory, sir?'

Redvers glared at him. 'With that bloody noncommittal report we've little choice. Unless you've picked up something else to support it, we'll have to look elsewhere. Welsh bastard! With a more positive report we could have gone to the coroner. We've got more than enough on our plate already — a murder inquiry is the last thing we need, and I didn't want this thing crawling all over the papers! I asked you — what've we got?'

Greybrook opened the file. He shook his head. 'Not a great deal, I'm afraid, sir. First of all, we can't turn up any information on the shotgun. There's no evidence of ownership on Andrews's part. Indeed . . .' He faltered briefly. 'There's one report that suggests the weapon might have been used in a robbery in Sunderland two years ago.'

'What? How the hell can we know that?'

'It seems the weapon might briefly have been in the possession of the Durham police, sir.'

Redvers stared at him, his grey hair bristling. 'Oh my God . . . I don't want to know, Greybrook. You're not seriously suggesting we picked up that shotgun two years ago and then allowed it to get back into circulation?'

'We can't be sure, sir.'

'Bloody hell!' Redvers scratched at his cheek with a fierce anger. 'I want a check on that. We get a weapon used in a robbery and lose it, so it gets into the hands of some other murderous villain? My neck could be in a noose on this, Greybrook. Get an investigation started!'

'The trail is pretty cold, sir. The weapon went missing shortly after it was brought in, so I'm told.'

Redvers let out a frustrated bellow and thumped his fist on the table. He was silent for a few moments, breathing heavily, then he nodded. 'All right, what else have we got?' Greybrook hesitated. 'We've got a report on the fingerprints, sir.'

'And?'

'There was a crate of wine on the back doorstep. We've got a print on that, though it's not a good one. Got caught in the rain. There was a bottle and glass in the kitchen, on the worktop. Andrews's prints are on both, but there's someone else's as well.'

'Are those prints matched up anywhere else in the house?'

'Not that we've been able to find. Someone other than Andrews was in the kitchen — we can be sure of that, and the bottle and glass certainly carry two sets of prints only. Elsewhere, well, there's plenty of Andrews's of course, and others . . .'

'Have you picked up any prints you can identify?' Greybrook hesitated. 'Only one set, sir, apart from Andrews's.'

'In the house?'

'Yes, sir, in the study.'

'Whose?'

'Yours.'

Greybrook kept his head up, holding Redvers's glance.

The Chief Superintendent's eyes were cold, but little devils of anger seemed to dance in them as he glared at Greybrook. There was a moment when it seemed he might explode, but the moment passed and Redvers controlled himself to sneer. 'I imagine we'll find your prints in the house too, Greybrook, as an investigating officer.'

'I would doubt that, sir . . . I'm very careful.'

The room was still, apart from the fly buzzing at the window. Redvers was struggling with his thoughts, trying to suppress a surging anger. But Greybrook suspected there was an element of panic also, that made him curb himself in case he said too much. Redvers had no intention of explaining himself to a junior officer. 'All right, is there anything else? Anything missing?'

'Nothing obvious, sir. But we can't be sure. Certainly there was no ransacking of the place. On the other hand . . .'

'Yes?'

'There's something odd about one of the photographs taken by the police photographer.'

'What do you mean?' Redvers asked gruffly.

'When he arrived — before I knew you were coming, sir he took a couple of shots of the room. Now it might have been a trick of the light . . . you know, a flash bounces gleams off polished surfaces, but in one print it looks as though there's something white on top of the drinks cabinet. But I've checked it out: there's nothing on the cabinet itself.'

'It must be what you say,' Redvers said slowly. 'A trick of the light.'

'I just wondered, sir, whether you'd seen anything there, when you made your inspection of the room.'

Redvers paused. 'There was nothing on the cabinet . . . nothing I recall seeing.' He paused, clearly wanting to move on, and eyeing Greybrook distrustfully. 'So what about it, then? If we go along with Evans's report as it stands, we'll have to discount suicide. Do you have any thoughts on what happened?'

Greybrook looked at his hands. He shrugged. 'It can only be a loose theory, sir. We don't have the evidence yet. But the back door was open. Someone could have walked in, looking to burgle the house, been disturbed, tried to force Andrews to come up with some money and then the trigger got pulled. An accident, maybe; perhaps Andrews tried to grab the gun. There was no sign of any real struggle, but with a shotgun muzzle under your chin . . .'

'But nothing was taken.'

'After the gun went off, panic. He could have run out, scared at what he'd done.'

Redvers turned away, locked his hands behind his back and stared out of the window again. He said nothing for several minutes. At last, Greybrook asked, 'Do you want to see the photographs of the sitting room, sir?'

Redvers remained still for several long seconds. Then he shook his head. He turned, and stared coldly at Greybrook. 'You're moving to a new job. Private security firm, I understand, Greybrook.'

'Yes, sir.'

'When do you leave us?'

'I leave for Merseyside in three weeks.'

'Three weeks . . .' The grey skullcap of hair inclined slowly, nodding. 'Right. I'm stepping out of this investigation, Greybrook, and leaving it to you. But I'll be watching you. Three weeks . . . I want it cleared up before you go. Cleared up — or buried. You hear what I say?'

Greybrook heard. And understood.

* * *

Arnold stood at the reception desk at Aykley Heads and waited until the smart young woman in uniform smiled at him and asked if she could help.

'I have an appointment with Chief Superintendent Redvers.'

'Ah, yes, your name is . . . Mr Landon? Good, I'll see if he's free.'

She turned her attention to the switchboard. Arnold turned his attention to the small puddle of rainwater collecting at his feet. After leaving Jane Wilson at the hospital he had driven south to Durham and the clouds had opened. He'd been forced to use the public car park at Aykley Heads, which meant a short walk in the rain but it had been enough to make him wish he'd brought a raincoat. His jacket was damp, his trousers limp and sodden, after the sudden cloudburst.

'If you'd just like to take a seat and wait for a few moments someone will come down to escort you to the Chief Superintendent's office,' the young woman said, smiling a dazzling, police relationship smile.

Arnold did not sit down; he felt too damp and uncomfortable to do so. He had not long to wait, however, before a young cadet marched towards him and asked his name.

'Follow me, sir.'

They marched briskly up the stairs, the cadet saluting smartly as they passed a uniformed senior officer and proceeded along the corridor on the floor above. The cadet tapped on the glass door: Arnold entered the ante-room beyond. The woman sitting there smiled.

'Can you wait a moment? The Chief Superintendent is on the phone.'

The voice was a dull murmur from inside the office, but the intonation suggested to Arnold that he had not come at an auspicious time — there was an angry belligerence about the voice inside. Redvers was having some sort of argument over the phone and a few moments later there was a crashing sound.

The lady at the desk was clearly used to Redvers and the mayhem he committed on telephones. She smiled sweetly. 'You can go in now, I think, Mr Landon.'

A few moments later Arnold found himself facing Chief Superintendent Redvers. The man did not seem pleased to see him, and there were angry stains on his cheeks, the residue of the argument he had had over the phone. Arnold glanced at it: it was insecurely placed on its cradle, as though it had been banged down in temper.

'Mr Landon. Now what was it . . .' Redvers glanced at his diary, and then stiffened. He sat down, waved Arnold to a chair, and as Arnold lowered himself uncomfortably into it, Redvers said, 'You wanted something belonging to the man who . . . died at Bodicote Barn House.'

'That's right, Chief Superintendent.'

'What exactly is it you want?'

'Mr Andrews was working on a manuscript, to be published by Peter Aspen of Newcastle. Mr Aspen has his original notes and outlines, but the material itself would have been in the study. I've now been commissioned to carry on with the work and complete it for publication. Mr Aspen tells me there's a problem, in that the material is now held by the police and . . .'

'And you want it released.' Redvers leaned back in his chair, and folded his hands over his stomach. 'I'm afraid you've had a wasted journey, Mr Landon.'

'I'm sorry—'

'It's out of the question. The papers cannot be released to you. They form part of our investigations into the death of Mr Andrews. I'm sure you'll understand that.'

Arnold frowned. 'Forgive me, but I'm afraid I can't see why you need to hang on to the papers of a man who shot himself. They can have no bearing on—'

'We haven't said he shot himself,' Redvers interrupted. 'That's newspaper speculation, nothing more.'

'But the papers—'

'Cannot be released.' Redvers scowled at Arnold and ran a hand over his bullet-shaped skull, rasping his fingers through the short grey hair. His mouth was twisted sourly. 'I think you must have heard me first time, Mr Landon. And why you should want to get into the kind of muckraking activity that Andrews was involved in I can't imagine. Landon . . .' He paused thoughtfully, frowning as the name began to mean something to him. 'I've come across your name, surely. Landon . . . Weren't you involved in that business up at St Michael's Church?' He grunted when he saw the expression on Arnold's face. 'Right! All the more reason for me to refuse you access to those papers, dammit!'

Arnold was annoyed. The 'involvement' at St Michael's Church had made his name well known, but it had been innocent enough, and not sought after. He was moved to protest. 'Refusing me access is one thing, Chief Superintendent, if it's connected with your investigations, but I seem to detect you have other reasons to want to withhold property which is not yours to keep . . . and probably belongs to Peter Aspen in any case, in view of the advance he paid to Andrews!'

'What are you trying to say?' Redvers demanded belligerently.

'I'm trying to say nothing. I'm simply asking for access to papers relating to the work Andrews was doing on the Savoyards—'

'The who?'

Patiently Arnold explained. 'Andrews was working on a book about the Savoyards in Edward I's reign, and in particular Master James of St Georges.'

Redvers's eyes widened. 'Who the hell was he?'

'Does it matter?' Arnold asked wearily. 'I've been commissioned to complete the book. Now if it figures in your investigations — though I can't for the life of me see how — all right, I'll wait. But for how long? And in any case, what possible bearing—'

'The Savoyards.' Redvers was frowning, deep in thought.

There was a certain doubt around his mouth now, and his eyes were slitted, as though he were indulging in calculations he wanted to keep to himself. He drummed his fingers on the table in front of him. Arnold waited. At last, Redvers made up his mind. He even managed to raise a smile, or what passed for one, a wolfish grimace that vanished almost as soon as it was displayed.

'I have a feeling we've been at cross purposes, Mr Landon,' Redvers announced. It was as near to an apology as Arnold would get. 'We've been talking about different things, it seems. I think, in the circumstances, you'd better see Detective Inspector Greybrook.' He paused. 'Yes, Greybrook is the one to handle this . . .'

* * *

Detective Inspector Greybrook was about fifty years of age. He was tall, spare of frame and gave the impression of fitness. He walked lightly, like a cat, and indeed exuded the kind of wariness that Arnold noted among felines. He was quietly spoken and polite — a significant contrast to Chief Superintendent Redvers. Unlike his superior officer he did not show his emotions in his face: there was a control about him which made Arnold think he would not make friends easily, and would be a difficult man to know. There was also an odd tension about the man: his grey eyes were quick-moving, calculating, weighing words and movements and intentions. He would be an efficient policeman, Arnold guessed; one who would be committed to the task in hand.

'Sit down, Mr Landon. I understand you want access to Mr Andrews's papers. For what reason?'

Arnold explained again. When he had finished, Greybrook asked quietly, 'Chief Inspector Redvers was unwilling to give you access?'

'It seems so. I can't understand why. But he did say at the end that we were at cross purposes.'

'I see.' Greybrook sat down opposite Arnold and began to play with a pencil. Uncomfortable in his wet trousers, and steaming slightly in the warmth of the room, Arnold waited. 'The material you want to see relates to—'

'A study of the Savoyards.'

'And the Chief Inspector thought you wanted the other material. And didn't want to give it to you.'

'I didn't even know there was other material. At least—'

'Yes?' The grey eyes were fixed intently on him.

'Well, I had heard that Andrews had been commissioned to do two books. By Peter Aspen.'

'Aspen. Ah yes . . .' Greybrook lowered his head, as though he wanted Arnold to read nothing in his eyes. 'Do you know what the other book was about?'

'Not really.'

'Well, I'm certain Mr Aspen will be able to tell you. I don't understand such things myself. However . . .' He grimaced, as though he was finding it difficult to find the right words. 'I find myself in a difficult situation, Mr Landon. The investigation into Andrews's death continues, but we don't at this stage have much to go on. It could be there *is* something in the material we now hold—'

'On the Savoyards? Surely not!'

'Probably not, I agree. But I can't be sure. I'll need to look, get a view of the contents. I've already taken a preliminary glance at the other material. I have a view . . .'

He paused, staring vaguely past Arnold, out of the window. The rainstorm had passed over, and late evening sunlight filtered weakly into the room. The pencil in Greybrook's hands was turned, over and over, rhythmically, as Arnold waited. At last, Greybrook seemed to reach a decision.

'All right, Mr Landon, I wonder whether we could come to some sort of agreement? Give me a few days to look over the Savoyard material, and then I hope I'll be able to let you have it. You can do your worst with it then.' He smiled, but it lacked warmth or mirth: there was a preoccupied air about the man that made the smile almost meaningless. 'Meanwhile . . . I hope I can be frank, Mr Landon?'

'Of course,' Arnold said, puzzled.

'I wouldn't want this to go further than you and me at this stage. I'm hoping you'll respect my confidence. The fact is, I've looked at the other material . . . and I get the impression there's something missing. I don't want to do anything about it, formally, at this stage. I won't explain my reasons, Mr Landon.' Again the edgy smile came and went. 'Let me just say I'd appreciate it if you could ask Mr Aspen, when you see him, just what the book is intended to cover.'

'I don't understand.'

Greybrook hesitated. 'Well, specifically, ask him if it's intended to deal with . . . any local . . . colour.'

'Durham?'

'Durham, Northumberland . . . the North,' Greybrook replied vaguely. 'Could you do that for me? If you can find out, perhaps we could have a word. By then, I imagine, I would be able to release the Savoyard material. Like you, I can't really see it's relevant to Andrews's death. Whereas . . .'

He left the rest unsaid. But Arnold was left with the clear impression that the mysterious 'occultish' book, as Ben Gibson had described it, might well have had some connection with the death of the man in Bodicote Barn House.

3

It was several days before Arnold was able to make arrangements to meet Peter Aspen. It proved difficult to arrange a mutually convenient time: Aspen was in London on the first two occasions Arnold was available, and thereafter a planning inquiry kept Arnold so busy he was unable to think of anything else.

The Senior Planning Officer was making life difficult also.

He disapproved violently of Arnold's pursuit of his own personal interests, not least because there had been occasions both during his time and in that of his predecessor when unwelcome publicity had been visited on the department. He was clearly of the opinion that the best way to make Arnold toe the line of departmental policy — his policy — of low profile endeavour, was to keep Arnold extremely busy. The workload schedules were therefore geared to leave Arnold with as little time to think as possible. It was a policy also designed to keep him in the office.

He found it inhibiting. There were various tasks that demanded site inspection and, where this opportunity was denied him, it meant he was working with rather less information than he required for some of the files. He had tried to fix an interview with the Senior Planning Officer to discuss the matter, but that gentleman had a disconcerting habit of avoiding personal confrontations with his staff by fixing an appointment several days in advance and then not being available when the time came. It was a good system: painful interviews could be delayed almost permanently in this way.

Consequently, it was a Friday evening before Arnold was able to get free of his work schedules and discover, coincidentally, that Peter Aspen was free to see him in Newcastle. Arnold had made no contact with Jane Wilson and he hesitated over the thought that he had been churlish not to tell her what was happening — or rather, not happening. He toyed with the idea of phoning her now that he had arranged to go to Newcastle, but finally discarded it. Their arrangement was that he would get in touch if he needed help; he had no idea yet what help he might need.

He left Morpeth at six and took the A1 south to Newcastle. The air was heavy and muggy; there was the occasional distant growl of thunder and in the dark sky above the sea pale lightning flickered and glowed, illuminating the surly horizon. He had a slight headache — probably presaging the storm. It could also have been the result of his workload, and the frustration that went with it. In many ways it would be a relief to do something different and undertake the work on the Savoyards. There was also the thought that he would be able to spend the weekend working out in the open, at Flint, or Harlech, or Conwy. The traffic flooding out of Newcastle was heavy, but running south into the city it was relatively light. Arnold had arranged to meet Aspen at his office just off the Shields Road, so he swung left away from the city centre and drove through some back streets until he was heading for Byker. As the shop fronts began to thin he checked on the address Aspen had given him. He found the place without too much difficulty.

It was not as grand as he had thought it might be. Publishing, he had been told, was a business for gentlemen. Peter Aspen had all the appearances of a gentleman: well-cut suits, a genteel manner, but the offices he used were elderly, shabby, and not in the best part of town. The building had been erected in the thirties. From the upper storeys, there was probably a view of the rusting gantries at the docks, but the exterior of the building was grey and uninspiring, paint peeling from the window frames, with the sign outside lacking the *P* in the owner's name.

Arnold parked his car with some trepidation in a side street. He hoped his radio would still be intact when he re-emerged from the offices of Aspen Publishing Ltd.

The entrance foyer was rather better furbished than he had expected. An elderly lady with a Gateshead accent and spectacles in which one lens was cracked, greeted him. 'Me grandson,' she said, indicating the cracked lens. 'Bring him in sometimes, babysittin', like. The boss don't mind — seems to like the little 'un. Can I help you, hinny?'

'I have an appointment with Mr Aspen.'

'Oh aye, the boss. I'll just make sure he's in. I'm off in a moment but I think he's stayin' on for to see you.' She buzzed the phone. 'There's a gentleman here to see yer, pet. Shall I send him up?'

She nodded, replaced the phone, and readjusted her glasses. 'He says you can go on up. First floor — his name's on the door. Lovely man, Mr Aspen. Wonderful fond of kiddies, he is. See you, hinny.'

Arnold made his way up the stairs to the first floor. The glass in the door at the end of the corridor bore the legend: Peter Aspen, Managing Director. Arnold tapped on the door and went in.

Peter Aspen was alone in the book-lined room, as elegantly dressed as before. He was seated behind a leather-topped desk, reading a manuscript. He looked up as Arnold entered and he sighed, tossing the manuscript to one side on his desk. 'Yet another Geordie dialect story. A charmless accent, anyhow. Someone ought to have cottoned on to the fact that they're ten a penny now. Glad you could make it, Mr Landon. Please take a seat. Would you care for a drink?'

So it was still a gentleman's profession, Arnold thought. 'Anything you've got,' he suggested.

'I can offer you a reasonable malt.'

'Thanks very much.'

Aspen concentrated on pouring the golden liquid into two small glasses. He handed one to Arnold. 'Mud in your eye.'

'Of course,' Arnold muttered, and sipped gingerly at the fiery whisky.

Peter Aspen slid elegantly into a Louis Quinze chair beside Arnold and smiled genially. 'So, how have you got on, then?'

Arnold shook his head. 'Not too well, I'm afraid. The police won't release the materials until they've had a chance to discount them from their investigations.'

'Absurd, isn't it? Did they give you a timescale?'

'I'm afraid not.'

'Ah well, not to worry. I have Andrews's notes and outlines. I've put them in that box file over there. You can take them with you and see what you make of them. I'm beginning to wonder whether we shouldn't even discard the lot and give you free rein to start from scratch. We might get a more effective book that way.'

'I don't pretend to be an expert,' Arnold said carefully. 'I think the notes should prove useful.'

'I suppose so . . . but you already know a fair bit about Master James of St Georges, don't you?'

Arnold shrugged self-deprecatingly. 'I've read a great deal about the mediaeval master masons. I have a view, also, though there are no records I'm aware of, that Edward I met Master James for the first time at St Georges d'Espéranche on Edward's return from the Crusade. It's generally known, certainly, that Master James had been recruited, by 1278, to ordain the works of the castles in Wales.'

'Andrews was of the opinion he had a hand in the whole chain.'

'I'm not too certain about that. He was employed throughout the second Welsh war and stayed with Edward until he was summoned to Gascony in 1287. He was certainly responsible for Beaumaris on Anglesey, and the building contracts at Conwy show he was allocating work to teams of masons. He employed a number of Savoyards: there were important English masons like Walter of Hereford around, but the Savoyards were the elite of the men employed in castle building.'

'How will you be able to find out whether Master James was involved — other than from the records, I mean?' Aspen asked.

'Design,' Arnold said simply. 'By the thirteenth century the motte and bailey forms had been left behind. Curtain walls, flanking towers, polygonal enclosures, towered gatehouses — they all provide clues. In Edward's castles the old elements of keeps, towers, gatehouses and curtain walls were all employed but Master James developed them in more complex ways, without actually adopting any totally radical innovations.'

'Mmmm.' Peter Aspen sipped his whisky. 'Well, you seem to be *au fait* with the subject, anyway. No doubt you'll find a lot of the stuff Andrews did naïve and superficial — it may be you'll be able to bring a tighter control to the work.'

'My writing experience—'

'I told you,' Aspen smiled, 'don't worry about it. I can get it knocked into shape. Might even take a hand myself, if I think it's really interesting.'

Arnold hesitated. He sipped his whisky, feeling it burning his throat, and he coughed. Reluctantly he said, 'I was talking to . . . to Ben Gibson, in hospital. He was telling me that Andrews was actually working on two books for you.'

'That's right. Did I not mention it to you? I hardly think the other would be up your street, though. And in fact—' a cloud touched Aspen's eyes; he stroked his hollow cheeks unhappily — 'I've already spent money on that book, given an advance to Andrews and so on, and I'm beginning to regret I bothered. It's making a number of people unhappy.'

'Why?'

Aspen fluttered his hands evasively. 'Oh, you know how people are.'

'Ben said the book was "occultish".'

Aspen smiled. 'Hardly a precise definition. There are elements of the occult, I suppose . . .'

'So what's the theme of the book?' Arnold asked curiously.

'The Rosicrucians. Ken Andrews and I were . . . in contact from time to time, and at a dinner party in Durham one evening we got to talking about the Rosicrucians. I must have been a bit in my cups, or I wouldn't have commissioned it. But he was talking to me about the castle of Mont St-Jean, how the owner at the end of the last century recalled a family tradition about discovering a cellar where eight skeletons were found. Together with two shields and an iron coffer full of rings. Then in 1849 there was the unearthing of stone coffins in the neighbouring chateau of St Sabine . . .'

'What's that got to do with the Rosicrucians?'

'Well, they were probably deliberately planted there — it was all about lending a spurious antiquity to a relatively modern secret society, in this case the Brotherhood of the Rosy Cross. They wanted to claim descent from the Templar's, just as the Freemasons did. All really rather childish. But . . . well, Andrews considered there was a rather more sinister side to it all.'

'I can't say I know a great deal about the Rosicrucians,' Arnold said.

'Sort of second order Freemasonry,' Aspen suggested dismissively. 'But with a similar degree of opportunity for corruption.'

Arnold chose his words with care. 'Was Ken Andrews looking at that aspect . . . the corruption, I mean?'

Peter Aspen was silent for a moment. He seemed to be about to reply when he paused, his attention seemingly diverted. He frowned, cocking his head on one side. 'Did you hear something just then, Mr Landon?'

'Such as?'

'Mrs Langholme . . . the lady in reception . . . she'll have gone by now, I imagine,' Aspen said, almost to himself.

'She told me she was just about to leave.'

'Mmmm. Yes. Perhaps the door . . . what was it you were saying, Landon?'

'I was asking whether Andrews was researching into corruption in the Rosicrucians, and whether there was any local colour to the—'

Peter Aspen stood up abruptly. Startled, Arnold looked up at him, wondering what he had said to disturb the publisher.

'Excuse me a moment,' Aspen said. He looked agitated as he strode towards the door. He opened it, and stepped out into the corridor. The door was left slightly ajar, and Arnold heard Aspen calling out. 'Hello? Is there someone there?'

There was a short silence and then Arnold heard what the more sensitively attuned hearing of Peter Aspen had already picked up. Someone was coming up the stairs to the first floor. The one-lensed Mrs Langholme must have left the front door to the building unlocked.

* * *

The tread was heavy, and measured. The footsteps echoed on the empty stairs. They reached the corridor, and stopped. 'Aspen! So there you are! I'm glad I caught you.'

'Oh, it's you! I'm sorry, but it's not really convenient just now—'

'You can dispense with that bullshit, Aspen! I've been trying to get hold of you for days. Running off to London only delays this inevitable confrontation, my friend. It's time you and I had a talk — face to face.'

'Really, I'm serious. I have another appointment—' Arnold heard a short, explosively unpleasant laugh.

'To hell with that. Now I've got you, I intend talking plainly. You've been avoiding me, and avoiding this conversation. Don't you think I'm serious, you miserable little bastard?'

'I don't know how you got in,' Aspen protested in the corridor, 'but I must ask you to leave. I have nothing to say to you, no desire to have any convers—'

There was a sudden scuffling sound, and a gasp of surprise. Arnold rose to his feet in embarrassment as he thought he heard a brief whimper of pain.

Moreover, he was puzzled. Aspen's voice was clearly identifiable, but the other man's voice also sounded familiar. Out of context like this it was difficult to place, but he had heard it recently.

'Oh no you don't, you miserable little worm. You don't walk away. You don't turn your back on me! I've got you now, and you're going to listen to what I say. I warned you, like I warned that queer Andrews—'

'Please, you're hurting my arm!'

'Don't you understand? I'll break your bloody neck if you don't listen to what I've got to say. I warned you, I warned him, but there must be some stupid block in your mind as there was in his. So I'll say it again — and plainly, this time. I'm a busy man and a successful one. I've got a lot of important contacts, and I'm not afraid of using them. Moreover, if you keep going the way you are, I won't be the only one down on your neck.'

'Publishers have a duty—'

'Don't make me laugh! Duty? You're a backstreet tuppenny shyster who's never published a worthwhile book in his life! You're incapable of turning a decent quid, and you're just out to ruin honest reputations, spread innuendo about things you can't prove and couldn't prove in a million years. But the kind of rumour you'd be peddling can damage a man . . . and his business. I make no secret of that. So all you have to do . . . now . . . is tell me you're killing the project, and we can be friends.'

'But there's nothing—'

'I know different. I've seen some of the notes, damn you! You can't fool me with your whining. I'm warning you, kill the project or maybe what happened to Andrews could happen to you one dark night!'

'All right, all right! I'll do as you say, if you just let go my arm!'

There was a grunt, and another whimper. Arnold moved towards the door: the voice . . . he could almost put a name to it, but the name danced tantalizingly out of his reach.

'I think you've broken my wrist,' Aspen said complainingly. 'There's no need for this kind of behaviour. We could have talked it over like civilized human beings—'

'With you asking for some "compensation" for giving up the project,' the voice retorted sneeringly. 'You don't fool me. Both you and Andrews will have cooked this up at one of your effete cocktail parties, I've no doubt. The whole idea was to put the screws on, wasn't it? Pity it's all falling apart. Andrews's unfortunate demise has changed things, hasn't it? You've no real support now — and you haven't got the guts to carry it through by yourself. At least, you'd better not have the guts.'

'Please. Keep your voice down. And I've told you . . . I agree, I'll shelve the project.'

'Ditch, my friend, not shelve. Because there's two can play at that game.'

There was a short silence. Arnold stood at the door.

Aspen's voice was sullen. 'What's that supposed to mean?'

'I'll break every bone in your body if you publish that material. But maybe I'll leave you alive. Because there's other things I can do as well. There are skeletons . . . and skeletons, aren't there, Aspen?'

'I don't know what you're talking about.'

'I think you do. I told you . . . I have friends, important friends. Some of them have had their eye on you for some time. Certain activities up at Hamsterley Forest, for instance. You wouldn't like to have that sort of fun and games made public, would you?'

'I don't know what you're talking about!' Aspen blustered. 'And for God's sake, keep your voice down!'

‘Now the shoe’s on the other foot, and you don’t enjoy it, do you?’ the voice jeered.

And as he stepped into the half-open doorway Arnold recognized the voice at last . . . at the same time as he found himself staring eye to eye across a distance of fifteen feet with Councillor Sandy Bryman.

* * *

Bryman’s thickset brows drew together in an astonished frown. Peter Aspen was standing near him, leaning against the wall, nursing his left arm. Clearly, the shorter but more muscularly aggressive Bryman had seized his wrist, twisted his arm behind his back as he bullied him into submission in the corridor. But that was all forgotten now by Bryman as he gazed in bewilderment at the officer who serviced his planning committee.

‘Landon! What the bloody hell are you doing here?’ Arnold looked past him to Peter Aspen, almost in tears, gently massaging his wrist. ‘I might ask you the same question, Councillor,’ Arnold replied coldly.

Bryman stared at him grimly, then switched his attention to Aspen. He glared at the publisher for several seconds, and then turned slowly to stare at Arnold again. ‘What have *you* got to do with Aspen?’

‘I’m not certain it’s any of your business,’ Arnold replied with a boldness that surprised even himself. ‘But I don’t mind telling you. I’ve agreed to work on a mediaeval project for Mr Aspen.’

‘A med . . .’ Mad lights danced in Bryman’s eyes suddenly. He jerked a stubby thumb in Arnold’s direction, as though he wished it was thudding into an eyeball. ‘Are you involved with this thing too?’

‘What thing?’

Peter Aspen lurched away from the wall. ‘No, you’ve got it wrong, Bryman, he—’

‘If you are, I’ll have your job, Landon.’ Bryman was breathing heavily, almost insensate with a sudden surge of rage. ‘I’ve heard often enough you spend half your life interfering into other people's affairs, without getting on with your own job.'

'I resent that.'

'Resent away, my friend. I just thought you were an uncooperative bastard and too clever by half, but while I could ride that, I won't ride your poking your nose into my private or business affairs!'

'I told you, you've got it wrong!' Aspen insisted. 'I've asked Landon to work on an entirely different project. For God's sake, Bryman, you've said enough—'

The thickset man was hardly listening. He was glaring at Arnold with a barely veiled malevolence, and his lips were set tight above clenched teeth. He took two stiff steps forward. 'You were skulking in there, Landon. I've no doubt you heard most of what went on out here. So you'll be under no illusions. This is no game here. I want to be sure you'll know I'm serious. I don't brook interference in my affairs from anyone.'

'Bryman—' Peter Aspen moaned.

'Stay away from me, Landon; stay out of my way. If you don't . . . I'll break you! Just like I've broken others, in the past.'

His rage was drawn under control, slowly. He unclenched his fists, and Arnold felt the sweat cooling under his shirt as Bryman stepped back, turned and looked again at Aspen. 'And you . . . I've said enough to you. Do what you agreed . . . or you'll end up worse than Andrews!'

Bryman strode off, almost strutting, his heels echoing heavily in the corridor, and clumping down the stairs. Aspen sagged against the wall. His face was grey, drained of all colour.

'Are you all right?' Arnold asked. His own mouth was dry, and he was trembling slightly now the threat of violence was past.

'Just leave me alone, please,' Aspen replied, shaking his head. 'I'll be all right.' He staggered, belying his words, and suddenly his lean form seemed very frail. He held out a hand. 'Would you mind . . .'

Arnold took his arm and helped him back to his room.

Aspen gestured towards the bottle of malt whisky: Arnold poured him a stiff glass. Aspen took a hefty swallow, and shuddered. His eyes were bleary and defeated as he looked up at Arnold. 'I'll be all right, now. You . . . you'd better go.'

'If you're sure . . .'

'I'll be all right.'

Arnold nodded uncertainly and walked towards the door.

He had just reached it when Aspen called out, stopping him.

'Mr Landon, I'm sorry you got involved in that . . . unpleasant scene.' He was dragging around him some elements of whatever dignity was left to him. 'I . . . I think it would be as well if we . . . if we forgot the agreement we reached.'

Arnold frowned. 'I don't understand. The Savoyards . . . it's nothing to do with Bryman, is it?'

Aspen shook his head. 'No, it's not that. But that man . . .' His eyes glazed, hopelessly. 'I . . . I feel tired. I think I've had enough of the publishing game. It's time I went back south . . . The North, it's never really suited me.' He focused again on Arnold. 'I'm sorry . . . I hope you've not been put to too much trouble. But you do understand, don't you? I think things are better left well alone.'

'You want me to forget the Savoyard project? You no longer want to publish it?'

Peter Aspen nodded weakly.

There was little argument Arnold could raise. He nodded in his turn, and quietly closed the door behind him.

* * *

The following Monday morning a message came down to him from the Senior Planning Officer: he was required to attend at his office. Immediately.

Arnold made his way to the office. The Senior Planning Officer was in a state of some nervous tension. He was standing near the window, overlooking the car park, and his left hand gripped the chairback behind his desk. The knuckles were white: he had a horror of unpleasant scenes. He did not ask Arnold to sit down.

'Are your files up to date, Landon?'

'More or less,' Arnold replied. 'There are just two I haven't yet completed—'

'I presume Johnson could take them over from you without too much difficulty?'

'I imagine he could. Is there any particular reason—'

'In the public service, Landon, one must be like Caesar's wife — above suspicion. Trust is all; without trust, the whole service can collapse.'

'I'm not certain I understand what you're talking about,' Arnold said slowly.

'I am a man who trusts all,' the Senior Planning Officer said grandly, 'until I am let down. Thereafter, I am unable to trust the person in question again.'

'You'll have to be a bit more specific,' Arnold said quietly. 'Are you suggesting—'

The Senior Planning Officer waved an imperious hand. 'There's been a complaint, Mr Landon.'

'A complaint? About my work?'

'The complaint relates to the misapplication of expenses.'

'You can't be serious!'

'I am completely serious, Mr Landon. You will appreciate that a complaint of this nature and gravity cannot be ignored; it must be investigated. Accordingly, you will hand over your files to Mr Johnson.'

The Senior Planning Officer sniffed, his nostrils twitching unpleasantly. 'And I must explain to you that during the process of investigation, your presence in these offices would naturally be an undesirable embarrassment. You will, of course, continue to receive your pay, but, as from this moment, and until further notice, Mr Landon, you are suspended from all duties in this department!'

CHAPTER THREE

1

There was usually pickings to be had at the back of the Three Tuns. And if there was nothing there, it was only a short walk down to the Royal County. And across the road, overlooking the river at Elvet Bridge, there were sometimes leavings from the afternoon people who lunched there, and threw away half of what they bought.

Not that Foxy was very hungry.

He had set off from the gully feeling hollow and edgy, and it had been a long, tiring walk down into the city. But on the way he'd passed the college and there'd been some students on the grass and they'd left a couple of cans and a half-empty bottle of wine while they went off under the trees to do other things than eat. Foxy had giggled about that. There had been a time for him too, but that was long ago and long since gone. He'd picked up the cans and the bottle and walked across the field towards the cathedral on the skyline, drinking as he went.

The windfall had fortified him; warmed him, and emboldened him. He had clambered over a rickety fence and taken a short cut through a prim little garden. A woman had shouted at him when he blundered into the clothes line but he hadn't bothered to turn around. He'd shambled on into the avenue, and climbed the steep little rise until his breathing became laboured and he was getting pains in his chest, and then he stopped for a breather, leaning against a red, highly polished car.

That was when the man with a face the colour of his car, it seemed to Foxy, came out of the house. 'Hey, you! Get away from my car! What the hell are you doing around here . . . shove off, you filthy tramp!'

He had pushed at Foxy and Foxy had been pleased at the way the man had stepped back when Foxy bared his teeth and snarled at him. He wasn't to know Foxy didn't have the strength — or the inclination, for that matter — to raise a fist these days, but no one liked to see Foxy's black teeth bared. It did wonderful things to people.

With the liquor warm in his belly, Foxy wandered on happily, out of the avenue, and once he'd crossed the main road, to a blaring of car horns he was on the descent to the city.

It was a warm morning and there was the sound of bells in the air. It was probably a Sunday, he decided, but no matter: people ate out in the hotels on Saturday nights, and the bins at the back of the Three Tuns might contain some choice items. He wasn't all that hungry, but a tasty morsel here, a tasty morsel there . . .

He'd known what it was like to live in style. He remembered it vaguely, but it was a long time ago.

He tried the Three Tuns first, but there was someone parking his car in the street and he went into the hotel when he saw Foxy and shortly afterwards a young man in a uniform came out. 'You! Shove off! We're getting complaints. And stay away from those bins.'

There was only cabbage leaves anyway.

The Royal County looked like yielding nothing at first, but tucked away behind the gate he found another bottle, dropped by a late-night reveller. Students again, probably:

Saturday nights they didn't know how to handle their booze. Got drunk, walked out with bottles of Newcastle

Brown, left half of it to go to waste, unless Foxy or others of the fraternity happened along.

He finished the bottle. It gave him confidence, and more.

It was not that he minded students: it was merely that they didn't deserve all they had. You could tell, by the way they left food and drink lying around.

It didn't ought to be allowed.

There was something illogical in the thought, he knew that, for their leavings sustained him, but they didn't deserve it, just the same.

He crossed the road at the lights, confused by their changes but in the end ignoring them. Someone swore at him. He walked onto Elvet Bridge and leaned against the parapet, staring with glazed eyes at the skiffs moored outside the University Boat Club. He could make out, vaguely, young men in shorts preparing to take to the river. Students.

He shouted at them.

It sounded good. Swifts wheeled out from under the arch of the bridge, and his voice seemed to reverberate against the slow-moving waters of the river. He shouted again, adding those obscenities that still interested him, cursing the student brotherhood, and spitting into the water that was about to receive their boats.

He turned, leaning with his back against the parapet and gave a black-toothed grimace to three elderly women, walking across the bridge in their Sunday best, headed for the cathedral. They hurried past, and he began to mince after them, laughing hollowly, and chanting a half-forgotten hymn.

'*All things bright and beautiful,*

All creatures great and small . . .'

He had to repeat the lines. He'd forgotten the rest, and somehow, the tune didn't seem quite right either. He stopped, and returned to the parapet. The students were taking to the water.

'Bastards!' he shouted.

'All right, Foxy, that'll do. Don't you know it's Sunday?' Foxy swivelled his head with difficulty. There was a policeman standing behind him. He was tall and young and he sounded alright. The police never gave Foxy much trouble, if he behaved himself.

'It's the students,' he mumbled.

'Yes, it's always the students, but I think you'd better move on. We've been having complaints, Foxy. What are you doing down here on a Sunday, anyway? You're better off back on the hill, so come on, move on away now, laddie.'

Sunday. Not often he came on a Sunday. 'Been having bad dreams,' he mumbled.

'Happens to us all, laddie. Come on now, turn around, across the bridge. I'll see you over at the lights, then away home, hey?'

'I . . . I didn't do it.'

'Sure you didn't,' the policeman soothed.

'He was like it when I was there.'

'Come on, now, down to the lights.'

Foxy did as he was told. But he had mentioned the dreams, and they were coming back to him now. There were intermittent flashes of terror in the darkness, and they disturbed him in the gully. It wasn't in the gully, it had been elsewhere, but there had been blood.

'There was blood,' he said.

They had reached the lights. The policeman was standing there, not touching Foxy — they rarely touched him — but holding out a warning hand, restraining him.

'There'll be more blood if you step out into the road before I tell you,' the policeman said.

'Not in the road. On his head. And on the wall . . . no, he didn't have a head . . .'

'You been trying to catch rabbits again, Foxy?' The policeman stepped forward. 'Come on, you can cross now but look lively.'

'Walls,' Foxy muttered. 'I didn't do it . . . but there was blood. And I get the bad dreams.'

They had reached the pavement. The policeman was staring at him. 'In the gully?' he asked. 'You mean there's blood in the gully, Foxy?'

Foxy was seized with a sudden impatience. 'I'm going home,' he muttered. 'Not in the gully. In the house.'

The policeman was walking beside him. His voice was quieter, more gentle. 'You getting bad dreams about blood on a wall, Foxy?'

'In a house. Going home now.'

He shambled away. He was suddenly nervous. There were eyes digging into his back. The black, blood-drenched dreams were coming back more forcibly, here in the bright morning, but there was the policeman too. They didn't hassle him much, the coppers, not if he behaved himself. But somehow he hadn't behaved himself. He couldn't talk to the police . . . it was dangerous.

He stopped, looked back hazily at the young policeman.

The copper was talking to himself, talking to his jacket lapel. There was a crackling noise, radio noise.

Foxy shook his head, turned, began to walk on up the hill. He should have stayed home; he shouldn't have gone down into the city. They were bad dreams.

'Foxy! Hold on a moment. I want a word with you, old man!'

An inexplicable terror gripped Foxy Fernlea. He shook his head, his wispy beard waving, and he shambled into a run.

* * *

'God almighty,' Detective Sergeant Eyre said disgustedly. 'Can't we get the window open? It smells like a pigsty in here!'

He stared at the filthy overcoat of the man slumped in the chair, wispy beard sunk on his chest, glazed eyes staring vacantly at the table and he shook his head. 'When the hell did he wash last?'

The constable who had radioed in shook his head. 'He lives rough, up on the hill.'

'He must scare off every animal down wind of him for miles,' Eyre replied. 'I've always wondered what a skunk would smell like — now I can guess. Anyway, what have you got so far?'

'Just nonsense, really. But he keeps talking about blood on a wall, and a man with no head, and bad dreams, and I thought . . .'

'Mmm. All right, son.' Eyre looked thoughtfully at the vagrant slumped in the chair. 'You did right, calling for a car. It'll have to be fumigated now, I imagine. We'll dock it out of your pay.'

'Sarge—'

'Wrap up, I'm not serious. But if I'm to talk to this guy in this atmosphere, it'd better be worth it, son! Where did you say this character lives?'

'In a gully. Up beyond Bodicote Farm. He's well enough known in Durham — been shambling around the city for years.'

'Yeah. All right.' Eyre paused thoughtfully. 'Get him a cup of tea, and see if you can arrange for fingerprinting. I don't think he'll stand on his rights.'

'No, he's pretty cooperative, is Foxy.'

'All right, get the tea.' Eyre eyed the vagrant in the chair. 'So it's Foxy, hey?'

When the constable had gone, Eyre hitched up a chair facing the man slumped beside the bare table. He stared at him, noting the rimed dirt on his cheeks, the paler areas around the eyes, the wispy beard. It was impossible to tell how old he was, but though years of alcohol had taken their toll the man was not a complete wreck. His wrists were bony, but he was lean, and wiry in build.

Eyre grimaced. 'Foxy . . . hey, Foxy . . . tell me about these dreams.'

* * *

An hour later Chief Superintendent Redvers stood in the doorway beside Eyre. The senior officer wrinkled his nose. He glared distastefully at Foxy Fernlea where he sat, an empty teacup in front of him, snoring gently as he snoozed, unburdened, in the chair.

'This is it?' Redvers snorted derisively.

'I think he was up at the house, sir,' Eyre replied stolidly.

'What's he had to say?'

'It's a garbled story, and difficult to make out. He keeps confusing his dreams with reality, I think. But apparently he's well known to officers on the beat in the city. A vagrant . . . always causing trouble, put one of our sergeants in hospital, a few years back, but apart from that conviction, nothing particularly serious. Just complaints from the public about his swearing and carrying on when he's had a drink.'

'He lives rough?'

'On the hill above Bodicote.'

Redvers bared his teeth in a grimace. 'Bodicote . . . and you say dreams . . . and reality. What's the reality?'

'As far as I can make out, he was up at Bodicote at some time or another. I think he saw the blood there, on the wall. I think he saw the dead man, Andrews. He's also been muttering about seeing someone up there, in the lane, but it's all confusing.'

Redvers's eyes were slitted malevolently. 'Seeing someone in the lane. He's bound to say that, isn't he? Even in his state, he'd want to suggest that someone else was up there. An automatic defensive reaction.' Redvers snorted derisively. 'They're all the same, these villains. Take us for fools. Dreams and reality, hey? Well, we'll just have to sort out the one from the other, won't we? You've arranged for his prints to be taken?'

'Yes, sir.'

'Right,' Redvers snarled decisively. 'I have a feeling we've made a breakthrough here. Get him washed, cleaned up. And sober. We'll hold him for questioning. And I want no bloody nonsense about lawyers either. Not that I can imagine he'd ask for one. For that matter, I doubt if he could get a lawyer to come within a mile of him!'

'Sir?'

Redvers swung around. Detective Inspector Greybrook was standing behind him in the corridor. 'I've just got back from Chester-le-Street, sir. I heard that—'

'You heard that we've pulled in a suspect in the Andrews killing.' There was a glitter of triumph in Redvers's malicious eyes. 'Yes. While you've been sitting on your arse doing God knows what in Chester-le-Street one of our innocent, wet-nosed young constables has pulled in the man who probably killed Andrews! It looks as though we'll get this case wrapped up before you leave us after all, Greybrook — but it'll be no bloody thanks to you!'

* * *

The police car stopped at Bodicote Farm and Greybrook got out with the young constable who had brought Foxy Fernlea into Aykley Heads. Greybrook looked around him. Bodicote Barn House was over the rim of the hill; across to the right was the drive leading to the Country Manor Hotel. Ahead of them the hill rose steeply, thinly scattered with alder and beech trees. Half a dozen sheep grazed on the hill, and a rabbit sat watching them from the shelter of the hedge, whiskers twitching, ready to bolt as soon as they moved.

Greybrook turned to the young constable. 'Show me.' The constable pointed ahead. 'There's a gully up there, sir. I used to play up there as a kid. We used to creep up on old Foxy, in fact: you know what kids are like. We used to throw old cans at him, and he'd come charging out, swearing like a maniac. We'd run like hell, then: we were pretty scared of him, I can tell you, but it was excitement, you know? And he never stood a chance of catching us.'

They walked up across the field. 'Does he have a record of violence?' Greybrook asked.

'Don't think so. Often enough in trouble, I believe but petty offences. On the beat we've been used to just controlling him, you know what I mean, sir? Moving him on when he gets offensive. There's been a few times, when he's drunk, when he started throwing things around—'

'Any thieving?'

'Not in my time, sir. But we were talking in the canteen . . . before you called me out, like . . . and the lads were saying when he was a bit younger he could be a bit of a handful. He put one of the sergeants in hospital once. But that was a few years back, now.'

They reached the crest of the hill. The constable extended his arm, pointing. 'That's the gully. As I recall, he's got a hide across there to the left.'

The gully was steep-sided, and thickly wooded with oak and ash, blackthorn and hornbeam. Although the undergrowth was dense with fern and tough grass, the path was clearly marked: Foxy Fernlea would have walked it a thousand times. There was the scent of garlic, trodden under their feet, and across to the left Greybrook could see a trail beaten out through the stems of the dark green wild garlic, possibly by badgers; deep among the trees he could hear pigeons calling, and the tumbling beck below them gave a soft, rushing sound on its way to the Wear.

Greybrook was forced to stoop several times as the canopy closed in on them. He snagged his jacket on a blackthorn, and he began to slip on a muddy stretch of the slope. They were not things which would have bothered Foxy; probably, he would not even have noticed them.

'Here it is. I wasn't far out.'

They were in a small clearing. The hide was crudely constructed, a lacing of branches, some still living and threading through older, bare branches that had been twisted and layered in a rough attempt to create a shelter. It had been roofed with turves, but many of them had dried and rotted away. The smell in the hide was familiar: it matched the stench of

Foxy Fernlea's person. There was a pile of old sacking, some ancient, torn newspapers, a scattering of tin cans.

Greybrook wandered about the site thoughtfully. A small area had been trampled down — Foxy had not bothered to move far once he collapsed in his home. There was a considerable amount of litter indiscriminately thrown aside a short distance from the hide, and Greybrook rooted among it with his foot in desultory fashion. The young constable watched him fervently, obviously interested to see a detective at work. Greybrook stepped back, at the edge of the thicker ferns. He heard the clink of glass against his feet and looked down. In the undergrowth there were numerous bottles and beer cans, some of them half buried in the long, dank grass. Greybrook turned them over with his foot, gingerly. They were scattered over a narrow radius, smashed, encrusted, filthy, mostly of ancient provenance.

One bottle glinted darkly. He stared at it, then bent down, inspected it without touching.

He straightened, and turned. The young constable was watching him.

'Did you take a statement from Fernlea?'

The young constable shook his head. 'No, sir. Detective Sergeant Eyre took a statement . . . of sorts, I guess.'

'Of sorts?'

'Well, Foxy was sort of incoherent when I was talking to him.'

'But you did talk to him. What did he have to say? Why did you bring him in?'

'He was muttering about blood, sir, and blood on a wall, and a man without a head . . . I'd heard that it's been decided Andrews wasn't a suicide, and it just clicked with me, the thought, I mean, that maybe . . .'

'So you brought him in. Did he have nothing else to say?' The constable shrugged.

'Not really. He did mutter at one point about having seen someone else up at the house, but it wasn't very clear.'

'Someone else?' Greybrook frowned. 'When? Before or after he went into the house?'

'I said, sir, he wasn't clear. He just said he'd seen someone else up there . . . and I presumed he was talking about Bodicote Barn House.'

Greybrook chewed his lip. The old man was saying he'd seen someone at the house, and yet Redvers — Redvers was already thinking of charging the vagrant with the murder. Why was Redvers in such a hurry? First, he was suggesting suicide. Now, he wanted to pin it on the old vagrant. It needed thinking about . . .

He took a pen out of his pocket and bent down. He inserted the pen into the mouth of the bottle and lifted it gingerly. He looked at it carefully as it glinted in the subdued light under the trees.

'What have you got there, sir?'

'A bottle of what was expensive brandy . . . the kind Ken Andrews had ordered in the case of wine and spirits up at Bodicote Barn House. I think we can go back to Aykley Heads now. We'll get a team up here to comb the place thoroughly.'

Under the trees there was a sudden whirring as a pheasant took to panicked flight.

* * *

The suspension irked Arnold. It was not merely the injustice of it, for he had been given no real intimation of the reasons for the suspension other than that it had something to do with an expenses 'fiddle'. It was made worse by the fact that he felt at a loose end: he was unwilling to stray too far from his house in Morpeth in case the Senior Planning Officer phoned him, and he was used to spending his weekdays working, so after he had tidied his garden the first day, he had nothing in particular to do.

He was also overcome with a certain feeling of shame.

He was not guilty of any expenses offence — unless it had been inadvertent, but he could not see how. Nevertheless, the fact of suspension, and the realization that the Senior Planning Officer could think he might be guilty, was enough to make him want to stay indoors and not be seen by the neighbours.

There was the additional annoyance that Peter Aspen had decided to have nothing more to do with the Savoyard project. Arnold had not spent a great deal of time or thought on the matter, because he had not been particularly attracted to it. However, now that it had been whisked away he was resentful, and regarded it as a lost opportunity to undertake an interesting piece of research.

The more he thought about it, the more resentful he became.

After two days of his suspension, hiding in the bungalow, he felt irritable and out of sorts. There was no word from Morpeth, and he felt that if he did not do something positive he would end up beating his head against the wall.

The Savoyard project would at least fill his time, exercise his mind, make him concentrate on something other than worrying about what mistakes he might have made in his expenses and mileage claims.

He drove into Newcastle and went to the public library. He was on good terms with the deputy librarian there, and had a ticket that would get him into the stack room and one of the carrels where he could work quietly by himself among the musty odour of old paper and dust. He managed to get hold of a copy of Simpson's *Castles in England and Wales,* and Brown's *English Castles.* He pored over them, noting the technique used to build the Welsh castles. It entailed inclined or sloping scaffolds — a common Savoyard technique, but one rarely adopted by the English masons of the time.

It was hardly conclusive, for mediaeval master masons were never afraid to copy other men's work. He left the carrel and spoke to the deputy librarian: within twenty minutes the librarian came up with a copy of Taylor's work on the castle of St Georges d'Espéranche. Arnold settled down to read it, and then made his own rough copy of sketches of Flint and Harlech castles.

It was late afternoon before he completed his notes. He yawned, stretched, and decided he deserved a cup of tea. It was only after he had left the library and was sitting in a cafe in a side street that he realized he hadn't worried about his suspension for at least three hours. But there was another guilt that worried him: he was here in Newcastle, and it had not yet crossed his mind that he should call in to tell Jane Wilson what had happened. She had generously offered her assistance, albeit after pressure from Ben Gibson, and Arnold had promised to get in touch if he needed help. Now, the very least he could do would be to call in and tell her the project was off and Aspen had no intention of publishing anything on the Savoyard project that Ken Andrews had started.

He finished his tea and set off down Grey Street towards the Quayside and the little shop and flat owned by Ben Gibson. It was five in the afternoon; the shop would be closing soon, so he hurried on, unwilling to disturb Jane Wilson after closing time. He would just call in, explain, and leave.

The dark little shop was empty of browsers. Jane Wilson was sitting on the high stool favoured by Ben Gibson beside the roll-top desk. She was reading a book. When she heard him enter she turned her head: she was wearing reading glasses perched on the end of her nose. It gave her an owlish, studious air.

'Hello,' he said lamely.

'Hello, yourself.' She removed the spectacles and put them on the desk, turning around on the stool. Her eyes were level with his, and she contemplated him for a few seconds as he stood there sheepishly.

'Cup of tea?'

'Just had one, thanks. I . . . I only called in to explain. About the Savoyard thing.'

'You've hit a snag?'

Arnold managed to smile slightly. 'Only that Aspen has decided to drop the project.'

'Drop it? Why?' she asked sharply.

Arnold shrugged. 'It's a complicated story. There was a row . . . with a councillor called Bryman. I think it was because of that.'

'What was the row about?'

'I don't know, really. But there were threats, and Bryman was getting violent. Aspen is . . . well, a delicate creature. He got scared, I think, and there were other odd threats . . . Anyway, it doesn't matter. The fact is the project is shelved.'

'I see.' Jane Wilson was watching him carefully, a slight frown on her face. 'So what are you doing in Newcastle, today?'

Arnold drew a long breath. 'Well, I was at a loose end, so I thought even if Aspen doesn't want a book, I could get some . . . fun, just looking up the stuff anyway. So I've been into the library.'

She paused. 'No work today?' she asked quietly.

'I . . . er . . .' Arnold hesitated. The matter was personal, worrying and hurtful. He had no particular friends, no one to confide in, because he had never needed other people. He was self-sufficient, a loner, with acquaintances, not friends. But now, suddenly, he wanted to talk. In spite of himself, the words rushed out. 'I've been suspended. They say I've been fiddling expense claims.'

'Who says?' she demanded sharply.

'I don't know.' Arnold shrugged. 'I can hazard a guess, though.'

'Someone you've crossed?'

'I think it might have been Councillor Bryman — the one who had the shouting match with Peter Aspen.'

She hesitated, then slid down from the stool to stand closer to him. 'And *have* you been fiddling expenses, Arnold Landon?'

'Certainly not!'

'No, I didn't think so. It's not in you,' she said thoughtfully. She turned, walked away from him and closed the door to the shop, locking it. She walked past him towards the back of the shop. 'Whether you've had one or not, you're going to have another cup of tea.'

Arnold felt low. Telling her of the suspension had been the result of an uncontrollable weakness; he felt a certain relief that he had told someone, and he appreciated her vote of confidence, but now he felt, oddly enough, more vulnerable, less capable of handling the problem. He followed her to the small kitchen at the back and watched her make the tea. She put two mugs on the table and when the tea was ready she poured it out silently. Then she motioned him to a chair and sat down herself, chin on hands, elbows on table.

'I'm glad you came. I've been a bit niggled with you.'

Arnold shrugged despondently.

'I thought you made it pretty obvious you didn't want my help but didn't have the guts to say so,' she continued. 'I wasn't so keen either, but Ben—'

'I know.'

'And then you didn't have the courtesy to get in touch . . . It annoyed me. And now I hear you've been suspended because of some ridiculous claim about fiddled expenses, Peter Aspen's backed off from the book because of threats, for God's sake. I mean, what the hell's going on? What's so important about the Savoyards that this Bryman character—'

'I don't think Bryman was angry about the Savoyards project. It was Andrews's other work . . . on the Rosicrucians. Bryman was hopping mad about it, wanted it stopped. And he seemed to think I was involved with it . . . which may be why he started the story about me fiddling expenses. It's really a chapter of accidents, people jumping to wrong conclusions—'

'But you're the one to suffer! Damn, the injustice of it all!' She was suddenly fuming with anger. 'And have you heard the other thing . . . about Foxy Fernlea?'

'Who?'

'A Durham vagrant, an eccentric, a bit loopy, but harmless. He's been around Durham for years. I've seen him often, he's one of the sights of the city—'

'I didn't know you were from Durham.'

'Well, I am, and I'm mad as hell that those idiots at Aykley Heads can even contemplate charging Foxy with the murder of Ken Andrews! I'm certain they'll never show he had a shotgun . . . I mean, a sawn-off shotgun, where the hell would Foxy get such a thing? And why would he want to kill Andrews? I tell you, it all smells to high heaven . . . that poor old tramp! And now I hear this man Bryman had it in for Andrews, and Aspen has chickened out of the project as a result. What the hell is going on?'

'Your guess is as good as mine.'

She sipped at her mug of tea, her temper still smouldering.

It brought a life and a light to her face that made Arnold forget her plainness, and he realized she was a determined woman who held strong principles. 'I get the impression you're going to do something about the Fernlea business,' he said wonderingly.

'Too damn right! I've started a petition in Durham; quite a few people are helping. For all his oddness, old Foxy was well liked. Perhaps liked isn't the right word,' she reconsidered, wrinkling her nose, 'but anyway, I'm not alone in suspecting the old man's being railroaded just because the police want to get a suspect . . . or maybe because there are other, more sinister reasons behind it all. So there's the petition . . . and there's more.'

'How do you mean?'

'I'm going to play detective.'

'Surely—'

'No, there's something odd about all this. The story at first was that Andrews committed suicide; then Foxy — an easy target — was hauled in. Now you tell me there are other people who didn't like Andrews. And the dead man himself . . . there was something funny about him. Various rumours have been circulating around Durham since his death.'

'About what?'

'Bit vague,' she replied, and sipped her tea. 'It sort of boils down to the generally held view he wasn't a nice man. Maybe, he even had some unpleasant sexual habits.'

'Oh,' Arnold muttered uneasily.

'Nothing specific, but . . . well, I've got a contact at Catterick. Ex-Army. Colonel. Friend of my father's, really. I'm going to have a word with him, see if he can tell me anything about Andrews. Durham has rumours, but mouths are also buttoned on detail. I just wonder . . . and what the hell, I've nothing else of importance to do. This shop won't keep me busy. How Uncle Ben makes a living from it—'

'I don't think he does, really. It's a hobby.'

'Hmmm. Anyway, that's what I'm going to do. Gallop to the rescue of old Foxy Fernlea. And you . . . you're going to bury your head in Savoyard materials, hey?'

Arnold nodded. He hesitated, then reached for his briefcase, opened it and took out the sketches he had made. 'I've made a start. You see this sketch of Flint Castle? See the two concentric drum towers? There's an absurd military explanation in Simpson's book for them — the suggestion that the idea was to drive attackers into the basement of the inner drum and pick them off at leisure. But if you consider the Tour de Constance in the crusader port of Aigues-Mortes, the Apulian castle of Lucera, and the Castel del Monte in Apulia, the answer is simple and obvious.'

'Tell me.'

'The purpose of the design was just to provide comfortable, warm, well-lit accommodation in the upper levels of the keep, with the inner drum open to the sky, like a small courtyard.'

Jane Wilson looked at the sketch and nodded. 'But what has that to do with—'

'Aigues-Mortes, Lucera and Castel del Monte were all built by Master James of St Georges.'

'Aha!'

'It's not conclusive,' Arnold hastened. 'But it's a start.'

Jane Wilson looked at him, a calculation in her glance. 'You think I'm being silly, looking into the Andrews thing, don't you?'

'I didn't say so—'

'When I was at Harlech, and the other castles, I took a lot of photographs. Could you use them?'

'Ah well, I suppose so, yes, they'd be useful save me going back—'

'I'll do you a deal. You turned me down last time but let's try again. You can bounce ideas about Master James and the Savoyards off me — try them on for size, so to speak. I do have quite an analytical mind, I've been told. In return, I'll bounce ideas about Andrews off you.'

'I don't think I can contribute much, really—'

'Are you going to turn me down again, Arnold Landon?' He was inclined to do so. But the last two days had been bad. He had felt lonely for the first time in his life, and she was the only person he had confided in. He shuddered at the thought of talking to others, exposing his feelings. He had blurted it out, strangely enough, to Jane Wilson. She now knew how he felt . . . and she could in reality lend some assistance to him, with the Savoyards.

As to the murder of Ken Andrews, he thought she was being absurd. The police knew their own job . . . but she was burning about his suspension. Fate was throwing them together in an odd way. Perhaps he should not resist the cooperation she was suggesting. There could be no harm in it; they would both be occupied; they could help each other.

He sighed unhappily. 'Well, if you think it would be useful . . .'

She stuck out a hand. 'Deal?'

'Deal.'

'Right, I'll go dig out those photographs.'

2

The photographs were indeed useful. She had taken a number of unusual external shots, and in her wanderings within the structures she had obtained a number of close-ups of the stone which were quite interesting to Arnold. In addition, before he had left the shop, she had demonstrated how useful she could be to his research.

'I know you pooh-pooh talk of Arthurian connections with Eleanor and Edward I,' she said, 'but there's no doubt that Caernarvon has strong links with a Roman past — the multi-angular towers and the dark stripes in the stonework. But there's also the eagles placed on the top of the Eagle Tower — you know, the one with triple turrets. They're all traditional links with Roman and with Arthurian symbols—'

'The eagle is also the symbol of the Count of Savoy,' Arnold replied thoughtfully.

'It's the point I wanted to make,' Jane said eagerly. 'It's all very well looking at structures and systems to discover links, but I think it's equally important to look for the small things, the minor details which will provide the clues. After all, people have always wanted to express themselves in a personal way, in small details, on even the most magnificent of structures.'

'Gargoyles on cathedrals, drawn from life,' Arnold agreed.

It had been a point he was in danger of overlooking. During the next two days Arnold filled his time by reading all he could on the Welsh castles. He discovered that a thousand men had laboured at Harlech in 1286, with the master masons at Beaumaris calling on two thousand labourers. He found documentation that showed the cost of building the twin towers at Harlech had been forty-five shillings per foot, each tower being fifty feet high. But he was frustrated in his quest for anything referring to Master James of St Georges. It was partly because of that frustration that he was somewhat less than honest when he received a telephone call from Aykley Heads. It was a woman's voice. 'Mr Landon?'

'That's right.'

'I understand you had requested access to certain papers held by us, belonging to Kenneth Andrews. I'm just ringing to say that if you still wish to see them, Detective Inspector Greybrook is now prepared to release them. If you would care to call . . .'

It was a moment's hesitation: Arnold should have told her he no longer held a commission from Peter Aspen to complete the book Andrews had been working on. Whether it would have made any difference he had no way of knowing, but he could guess that the offer of cooperation and access would possibly have been withdrawn had he been open and direct — the only person with any right to the papers was Peter Aspen.

On the other hand, after the scene with Councillor Bryman, Aspen was no longer interested in publishing anything connected with Andrews, and it was too good an opportunity to let slide. After that momentary hesitation, therefore, Arnold announced quickly that he was grateful for the opportunity to inspect the papers, and would pick them up at Aykley Heads that afternoon.

He left his bungalow at Morpeth and drove down to Durham at once, nervous that Greybrook might in some way discover in the meanwhile that the commission from Aspen had been withdrawn. In the event, he need not have worried. After a short wait at reception, Arnold was called upstairs to Greybrook's office.

'Sit down, Mr Landon,' Greybrook said courteously. 'Would you care for a cup of coffee?'

'No, thanks. I don't want to take up too much of your time. I just came to collect the Savoyard material . . .'

'Of course.' Greybrook's eyes were lidded thoughtfully. 'I've had a careful look at the Savoyard stuff and I think I can safely eliminate it from now on . . . as far as our investigations into Andrews's death are concerned, you understand.'

Arnold nodded. 'The gossip in Durham is, I believe, that you've arrested a suspect.'

There was a short pause. 'That's right,' Greybrook replied hesitantly. There must have been something in Arnold's tone that concerned him and put him on guard. He watched Arnold for a few seconds, then went on, 'I've looked at the material and I can see no harm in letting you have it for your researches. It's pretty turgid stuff . . . I don't know what you'll make of it.'

'I'm not sure myself,' Arnold admitted. 'It may well be I'll take an entirely different track, anyway.'

'Yes. Mr Andrews's tastes were . . . shall we say . . . somewhat esoteric. He was dearly interested in the . . . unusual.' Greybrook's glance flickered sideways towards the window and then back again to Arnold. His voice was suddenly quieter. 'Did you get anywhere with Peter Aspen?'

'Aspen? I don't understand.'

'You may recall,' Greybrook said patiently, 'I asked you to have a word with Aspen when you saw him, to discover what the other book — the Rosicrucian book — was supposed to cover. Whether it touched on local stuff.'

Arnold hesitated. He saw no real reason why Greybrook should not have asked Aspen himself, directly. He shrugged. 'I did start to ask him, but, well, we didn't get very far.'

'Why not?'

'We were . . . interrupted.' Arnold hesitated, reluctant to mention Bryman's assault on Peter Aspen and the result of the threats made.

'How do you mean . . . interrupted?' Greybrook was no fool: he was aware of the tension in Arnold.

'I . . . well . . . I'd asked him, but he was called outside, and later, well, I don't know whether it's much use you chasing this line of inquiry anyway.' He sighed. There was nothing else for it. 'Peter Aspen's dropping the Rosicrucian book. And the one on the Savoyards. He wants nothing more to do with Andrews's work.'

'Dropping it?' Greybrook sat straighter in his chair. 'Why would he do that? Is he under some sort of pressure from someone?'

Arnold wriggled. Councillor Bryman might well have been responsible for Arnold's suspension but Arnold could not be sure of that. He disliked the man, and was suspicious and resentful of him, but he was reluctant to get him into trouble. 'It seems to me, Inspector, it would be better if you talked to Peter Aspen yourself. You're more likely to get answers than I am.'

There was a long silence. Greybrook sat staring at Arnold, but it was as though he did not really see him. His mouth was stiff, uncompromising, and his eyes were shadowed, glazed, as though he were looking inward, screening his thoughts from Arnold, checking on facts, surmises, premises, and calculating just what he should say next.

He was a careful man.

'When you came into this office, Mr Landon, there was something in the way you spoke of our "suspect" that was odd.'

'Really?'

'I got the impression, shall we say, that you were not impressed by our arrest of Mr Fernlea.'

'I don't know Fernlea. I've no real opinion in the matter.'

'And yet there was something . . .' Greybrook paused. 'I'm aware there is a petition circulating in the city.' Arnold nodded. 'I believe there are people who say the old man — I don't know him, as I said, and have never come across him — is not the kind to go around killing people.' Greybrook nodded. Casually he asked, 'Do you know anyone connected with the petition?'

He was sharp, this policeman, Arnold thought. He shrugged. 'I know someone who's helping organize it. In fact . . .'

'Yes?'

'I think she's likely to go a bit further. She feels pretty strongly about it — says she's seen Fernlea around Durham for years and he's harmless.'

'You said, *do* something about it.'

'That's right,' Arnold replied reluctantly. 'Do some checking of her own.'

'An amateur sleuth?' Greybrook said, raising his eyebrows. 'Can't leave the police alone to do their job?' Arnold felt he had been indiscreet, and even disloyal. He shrugged unhappily.

Greybrook pushed back his chair slowly and rose to his feet. He walked to the window and stared out for a few minutes. In the growing silence Arnold shifted unhappily. 'The materials—'

Greybrook turned to face him. He was frowning. He seemed to be struggling with his own instincts. 'I'm going to take a chance, Mr Landon. I'm going to take you into my confidence.'

Arnold waited warily.

'You suggested I approach Peter Aspen myself about the Rosicrucian book. I'm reluctant to do that. The fact is . . .' He hesitated, chewing at his lip. 'The fact is, there are some things about the Andrews case that leave me . . . uneasy . . . I shouldn't be telling you this, but, well, I think the case against Foxy Fernlea is pretty weak.'

'But you're charging him?'

'He's being charged. We've got his prints on a bottle and glass found inside the house and also on a bottle found at his hide on the hill. That second bottle came from Bodicote

Barn House — so he was certainly up there. And he went in. But we can't make a connection between him and the murder weapon, and if the motive was burglary, all he took was a bottle of brandy and in any case burglary wasn't Fernlea's scene. He's just a vagrant. But he's being charged, and . . . and I'm a bit nervous.'

'You think he's been wrongly charged?'

Greybrook held up a hand. 'I didn't say that. It's just that the case is a bit . . . weak. And maybe we should be pursuing other lines of inquiry.'

'But why are you interested in the Rosicrucian book?' Arnold asked.

Greybrook leaned against the wall and folded his arms. His reluctance and wariness was increasing. He shook his head. 'I don't know. When you've been in the job as long as I have you develop . . . gut feelings. I don't want to . . . I can't explain my suspicions to you, because they may well be ill-founded, but I have the impression there's something missing from the Rosicrucian papers that I collected from Bodicote Barn House. I've read them, and they're in a scattered, disorganized state. Unlike the Savoyard stuff — which is there, by the way.' He gestured to a brown paper parcel tied with string, lying on his desk.

Arnold eyed it reluctantly. He was intrigued, but puzzled.

He could not work out why Greybrook was talking to him like this.

'If something is missing from the Rosicrucian papers,' Greybrook continued, 'it puts a different complexion on things. I need to know what is missing, because it might point a finger at someone. I don't know. That's why I asked you if you could find out whether any local material was contemplated in the book.'

'You still haven't explained why you couldn't ask Aspen directly.'

Greybrook hesitated. 'There are two reasons. The first is, Peter Aspen's name appears on a file held here at Aykley Heads.'

'A file?'

'Let's just say . . .' Something unpleasant was happening to Greybrook's mouth; it twisted in distaste and suppressed anger. 'Let's just say he's suspected of . . . certain malpractices.'

'I don't understand.'

'No matter. Going to him directly might cause problems. He might feel . . . threatened. He might react by using such influence as he might possess in Northern circles.'

Arnold frowned. Councillor Bryman had threatened Peter Aspen with exposure of some kind. It might be connected to the file at Aykley Heads that Greybrook had referred to, though how Bryman would know about the file was a puzzle to Arnold. Perhaps Greybrook was right: perhaps the Rosicrucian book did contain dangerous material. 'You said there were two reasons.'

Greybrook nodded. 'I'm now officially in charge of the investigation. But . . . that's not how it started out. Moreover, now we have charged Fernlea, if I start pushing in other directions it might be seen as . . . counterproductive.'

Arnold frowned. The man was uncomfortable. He was not being direct, but the hints were clearly there. Greybrook was under pressure, probably from above, to conform. Decisions had been made. He was not to rock any boats. Arnold hesitated. He wondered whether he should tell Greybrook about Bryman's threats to Aspen. He decided to keep his own counsel: it was all too circumstantial at the moment. 'You have a problem,' he agreed.

'And I need any help I can get,' Greybrook said frankly. 'I think the Fernlea case could blow up in our faces. And I'm the officer in charge. I could be the one who gets crucified if we've got it wrong . . .'

'I'm afraid I can't help over Aspen,' Arnold admitted after a short hesitation. 'Not since he's decided to drop the whole idea of the Rosicrucian book.'

Greybrook stared at him. 'You think Aspen has been scared off?'

'I suppose that's about the size of it.'

'So it looks as though there could be something in that material . . . All right, so you can't help me. I'll just have to pursue other lines of inquiry.' Greybrook paused and looked thoughtfully at Arnold. 'This pressure group in Durham . . . you said someone would be doing some digging. A friend of yours?'

'An acquaintance,' Arnold hastened.

'Called?'

Arnold hesitated. There seemed little harm in naming her to Greybrook. 'She's called Jane Wilson. She works temporarily in her uncle's bookshop on the Quayside in Newcastle, though she's from Durham, really. That's how she knows Fernlea.'

'Hmmm. All right, Mr Arnold . . . Can I ask you a favour? You can leave Peter Aspen to me, but if this Jane Wilson does turn anything up . . . I don't approve of amateur detectives, but you never know, and if she does find anything of interest, it would be helpful if you kept me informed. My own hands are virtually tied but I have a feeling there's something behind all this I can't put my finger on . . . so any information will be of assistance.'

He stood away from the wall and extended his hand.

Arnold rose, shook it, and then Greybrook turned aside, picked up the brown paper parcel and handed it to Arnold.

The door opened.

The heavy-faced, grizzled man framed in the doorway was startled by Arnold's presence. 'Greybrook. I didn't realize you had someone with you.'

Detective Inspector Greybrook had stiffened. He glanced at Arnold, and something in the glance made Arnold cling tightly to the parcel under his arm. 'Mr Landon was just leaving, sir.' Greybrook hesitated. 'This is Chief Superintendent Redvers.'

Arnold nodded nervously. 'We've met.' Redvers was staring at him, tugging at his military-style moustache, eyeing the parcel suspiciously.

'That's right.' Redvers agreed. His red-rimmed eyes narrowed. 'You work in Northumberland. In the Planning Department, as I recall. So what brings you to Durham?'

There was a short silence. Arnold did not know how to reply: he felt a palpable tension in the man standing behind the desk. At last Greybrook raised his chin with a hint of defiance. 'Mr Landon is picking up some of the work that the dead man — Andrews — was undertaking.'

'What work?' The question came like a whiplash.

'Ah . . . it's the book on the Savoyards,' Arnold said, clutching his parcel.

'Is that it?' Redvers demanded.

Arnold nodded.

Redvers was staring at it hungrily. It was as though he had a personal sense of ownership of the material, and did not want it to leave his possession. Arnold felt the man's fingers would be almost twitching.

'I've checked it out,' Greybrook said smoothly. 'I can't see it has any relevance to the Andrews killing. And now we've arrested Fernlea . . .'

There was almost a challenge in his tone. Redvers was glaring at him, but his glance kept slipping away, back to Arnold and to the parcel he held. Arnold felt the man wanted to overrule Greybrook, but for some reason was unable to bring himself to do so. Bad-temperedly Redvers said, 'I think it's a mistake handing out stuff that could be evidence—'

'As officer in charge of the investigation, sir, I don't think we need hold this material. It's unimportant. It is only the Savoyard material, after all.'

Redvers stared at Greybrook. He was pale around the mouth and a muscle twitched in his cheek; he was uncertain, not clear how he should react. There was an unspoken argument lying between the two policemen and Redvers clearly was reluctant to expose it. He decided it was better to step back, and not make an issue of it. 'As you said, Greybrook, you're the investigating officer. You must take responsibility.'

He turned his baleful glance at Arnold. 'And if we need the stuff again, we'll know where to find it, won't we?'

There was an underlying menace in his tone that made Arnold feel cold. He was pleased to escape from the office, and from Aykley Heads. He still had the parcel . . . but the nonsense was, he did not expect to gain a great deal from it in any case. It was work done by Andrews, and Arnold really believed in doing his own research.

But as he drove back north through the Tyne Tunnel he was not thinking of the Savoyard research material; rather, he wondered about the wary animosity in Chief Superintendent Redvers's glance, and the challenge that was clearly being thrown down by Detective Inspector Greybrook.

There was no love lost between the two men . . . but the tension in both had roots Arnold could not possibly comprehend.

3

The following morning he was surprised to get a phone call from Jane Wilson. He had been working on Andrews's Savoyard manuscript and papers; they were in reasonable order but contained little that was not already known to him. Indeed, there was a certain superficiality about most of the materials that suggested to Arnold the researcher was doing little more than a journeyman's job: it was not his field, and an understanding and knowledge of military history was not enough to make up for the lack of feeling and interest in Edward and his castles. Arnold concluded that here was an opportunity missed, but also recognized wryly that all enthusiasts thought so when confronted with another's work.

'So how are you getting on?' Jane asked. 'I thought I'd ring to find out.'

'I've got the materials from Aykley Heads,' Arnold replied. 'I'm working on them, but I think I'll have to go for another wander around North Wales. I've certainly got time enough, anyway.'

'No further news about your suspension?'

'Nothing at all.' The Senior Planning Officer was keeping his head down. He certainly would not want to proceed formally until he was sure of his facts: he was not a man who enjoyed confrontation of any kind.

'Did you find anything useful from the photographs I gave you?'

'They're interesting: odd angles you've used. Some of them are quite revealing.'

'Thank you, sir,' she said.

'I have a feeling, too, I'm missing something in them. I can't put my finger on it, but there's something, somewhere, in the photographs that strikes a chord for me . . . it keeps slipping away whenever I try to concentrate on it. You know what I mean?'

'I do,' she said ruefully. 'There are times when Queen Eleanor does exactly the same thing to me — move out of mental reach.'

Arnold paused for a moment. 'I — er — I hope you don't mind — maybe I shouldn't have done it—'

'Why so hesitant?'

'I gave your name to the police,' he blurted out.

'What the hell for?'

'I was asked,' he replied lamely. 'I mean, I was at Aykley Heads collecting the Savoyard stuff, and we got to talking about things, and Andrews's death, and the investigating officer, well, he asked me about the petition circulating in Durham protesting at Fernlea's arrest.'

'And you gave him my name?' she asked sharply. 'So now I'll get hassle and harassment?'

'No, no, I'm sure not. He seemed, well, almost sympathetic. He couldn't commit himself, of course, but I was left with the distinct impression he believes Fernlea was set up, and he's interested in finding out what really happened. So I told him you had decided to do some digging yourself.'

'This gets better and better! It's beginning to look as though you want to see me inside, Arnold Landon!'

Arnold took a deep breath. 'Look, I'm sorry, but it wasn't that kind of conversation. The man's worried: he thinks Fernlea is a scapegoat, he's got suspicions, he's under pressure — and he's certainly not going to try to stop you digging around. All he asks is, keep him informed. If you come up with anything, I think he'll pursue it. There's no love lost between him and his Chief Superintendent. And it's not a bad thing to have a friend at court. So don't worry.'

She was silent for a few seconds. Then she sighed. 'OK, you're forgiven. But if I get put inside I'll expect you to make up on the bread and water rations. Actually, it was about this I really rang you.'

'Bread and water rations?'

She laughed. 'No, I told you I had a contact . . . A Colonel Horspool. He's retired, ex-Army, old friend of my father. I've made an appointment to see him tomorrow at Richmond. I'm going to tap him about Andrews, see if he can find out anything interesting about him.'

'So how can I help?'

'You can come with me.'

Arnold hesitated. He had an odd, sinking feeling in his stomach. 'I'm not sure I want to be involved.'

'You've done this sort of thing before.'

And got into trouble because of it. 'It's not that. I've got this suspension on my mind . . . and there's the research. Anyway, I just don't see why you'd want me along.'

She snorted. 'It's quite simple. You have something in common with Colonel Horspool. He too is a crusty bachelor.'

'I'm not crusty!' Arnold protested.

'Well, you know what I mean. The fact is, Colonel Horspool is a pretty dry old stick. He has always had very firm views regarding the place of women in the order of things. He thinks we should all be in front of kitchen sinks — or if we have to be involved in any work, it should be in a menial capacity in the forces. He does not approve of women officers. He's a dear, really, terribly gallant and polite and all that sort of thing . . . but I have a feeling that when I start to question him, he may well dry up on me.'

'Because you're a woman?'

'Precisely. Antediluvian, isn't it? On the other hand, if you were to come along, it might be he'd open up.'

'About what?' Arnold asked doubtfully.

'How do I know?' she protested. 'Men's things. What do men gossip about when they talk of other men? I just don't know . . . but he might be just a little bit more open to you than to me. Ah . . . were you ever in the Army?'

'Only National Service. In the Gunners.'

'That'll do. Throw it in at some point. It'll help. Now then, where shall we meet?'

Arnold could not recall having agreed they should meet. But somehow, it was now all taken for granted.

* * *

Arnold picked Jane Wilson up at the small semi-detached house she owned on the edge of Framwellgate Moor. It was located on a small, modern estate on a sloping site, and the back garden faced south. He inspected the garden while he waited for her to get ready: the flowerbeds showed signs of careful tending, the lawn was neatly mown and edged, and the hedge of escallonia was pink with tiny flowers.

'Green fingers,' he said when she came out into the garden through the patio doors.

'It's a relaxation. But a bit of a problem now I'm looking after Uncle Ben's place. Ready to go?'

They drove out of Durham and picked up the motorway to Scotch Corner. Beyond that it was only a short run towards Catterick, where apparently Colonel Horspool had ended his Army career. Beyond Scotch Corner, Arnold pulled off the motorway and took the winding road to Richmond.

They could see Richmond Castle from some distance as they approached the town: set magnificently on a crag high above the River Swale, the Norman towers dominated the town and the cobbled marketplace. Arnold liked the North Yorkshire town — not just for the twelfth-century rectangular keep of the castle but also for the eighteenth-century Georgian theatre. Edmund Kean and William Macready had trod the boards there, and he felt the whole town had a sense and appreciation of its history.

'Colonel Horspool was in the Green Howards,' Jane said. 'Mention it to him; it'll help.'

The grey and green slated roofs of the town were glittering in the sunshine. The surrounding hills were a patchwork of green fields and banks of trees and the roar of the motorway was distant behind them on the light breeze. They drove into the banked, cobbled marketplace and under Jane's directions went past the river bridge, winding up among the trees beyond the crag until it opened up into a narrow, tree-lined drive. Through the trees Arnold caught glimpses of the rolling hills of Richmondshire, before they drew up in front of the red stone Georgian house with its elegant, symmetrical windows and handsome doorway. The sandstone lintels drew his attention, but Jane was tugging at his sleeve.

Colonel Horspool was standing to one side of the doorway.

He was tall, lean, elegant and white-moustached. He wore a hacking jacket of worn tweed and cavalry twill trousers. His face was tanned and lined but his eyes were a startling blue, his smile welcoming. He helped Jane from the car and shook her hand warmly, but made no attempt to embrace her.

'Colonel, may I introduce Arnold Landon?'

'Delighted, Mr Landon. Do come indoors: I've been pottering in the garden and need to wash my hands. Then we can settle down to a drink, hey? And you can bring me up to date with the news, Jane.'

'Indoors' for the Colonel meant, it transpired, a small covered terrace at the back of the house where clematis twined profusely over a wooden trellis. At the far end a wall had been built to keep out the wind. Through the old stone, the trunk of an ancient oak appeared and the wall had been built to accommodate it. A sensible way to treat age and beauty, Arnold considered. The Colonel must have noted his approval. 'Four hundred years old, it would seem. Thank God we don't last that long, hey?'

Colonel Horspool produced glasses and a bottle of chilled Chablis. They sat on the covered terrace and admired the wine, the garden, the tree and the view. The Colonel talked for a while about Jane's father — whom he had not seen for seven years before he died — and it was at least twenty minutes before Jane finally got around to asking for the old man's help.

'It's a bit of an unusual request, Colonel Horspool, but I was wondering whether you'd ever come across a man called Andrews — Ken Andrews — at Catterick. I understand he held a commission there. From what I gather in Durham he was a major when he retired.'

'In the Howards?' Colonel Horspool screwed up his blue eyes in thought. 'I'd have to have a think about that. Name's familiar. And yet . . .' He glanced uncertainly at Arnold and he appeared vaguely uneasy. He pursed his lips and nodded. 'Enjoy your drink a while: I'll just pop upstairs and get out me manual. Might be something there to jog the old memory. Won't be a few moments.'

Arnold sipped his wine.

'You haven't mentioned you were in the Royal Artillery,' Jane whispered.

'Is it important?'

'He can be an awkward old cuss.'

'I found him charming,' Arnold protested.

'*Two* awkward old cusses!'

It was several minutes before Colonel Horspool returned.

He did not look at Jane when he came back to the terrace. He sighed, sat down and picked up his glass. 'Always had a fondness for white wine in the mess. We drank quite a bit of it there.'

'Was Major Andrews a white wine drinker?' Jane asked, unwilling to be diverted.

The Colonel frowned at her lack of subtlety. 'Don't know. Can't say I recall him too well,' he replied gruffly.

'He was in the regiment a short while only. Not popular in the mess. Left about eight years ago, I seem to recall, maybe a bit later. What do you want to know about him?'

'Anything, really,' Jane said. 'He's dead, you see, and they've arrested an old vagrant for his murder, and I don't think it's right, so I was trying to find out a bit more about the major. I thought you might have known him—'

'Knew him, yes, but not well, not really. Dead, you say. Killed. Not surprised.' Colonel Horspool scowled. 'Didn't like the man.' He peered at Jane Wilson for several seconds and then shook his head. 'Don't think I can help you much, my dear.'

'Why didn't you like him, Colonel?'

Horspool ignored her. He turned to Arnold. 'You an Army man, Mr Landon?'

'A brief stay in the Royal Artillery,' Arnold replied, anxious to avoid a kick from Jane. 'But merely a locating regiment: nothing with the traditions of the Green Howards. I can understand why you retired here to Richmond: isn't the regimental museum here in the town?'

Colonel Horspool almost beamed with pleasure. 'That's right. It's housed in part of the old church by the market square. The Green Howards,' he intoned, almost in reproof at Jane as though she should apologize for being a woman, 'have celebrated history. They were raised in 1688 to fight for William of Orange against James II. The regimental museum still houses some of the arms and equipment from that time.'

Jane Wilson stared at the Colonel for a few seconds and then she set down her glass. She looked at Arnold meaningfully, then rose to her feet, smiling sweetly. 'Why don't I go and make us a nice cup of tea?'

Colonel Horspool struggled to his feet. 'Splendid idea, Jane. No taste for good wine, hey? The kitchen's just through there. You'll find all the makings.'

When she had left them Colonel Horspool sat back in his chair and helped himself to another glass of wine. 'That's better,' he said, after taking a healthy pull at his glass.

'Sir?'

Colonel Horspool nodded his head in the direction of the kitchen. 'Sensible girl, Jane Wilson. Her father was a splendid chap . . . She's got a lot of his sense. But she's a gal, right? Some things you can't talk about. Not done. Difficult. Men's stuff.'

'I see,' Arnold replied, not seeing at all.

Horspool scowled. 'The Howards were my life, you know. Splendid regiment. Splendid men. But even the best get a rotten apple from time to time. Best to kick them out. Make them pay. But sometimes, best to keep it quiet.'

'Are you talking about Major Andrews, sir?'

Colonel Horspool nodded. 'The very one. When Jane mentioned his name I thought it was the one. Went upstairs to check, make sure — and gain some time to think. He's been killed, you say? Not surprised. I'd have killed him if I could have got my hands on him. Never liked the chap. But had to keep it quiet, didn't we?'

'Keep what quiet, Colonel?'

Colonel Horspool put down his glass carefully. He glanced towards the kitchen. 'I don't really approve of women doing the kind of thing she's up to . . . sniffin' at the past. Nasty things can turn up: damage a young gel's sensibilities, you know? And it was a bad business, you see.

He was silent for a while. Arnold hesitated. 'Was Major Andrews cashiered . . . court-martialled?'

Horspool shook his head. He stared gloomily at his old oak bole. 'No. He should have been. Should have been shot. But the scandal . . . and there was the problem of proof. No it was decided — at a high level — to hush the thing up. Too many people involved. He wasn't alone, you see. There were two others with him. It was all kept under wraps. They resigned their commissions, went back to civvy street. And the regiment was saved from scandal — the worst sort of scandal.'

'Money?' Arnold asked. 'Did he have his fingers in the till?'

'Not that,' the Colonel replied grimly. 'He couldn't keep his hands off young recruits!'

* * *

Below the marketplace the Swale tumbled noisily over the grey flat rocks and boiled whitely under the bridge. The track Arnold and Jane walked was dry and dusty under the protection of the hedge and the guard rail was red with newly painted undercoat. A squirrel darted across the path in front of them, yammered brief defiance as they advanced towards him and then leapt for the safety of a sycamore. Arnold watched him, then looked upwards to the aching blue of the sky. 'It was bad news for the regiment, he said.

'Bad news for me, too,' Jane Wilson grumbled 'Why the hell couldn't he say it in front of me? Does he think I'm a little girl?'

'Some men don't change their views or attitudes in a lifetime. Besides, you ought to feel flattered that he was so protective of your sensibilities.'

Jane snorted scornfully. 'I have heard of people with homosexual and paedophilic tendencies before now.'

'I don't doubt it. But that doesn't mean old Horspool would be comfortable telling you about Andrews.'

'So what exactly was it all about, then?' she persisted. Arnold pointed to a wooden seat above the river. They walked across the grass and sat down. Arnold tossed a stone into the white water. 'He didn't tell me the full story, of course: you weren't out long enough.'

'I was curious.'

'Maybe so. But I'd have learned more if you'd stayed out longer. What he did tell me was that Andrews joined the Green Howards as a major after a career in some other regiment, and lasted just three years there. Horspool didn't tell me how it all blew up, but it seems that there had been some complaints from one or two new recruits. They felt they'd been propositioned. When an investigation was undertaken the position was suspected to be more serious: there was a view that some of the young men had in fact responded — either out of inclination, or because of pressure from a senior officer.'

'You're not serious!'

'I am. He was — and the situation was! Homosexuality occurs in the armed forces: that's common enough knowledge even though the War Office tries to ignore it and hush it up. But no one wants it to become a scandal. And it seems Andrews didn't confine his attentions to young recruits alone. There was talk of rent boys, as well.'

'Rent boys?'

'Young male prostitutes. Some as young as twelve years of age. Andrews was involved, along with two other officers. Horspool wasn't clear whether Andrews was an active homosexual, or merely a procurer for others. Either way, it was nasty. But the Green Howards didn't really want to know. Once the suspicion emerged, the three men were quietly advised that it would be in their own best interests to resign. They did . . . That's when you came in from the kitchen.'

'You mean there was more?' Jane asked.

'I'm not sure,' Arnold replied. 'There was something else Horspool wanted to say, but your return inhibited him. Anyway, he suggested I give him a ring in a few days. He wants to look up some records.'

'Will you do that? And let me know?'

Arnold nodded. He was thinking back to snippets of information he had picked up from Greybrook, and from Councillor Bryman. It was possible there was a connection, but there was no point in discussing it now. He would wait until Colonel Horspool came out with a little more information: if there was any more information he could give that would be useful to Jane Wilson.

'So that's it?'

'That's it' Arnold agreed. 'I don't know whether you think our journey was worthwhile. All you've discovered is that Andrews had queer tastes. Maybe he made advances to your vagrant?'

'That's not funny.'

'No. It wasn't. I'm sorry. Anyway, I think we can head back north, now.'

'No,' Jane Wilson said firmly. 'You've put yourself out for me. The least I can do is walk you around Richmond and then buy you dinner at the Queen's Head. And after the way I've been treated by the kindly Colonel Horspool, I shall be mortally offended if you refuse.'

It did not seem that Arnold had any choice.

CHAPTER FOUR

1

The telephone call Arnold had been waiting for, and yet dreaded, came next morning. The girl on the switchboard at the office sounded sympathetic.

'Mr Landon? The Senior Planning Officer has asked if you can attend at his office this afternoon at two.'

'I'll be there,' Arnold replied grimly.

Driving to the office was an odd experience. He was not hugely enamoured of his job: it possessed the advantage of allowing him some little licence to pursue his major interests in wood and stone, but there was little more that he found attractive about it. He seemed doomed to work with unsympathetic senior officers and there was clearly no possibility of promotion: he was aware that the councillors on the Planning Committee thought him an odd fish, and there had been occasions when he had been warned that if he did not avoid controversy his job could be at risk.

Nevertheless, he had a leaden feeling in his chest as he drove to the office on this occasion: he felt as though he were heading for a confrontation he did not seek. He had no idea what to expect, for no formal charges had been made to him. The Senior Planning Officer had given no details, other than to say a complaint had been levelled against him.

It was likely Arnold would hear the worst today.

He was kept waiting in the outer office for at least ten minutes. He suspected that the Senior Planning Officer was dreading the interview as much as he — good relationships with the personnel were not the Senior Planning Officer's forte, and he hated 'difficulties'. When at last he was called in, however, Arnold was surprised to see that the Senior Planning Officer was not alone: he was flanked and supported by the Chairman of the Planning Committee.

Tom Ellsbury was in his late sixties. He claimed descent from a noted Labour politician but success in his business enterprises had led him into the political realms of the High Tories. He was a plump, good-natured man who always dressed in a somewhat outdated, natty fashion. He was not a confident man; when he became nervous he began to sweat and was inclined to mop at his brow with a startlingly red handkerchief, chosen to match the rose he always wore in his buttonhole.

He knew Arnold well enough; he did not acknowledge him nor meet Arnold's glance on this occasion and when the Senior Planning Officer invited Arnold to take a seat in front of the desk Ellsbury kept his head down, contemplating the bottom button of his waistcoat. His pudgy hands were clasping his knees.

'Well, then, Landon, thank you for coming in. I'm sorry for the short notice, but this was the only time Mr Ellsbury could make it, and I thought it best that we shouldn't drag this on too long. I'm sure you'd agree we need to deal with the matter as quickly as possible.'

'Most certainly,' Arnold said quietly.

The Senior Planning Officer glanced at him nervously, and hesitated. 'Well, we'll get on, then.' He opened the file in front of him and stared at the papers it contained. He picked up the top sheet. 'Is this claim form in your handwriting?'

Arnold took the proffered sheet, and glanced at it. 'That's right. And that's my signature.'

'Are the details accurate?'

'You mean the mileage, and the hours spent? Well, yes, I would think so because I'm pretty careful about such things.'

'The mileage from Morpeth is out by about twenty miles,' the Senior Planning Officer commented.

Arnold stared at him. 'What do you mean, it's "out"?'

'The distance from the office to Deepdale Farm is approximately twenty-eight miles. The claim, which you signed — it is your signature, isn't it?'

'Yes, I've already said so.'

'The claim is for sixty-seven miles. How do you account for that?'

Arnold stared at him, and then looked at Tom Ellsbury. 'It's my practice,' he answered slowly, 'to note my actual car mileage when I'm out in the field.'

'Are you saying our calculations are wrong?'

'No.' Arnold shook his head. 'But that figure on my claim form shows the actual miles driven.'

'It seems you over-claimed, Landon.'

'No.' Arnold wrinkled his brow, thinking hard. 'I think you'll find I would have gone elsewhere, in addition to Deepdale Farm. As far as I recall, I went north a few miles to Holtern House, since it was in the same area. I actually saved the authority money,' he added drily, 'by dealing with two files at the same time. I think you'll also find I worked rather longer than eight hours that day, but made no claim for overtime.'

The Senior Planning Officer expelled air through his nose in a delicate snorting sound. He picked up a second sheet and showed it to Arnold, disdainfully. 'And this claim?'

'Alston. A planning symposium and conference.'

'Alston is in Cumbria. It's outside our area.'

'You asked me to attend, sir. As I recall, you didn't feel . . . up to making the trip. It was the day after the Town Planning Institute dinner: I believe you attended. So I went to Alston instead. I was the most junior there: all the others were senior officers. Northumberland was the only county not represented by a senior officer.'

The Senior Planning Officer scowled. 'You stayed overnight on that occasion, and claimed the higher rate of subsistence?'

Arnold looked at Tom Ellsbury: the politician still kept his head down. 'I think both you and the Chairman will agree that the county has certain rules regarding expenses. One of them is that where an officer attends a conference with senior officers he is entitled to claim the rate applicable to them.'

'That assumes he is with his *own* senior officer!'

'*My* senior officer didn't go,' Arnold snapped. 'And I think you'll find my interpretation of the rules is correct.'

Tom Ellsbury wriggled in his chair. He glanced at the Senior Planning Officer uncertainly. 'Do we have to go all through these sheets? Can't we get to the main business?'

The Senior Planning Officer's cheeks turned a delicate shade of pink. 'Of course, Chairman. I merely wanted to give Mr Landon a fair hearing in your presence. I also wished to demonstrate on the part of Mr Landon a . . . *modus operandi*, if you understand me. For instance, although it's only a matter of a three-mile discrepancy on this sheet, it underlines a regular pattern of overcharging.'

Arnold leaned forward to look at the claim form. 'There were roadworks on the A1 for seven weeks. You may recall, sir, a detour past Felton was necessary at that time. A three-mile detour.'

The Senior Planning Officer waved a negligent hand. 'That may be so, but it doesn't destroy the feeling we have that there has been a certain . . . looseness of accounting over a period of time—'

'You'll have to explain that,' Arnold said angrily. 'My records are accurate, as any check in my desk diary will show.'

'Your desk diary. Yes.' The Senior Planning Officer smiled thinly. He glanced knowingly at Tom Ellsbury; the Chairman of the Planning Committee pursed his lips. The Senior Planning Officer turned back to Arnold. 'Your desk diary. Have you brought it with you?' the Senior Planning Officer asked silkily.

'I haven't got it with me, but I can fetch it. My diary remains on my desk,' Arnold replied. 'You know that's common practice — it enables you, or other officers, to check where I might be if I'm not in the office.'

'Quite.'

'So?'

'So why have you removed it?'

There were two burning spots in the Senior Planning Officer's cheeks now. He sat up straighter as Arnold glared at him. 'I have not removed my diary,' Arnold said angrily. 'When you told me to leave the premises under suspension I did not return to my office. The diary is still there.'

'That is not so.'

Arnold was silent. Tom Ellsbury shifted again in his chair and cleared his throat. 'You're saying your desk diary, which contains details of your work schedule and your activities outside the office, was still on your desk when you left?'

'That's exactly what I'm saying!'

'It seems odd,' the Senior Planning Officer pronounced with a doubtful sniff, 'that the record of your appointments, which would substantiate — or otherwise, of course — your movements, should have disappeared. You are the only person who would have any interest in taking the diary away.'

'I had no reason to take it.'

'Nor would anyone else, surely?'

Arnold opened his mouth, then closed it again. He was beginning to see the way the wind was blowing. He waited.

'Get on, get on,' Ellsbury suddenly said in an uncharacteristic burst of testiness. 'The main charge, if you please!' The Senior Planning Officer cleared his throat. 'You'll be aware, Mr Landon, I've been unhappy about your work for some time.'

'I was not.'

'Well, unhappy about certain other things that seem to impinge on your work, and bring unwelcome publicity to the department.'

‘My own interests, carried out in my spare time, are my affair,’ Arnold insisted.

‘If they are carried out in your own time, yes,’ the Senior Planning Officer agreed. ‘But I have here another claim form. It has been signed by you. It details mileage and overnight stay at Spittal, near Berwick.’

‘On Planning Department business,’ Arnold replied. ‘It was May . . . late May, I recall.’

The Senior Planning Officer smiled thinly. ‘Yes, your memory is sound. Unfortunately, it’s not as sound as it would seem. Can you explain what you were doing at Chesters Fort that same afternoon, at four o’clock, and how you could possibly have got to Chesters from Spittal by that time, when you were supposed to be undertaking a site inspection on the coastal walls?’

There was a long silence. Arnold stared at the two men facing him. The leaden feeling in his chest had gone. Now he was aware of a burning sensation, as the anger in him began to grow.

‘Who says I was at Chesters Fort that day?’

‘Do you deny being there?’

‘I certainly do!’

‘Come now, Landon, let’s not be so hasty! There may well have been a good reason for your going down there from Spittal, and then back again.’ Tom Ellsbury’s tone was uneasy, as though he was hoping Arnold could come up with a reasonable explanation, and avoid all this unpleasantness.

‘I was not at Chesters on that occasion — nor any, in recent years, at four in the afternoon. My diary—’

‘Which is missing,’ the Senior Planning Officer snapped. ‘Conveniently, it seems to me.’

‘Very conveniently!’ Arnold replied hotly. ‘But I don’t have it. And you still haven’t told me who says I was at Chesters that day.’

The Senior Planning Officer extracted a memorandum sheet from his file. He held it gingerly, between finger and thumb. ‘I have a deposition here.’

‘From whom?’

The Senior Planning Officer ignored the question. He passed the sheet to Lansbury who looked at it, nodded, and gave it back.

‘There is also a witness to the deposition — a confirmation of its accuracy. You were seen at Chesters Landon seen not by one but by two people.’

‘And one of them was a member of the Planning Committee.’ Tom Ellsbury glowered.

‘I think I should be entitled to see the deposition,’ Arnold said.

The Senior Planning Officer hurriedly slipped it back into his folder. ‘I don’t think we need go that far yet. Suffice it to say, the Chairman and I are both satisfied that the statement was made *bona fides*. The fact that you took your diary—’

‘I did not!’

‘-so we cannot check your movements accurately, is a pity. But there you are.’ The Senior Planning Officer took a deep breath. ‘The fact is, Landon, we are not malicious. If you are prepared to admit that your returns are — shall we say, inaccurate — well, let’s make the point that both I and the Chairman are anxious to avoid scandal. We certainly would not wish to take legal action, call the police in, that sort of thing. Scandals are to be avoided at all cost. So if you are prepared to make a clean breast of things, we will ensure that no prosecution is brought.’

‘Prosecution? You must be crazy!’

The Senior Planning Officer frowned, and lowered his tones as though he was dealing with a recalcitrant child. ‘I’ll overlook that outburst, Landon. But we must insist that you admit these . . . peccadilloes, and any others on your conscience. We for our part will promise not to prosecute if you make a clean breast of it. In the interests of the department.’ He licked his lips, and glanced towards Ellsbury. ‘You will naturally have to resign. But we would allow you the usual notice, with pay. After all, we don’t want scandal—’

'Scandal!' Arnold was almost beside himself with fury. 'You don't really expect me to go along with this charade, do you? You may well have reasons not to want me in your department, and there may be people who want to get me thrown out, but I've no intention of resigning. If you think you have a case against me for fiddling my expenses and overcharging on my claim forms you can damn well bring it! As for your deposition — it's a pack of lies! I was at Spittal, I never came south to Chesters Fort. I would have no reason to do so—'

'Your obsession with ancient stonework—'

'That has nothing to do with it. I was working at Spittal. I'm sorry, Chairman, but this won't do. I insist on knowing the names of the signatories to the deposition, and I deny the accuracy of its contents.'

'You're making things very difficult for us, Landon,' the Senior Planning Officer said bitterly. 'But if you insist on dragging all this out into the open, you'll be the one to lose. We're offering you a quiet route out of the department. If you continue to take another line, we'll be forced to prosecute.'

'At least I'll then know exactly who signed that statement — and maybe I'll find out why.'

'Then there's little more to be said,' the Senior Planning Officer announced stiffly.

'You're not going to show me the statement?'

Tom Ellsbury ran a nervous hand over his bald pate. He was beginning to sweat. He looked doubtfully at the Senior Planning Officer. 'I think this is as far as we can go today. We'll need to see the Chief Executive — he's the chief legal officer, after all. We'll need his advice. About whether we prosecute, you know.'

The Senior Planning Officer's mouth was like granite. 'I agree, Chairman. In the meanwhile, we'll retain this document.' He turned a baleful glance on Arnold. 'If we decide to prosecute, naturally you will be given copies of the documentation. In the meanwhile, until we have taken advice from the Chief Executive, matters must remain as they are, in the face of your intransigence.'

‘Intransigent because I won’t lie down with my feet in the air when you snap your fingers?’ Arnold said. ‘What the hell is going on here?’

‘I think enough has been said,’ the Senior Planning Officer replied coldly. ‘I will just add one thing. If it is shown that you were elsewhere than where you claimed to be — at Spittal — we will be justified in summarily terminating your employment with us. You could have taken the chance to go quietly. Publicity and scandal will make your going less pleasant — and certainly less remunerative!’

Arnold stood up. ‘And in the meanwhile?’

‘In the meanwhile,’ the Senior Planning Officer stated icily, ‘I think it is best if you remain away from the office. Your suspension, Mr Landon, remains in effect, *sine die*.’

2

Arnold stared moodily at the sketches he had made of Harlech and Flint castles. Spread out beside them he had the photographs of Harlech taken by Jane Wilson. He had told her there was something in the photographs that should have fired him, but he simply could not concentrate sufficiently to pin it down. The discussion with Ellsbury and the Senior Planning Officer had left an unpleasant taste in his mouth. He was convinced there had been nothing wrong with his mileage and expenses claims. Moreover, if there were any discrepancies they were in favour of the authority: he did not in fact always claim what he was entitled to by way of expenses.

But there was also the matter of his desk diary. It was beginning to look as though he was being set up quite deliberately. Someone had taken the trouble to remove the diary so that the claims could not be substantiated. But he could think of no other officer who might have wished to get rid of him from the department. He was blocking nobody's promotion; he kept very much to himself; he wasn't aware he was seen as a threat to anyone.

Except, maybe, Councillor Bryman.

The man's attitude towards Peter Aspen had been vicious and menacing. Bryman was on the Planning Committee; he visited the department from time to time; he knew where Arnold's office was. It was just possible that Bryman was vindictive enough to set up this false claim — maybe as a warning, maybe to demonstrate to Arnold how powerful he was. As for the Senior Planning Officer, it would not have been beyond his wit to set it up either, for he had seen Arnold as a problem from the moment he had taken up the job. Getting rid of Arnold Landon would be something the Senior Planning Officer would regard as desirable: he would smile in the mornings.

He left the sketches and photographs and prowled around his bungalow. The more he thought about it, the more convinced he became that Bryman was behind the suspension decision. It was a way of giving Arnold Landon something to think about other than the researches of Ken Andrews. But what was bothering Bryman, anyway? What was there in Andrews's work that worried him, and caused him to make threats against Peter Aspen?

He had forced Aspen to drop the Rosicrucian book. Arnold was damned if Bryman was going to force Arnold Landon into a corner, frightened to touch anything connected with the dead man at Bodicote Barn House.

The phone rang.

'Mr Landon?'

'That's right.'

'Horspool here. I hope I'm not disturbing you?'

'Not at all. I'm not doing anything in particular,' Arnold said bitterly.

'Ah. Yes. Well, I did say, old chap, that if you got in touch in a few days I might have something for you.' He cleared his throat noisily. 'Have to go away for a couple of days now, though — nephew of mine in the Somersets. But I got along rather faster than I expected, so I thought I'd give you a ring. I knew there was something else about that damned Andrews chap.'

'Something else?'

'That's right. I told you the Green Howards weren't keen on scandals. Fact is, of course, the kind of thing that blew up over Andrews would have been difficult to hush up. I mean, forcin' a chap to resign . . . he could have been sticky, refused, dared us to produce our proof and that sort of thing. But it was never necessary.'

'Why was that?' Arnold asked.

'Well, we sort of got rid of him on other grounds. The other two characters — they were weak sort of fellers, only too glad to take the chance to resign quietly when it all came out. I mean, they couldn't have kept their heads up in the mess and all that sort of thing. But Andrews, he was tougher — he might have been stubborn enough to stick it out. Because there was no real hard proof, if you understand me. Rumour, gossip, that sort of thing. Nothing in flagrante, so to speak.'

'So how did you force him to resign?'

'Well, the second in command had a connection in the Advocate General's office . . . old school chum. They were having a chat, and to cut a long story short, they managed to dig around in the records and they came up with somethin' interesting.'

'Yes?'

'Andrews had changed his name.'

'You mean before he entered the Army.'

'That's the ticket.'

'But what difference could that make?' Arnold asked, puzzled.

Colonel Horspool snorted in satisfaction. 'Ah, but that's it. All the difference in the world. It wasn't just his name he changed; he changed his background too. And managed to forget that he'd spent some time in Exeter Gaol, to boot.'

'For what offence?'

'Can't say, old chap. Maybe something to do with his sex life — but I was on the periphery of all this, and one didn't ask too many questions. Anyway, Andrews got the boot, not because of the corruption thing, but because he'd falsified his records to get into the Army in the first place. So out he went — but you know, it shows what a bounder the chap was. I mean, he didn't move far, did he? Set up in Durham, mingled in the right social set — though not the Army people — got on with his damned odd stories. Not that I ever thought much about his military histories. But then, perhaps I was biased. Didn't like the chap . . . didn't like his books. Follows, don't it?'

'Is there anything else you've been able to find out about him, sir?'

''Fraid not. Except he lived in Exeter when he was jailed. As for the rest, well, he wasn't well liked. And I mean, with that sort of background, I wouldn't be at all surprised if someone saw fit to do him in.'

'Colonel, I'm grateful for your trouble. I'm sure Jane Wilson will be pleased—'

'Ah well, don't like the idea of talking about such stuff with a gel, you know. But you and Jane — you friends, then?'

Arnold hesitated. 'Acquaintances, really.'

'Plain gel. But bright. Don't like 'em too bright, myself. Never did. Not that it matters too much these days. Past it, hey?'

'I wouldn't say she was plain,' Arnold said, surprised at himself.

'That's as may be. Anyway, I have to get off down south. Glad I was able to help, Mr Landon—'

'Oh, Colonel, before you ring off . . . Can you tell me the name Andrews used before he falsified his papers?'

'Oh yes, of course. Something like Haughton, or Horton . . . something like that. Give my best to young Jane, then, will you?'

Arnold promised to do so, when next he saw her.

* * *

He called on her the next morning, at the bookshop on the Quayside.

It was a bright and sunny day and the traffic was heavy.

The waters of the Tyne were black under the sunlight and some Japanese tourists were busying themselves with their inevitable cameras, taking a succession of identical shots against the background of the arching Tyne Bridge.

There were a few people browsing in the shop when Arnold entered. Jane was attending to a customer and smiled at him. Arnold was prepared to wait. He moved to the back of the shop among the dusty volumes and browsed, admiring some photographs of fourteenth-century dovecotes in a yellowing tome with foxed binding. After a while he was aware that she was standing beside him.

'Two thousand doves,' he said. 'Amazing, isn't it? The landowners used to vie with each other for the most magnificent stone structures. That was when the birds were still bred for food, of course — before the dovecotes became ornamental appendages to stylized gardens.'

'Amazing,' she agreed. 'I'm closing for lunch. You wanted to see me?'

'Colonel Horspool's been in touch.'

She had obtained some sandwiches from a delicatessen along the hill and was prepared to share them with Arnold; she made a flask of tea and after she had locked the shop they walked along the Quayside to the market walls. They sat down on the stonework, legs dangling over the edge above the black Tyne water and she offered him a sandwich.

'How's Ben?' Arnold asked.

'He's up and about. He should be home soon. But he'll have to take it easy.'

'Will you stay on?'

'For a while, I Suppose, until he's able to steady himself.' She munched on her sandwich. 'So what did the Colonel have to say?'

Arnold explained.

'So he'd been in gaol, this Haughton character?' she mused. 'In Exeter . . . It's likely, then, that we could get hold of his records.'

'I doubt it. The conviction would have been spent. You can't get access.'

'But if it was Exeter Gaol, the chances are there would have been something in the local papers — particularly if it was a sexual offence.'

'Maybe.'

'We could have a look.'

'To what purpose?'

'I told you,' she said firmly. 'If the police don't want to look into his past, I do. I'm not happy — and there's a few of us in Durham who aren't — about old Foxy being railroaded. He's not capable of raising a defence for himself. Besides, I'm beginning to get rather interested in this Andrews. He doesn't sound to me like a very pleasant character. He could have enemies. So . . .' She glanced at him quizzically, squinting in the sunshine and smiling. 'You fancy a trip to Exeter?'

It was ridiculous. He would normally have refused. But dancing at the back of his mind was the thought that she was right: Andrews, or Haughton, or whatever he was called would certainly have had enemies — and one of them would seem to have been Councillor Bryman.

Bryman was a man capable of making enemies — and perhaps of seeing enemies even where they did not exist.

'Why not?' Arnold replied with a shrug. 'I've nothing else to do.'

'I like decisive men,' she said.

3

It was a long drive to make from Northumberland to Exeter, but they concluded they might need the car when they were there, so they opted against the tram. They decided to set off early in the morning: Arnold called for Jane Wilson at her Framwellgate Moor bungalow and they drove to Scotch Corner, took the A66 towards Brough and crossed the Pennines towards Tebay. There they picked up the M6 running south. In the brightness of the morning the massive fells were grey-brown, speckled with sheep, and an RAF fighter screamed along the winding valley only two hundred feet above their heads: Arnold kept a steady pace while lorries thundered past on the half-empty motorway.

They stopped north of Lancaster for coffee and then pressed on, down through Lancashire and into the Midlands. Jane had brought some tapes with her — 'I hate the pop music they play constantly on the radio' — so Arnold found himself listening to arias by Placido Domingo and Pavarotti for a large part of the journey. He was not addicted to opera the way she clearly was, and in the late afternoon she relented, allowing him to turn on the radio for the news and current affairs programmes.

They had decided to take no lunch, but Arnold had booked ahead for them in Exeter, and when they arrived in the early evening they were able to go to their rooms, take a relaxing shower and meet again in the dining room of their hotel.

Arnold was not used to spending much time in the company of women. He had always been wary of them; as a young man rather too shy to deal with the kind of badinage other young men seemed to use, and later, his urge to follow in the footsteps his father had carved out for him took him away from the kind of social situations where he would develop an ease with the other sex.

He did not find Jane difficult to get on with.

There was a refreshing directness about her that he liked; he privately felt she was on a wild goose chase with no clear aim in view but he admired her persistence; and she had a sharp intellect. During the journey down she had talked more about her own obsessions, the fourteenth century, the Arthurian romances, Queen Eleanor and the way she had held on to her husband's affection for almost forty years.

'You know, when she died, he was grief-stricken. He built three separate tombs for her — Lincoln, Blackfriars in London, and the main one in Westminster Abbey, and there were the twelve Eleanor crosses — one for every point at which the funeral cortege stopped.' She looked at him mischievously. 'Do you think husbands are so romantic these days?'

'I imagine they don't have the money.'

'She was wealthy enough.'

'So I understand. Guisborough's *Chronicle* has the couplet: *The King he wants to get our gold, The Queen would like our lands to hold.*'

'She was much maligned,' Jane protested. 'By men.'

'Aren't all women?'

He had never found it so easy to relax in a woman's company.

* * *

The following day they decided to split up, to conduct their lines of inquiry separately. Arnold busied himself in the newspaper library, ploughing his way back through newspaper files for the court reports. Jane went a different route: checking on births and deaths, family names and seeking the advice of a history professor at the university with whom she claimed some distant acquaintance.

For Arnold the day proved frustrating. He was not terribly interested in reading sordid court cases in old newspapers and felt he could be spending his time rather better. And although he searched meticulously, he came across no cases involving the names the Colonel had suggested. At lunchtime he took a break and wandered down into Fore Street to the bridge over the Exe, where they had discovered the ruins of a Roman bridge some distance from the present stream. He strolled around it for a while until his conscience pricked him, and then he made his way back to the newspapers.

It was four in the afternoon before he came across a possibility. He sat back and thought about it, felt the stiffness of his joints, and decided to give up for the day. He had arranged to meet Jane back in the hotel at six, so he decided to make use of the rest of his time by taking a look at Exeter's underground passages.

He spent a pleasant hour there, inspecting the extraordinary system of tunnels, stone built in part, cut through the rock elsewhere, a series of conduits cut to bring water to Exeter from the springs in the Longbrook Valley. It was a fascinating and steamy-breathed journey through the ancient roots of the city; silence descended a yard from the entrance.

When he emerged at Princesshay he heard his name called.

It was Jane Wilson. She was standing at the exit, waiting for him. 'I thought I'd find you down here. I tried the newspaper library and they said you'd gone; then the hotel, but they said you hadn't got back. So I sat down and thought . . . and I guessed you'd head for here or the cathedral.'

Feeling vaguely guilty, he made his way back up to the street. 'I was getting nowhere — though I came across one possibility. So I took time off.'

'Mmmm. Well, I'm not surprised. I've got the feeling we've been chasing shadows. You said the Colonel told you Andrews's name was Haughton?'

'Right. But in fact—'

'I think he was wrong or you misheard the name.'

'Yes, I was about to say—'

'Either you didn't hear Colonel Horspool correctly, or he got it wrong from the records. My guess is Andrews wasn't called Haughton at all — the name was Orton. I've checked the birth records in Exeter and there just isn't anyone—'

'That's my point. I've checked the newspaper reports. There is no Haughton. But there is an Orton, sent inside at Exeter. A young man.'

'The offence?'

'The kind of thing Colonel Horspool would not mention in the presence of young ladies,' Arnold said.

'A sexual offence?'

'Young girls.'

Jane expelled her breath thoughtfully. 'A young man. Orton; a sexual offence. Unlikely there'd be two of these people.'

Arnold nodded. The coincidence would be too great. Maybe Colonel Horspool had got the name wrong. 'There's one thing more, which clinches it for me, really. This Orton character's name is given in the newspapers as Kenneth Andrew Orton. It's an odd fact, but it seems when people change their names they display a remarkable lack of imagination.'

'Did the newspaper account give any address?'

Arnold nodded again. 'Kenneth Andrew Orton of 15 St David's Hill. I don't know where that is.'

'I do. It's on the way to the university. It's walking distance from here — just above the railway station.'

They walked back up Fore Street as she explained how the history professor — an expert on Exeter — had been most helpful. He had produced census returns for her, but there had been no report of anyone called Haughton, of the right age, in the town at the relevant time. She had come away virtually empty-handed, though now that Arnold had found this possibility she could go back with a rather more specific request. If it was necessary. The first thing they could do would be to make inquiries at St David's Hill.

The city was clearing as the evening approached, shops closing and traffic pouring down Fore Street and out towards Haldon. At the top of the hill they turned left and crossed the old Iron Bridge. Down below them Arnold could see the ancient catacombs that were still a tourist attraction in Exeter — though few cared to enter them.

St David's Hill was an amalgam of eighteenth- and nineteenth-century, four-storey houses, blank-faced, iron-gated, with overgrown front gardens. Some were now used as offices; others had been split up into flats.

'So what do we do now?'

'We make inquiries,' she said determinedly.

The first two houses they called at echoed to the sound of their knocking but no one responded. At the third attempt they met a young woman, harassed by a child at her side. She suggested that there was only one house where they might get assistance: only one family would seem to have lived in St David's Hill consistently for a lengthy period of time: the rest of the inhabitants were relatively recent arrivals in flats that were subject to a fluctuating occupancy.

'There's a family — the Hargreaves — have lived along here for fifty years. The old girl might be able to help.' She couldn't. She was a long time coming to the door, and her attitude was unhelpful: she wanted to watch *Coronation Street* on television, and although Jane suggested it would not start for another hour or so it made no difference.

'Anyway,' the old woman said, 'I was never much interested in the neighbours. Old Annie Fellwood now, she was different. Always knew everything about everyone. Couldn't keep her nose out of other people's business. Aye, Annie Fellwood is the one you want to talk to.'

‘Where would we find her?’ Jane asked.

‘She moved out of St David’s Hill twenty years ago. Didn’t go far though — her mother lived round the back there.’

‘Around the back?’

The old lady began to close the heavy door. ‘Aye, that’s right. Ask around the back. She always liked a good gossip.’

‘But where around the back?’

‘Little Silver, that’s where she lives, Annie Fellwood. In Little Silver.’

The door was slammed shut with a decisive banging sound.

* * *

They found the narrow lane that led into Little Silver halfway along St David’s Hill.

Some attempt had been made to retain the character of the footpath. Old iron lamp-posts were still placed at strategic intervals along the lane; its high sides were of warm old brick, the protective rear walls of enclosed Victorian gardens backing on to the four-storey houses on the hill. The walls themselves were draped with escaping Virginia creeper, clematis and ivy — one magnificent specimen of honeysuckle made Arnold realize, from its profusion, how much more encouraging the south-west climate was to plants. Not that he would trade his northern hills for the softer, rounder contours of the Devon countryside.

When they finally found Annie Fellwood it was in a small garden of lupins, hollyhocks, roses, garlic and aubretia. Little Silver was a tiny, wall-locked area, quiet, sunlit and cottagey in its atmosphere. Annie Fellwood was perhaps sixty years of age. She was dressed in a faded flower-patterned dress and gumboots. Her hair was grey and straggly; where it kept falling in her eyes she had brushed it back with a grimy hand, so streaks of dirt ran across her forehead and cheek. She struggled to her feet when they approached and dropped her trowel, as though glad of the interruption.

'Bloody aphids.'

'I beg your pardon?' Jane Wilson said.

'Greenfly. On my roses. The garlic is supposed to keep them off. I think washing-up liquid is better.'

'I'm sure it is,' Jane said uncertainly. 'Are . . . are you Annie Fellwood?'

'Have been for sixty years. Who are you? Not local.'

'That's right. We're from the North of England, in fact.'

'Long way from home.' She peered at them suspiciously. 'You lookin' for me, then?'

'Only to have a chat,' Arnold offered. 'We're actually trying to trace someone who lived in St David's Hill.'

'When?'

'Quite a while ago. In the late fifties, or early sixties.'

Annie Fellwood grunted, and wiped a grimy hand across her forehead. 'Huh. Not many can tell you about those days.'

'But you can, we understand. You lived in St David's Hill then?'

'That's right, m'dear. Didn't come round here to Little Silver till me mother was took ill — that was in 1970. So who was it you wanted to know about?'

'A man called . . . Kenneth Andrew Orton.'

There was a short silence. The old lady had screwed up her eyes to stare at Arnold. Above their heads a pigeon swooped and in the silence Arnold was suddenly aware of the house martins that had started their evening feast, wheeling and darting to pick up insects on the wing.

'Orton. What you interested in him for?' Annie Fellwood asked. 'He been in trouble again?'

'He's dead,' Jane replied.

Annie Fellwood snorted. 'Comes to us all.'

'You said . . . trouble *again.*'

'Bad lot he was. Always.'

'You knew him?' Arnold asked.

'Oh, I knew him all right. Leastways, knew about him. He never bothered me, of course — he'd have got something for his pains if he'd tried, I'll tell you. Bad lot. They tried to say, of course, that it was all because of his background. But the story is his old man wasn't much better. Never remember him, mind you: just what people told me over the years.'

'What was odd about his background, then?' Arnold asked.

Annie Fellwood scratched her greying head and waddled forward to the white-painted gate. She leaned forward, resting her broad tanned forearms on the gatepost. 'He was an orphan.'

'He didn't know his parents?'

'No, not that. They was killed . . . died in a fire in the terrace house they lived in. Some said maybe he started it with matches, but I don't think that was much other than malicious gossip. Story is his old man was a drunkard maybe had a bit too much. Smokin' in bed, I dunno.'

'How old was Orton then?' Jane asked.

'Fourteen, fifteen maybe, I'm not sure. But that was when he came to live in St David's Hill. Got took in by the Ellands. They was cousins, see. And she was very good to him, was Sally Elland. She had kids of her own, you know, and Ken Orton wasn't her responsibility, but she took him in and looked after him. Even took him back in after the trouble.'

'When he was jailed, you mean?'

'Ar, you know about that, then? That's right. It was a bit of a funny business, mind. Sally Elland had two kids, and Ken Orton and the boy — Barry he was called — they were always together. Barry was a bit younger than Ken Orton, and a bit of a tearaway even when he was a kid. Anyway, there was talk that when the police caught them down at the meadows there was something funny going on and Barry was involved. He was about sixteen then, Ken Orton was about twenty. I seem to remember the gossip was Orton had sort of led Barry Elland on, so he got off with a warning. Orton now, that was different. He got about eighteen months, I think.'

'What sort of man was he?'

'Didn't like him. Never paid much attention, of course, was older than him. But if he hadn't been that way, and he'd tried his funny stuff with me, I'd have torn them off him!'

Arnold was inclined to believe her, when he stared at her meaty hands. 'What happened to Mrs Elland?'

'Oh, she's been dead these years now. Unhappy, she was — not a good life. She was a widow, see, and she couldn't cope with the two boys. The girl now, she was different — quiet, little mouse of a kid, as I recall. Afraid of her own shadow. But Barry Elland made up for that — and he gave his mother trouble as he grew up. What with Ken Orton as well, she had her hands full. No wonder she died young. Forty-five, thereabouts.'

'There are no Ellands in St David's Hill now?'

Annie Fellwood shook her head. 'No. After Sally Elland died the kids moved out. You said late 'fifties . . . you got that wrong. Ken Orton got took in about 1962. He was put inside in 1968.'

'You're right,' Arnold said. 'You have a good memory for dates.'

'Aye. But Sally Elland died in 1970, same year I moved to Little Silver. But the two boys — they had already moved away from Exeter then.'

'Together?'

'No, not as I recall. They went their separate ways. Now let me think . . . Ken Orton, I don't know, he went up north somewhere. Never heard of him again around here. Nobody missed him. Bad lot. Barry Elland, now what happened to him?' The old woman contemplated her grimy fingernails, broken and scarred with thorns. 'Aye, that's right, I remember now. Didn't he go north as well — Manchester way? That's right,' she added triumphantly,' I do recall. Manchester it was. There was someone here a few years later, talking about him. Didn't mend his ways, did young Barry. Got into trouble with the police in Manchester. Maybe he escaped down here, but he was in bad up there. Can't remember what it was about, though.'

'Was Orton with him?'

'No, don't think so. They didn't go off together; and there was a bit of a fuss around the time of Sally Elland's death.'

'Fuss? How do you mean?'

Annie Fellwood shrugged. 'Never got to hear the rights of it. All I can say is there was a big quarrel in the house: shouting and screaming. Ken Orton left shortly after that and Barry wasn't long in going either. Sally Elland died soon after. Pneumonia. Broken heart, some said. Only the girl turned up at the funeral. No sign of those boys. And the girl . . . what was she called? Susan . . . Sue Elland, that was her. Downtrodden kind of girl she was. Pretty face she had but always kept close to her mother, like. And after Sally Elland died, I suppose there was nothing — and no one — for her in Exeter.'

'So where did she go?'

'You almost got to go up country from here, don't you? I mean, what Devonian wants to go to Cornwall? Funny down there, they are. No, she left Exeter — went up to Bristol, I heard. Indeed, she must have smartened herself up somewhat, if you ask me, because I did hear she got married. Came back here with him once. Didn't see her, but he was pointed out to me in the corner shop one day. Quiet sort of chap; didn't have much to say for himself.' She squinted at Arnold again. 'Dead, you say . . . Ken Orton. Good riddance, I think. Dirty bugger, he was.'

* * *

After dinner Jane suggested they go down to the Exe and walk along the river bank past the maritime museum. The evening was pleasant: dusk was approaching, the city was quiet and the canal basin where the old craft were crammed was empty of people. Behind them stood the old warehouses that had been given a new lease of life by television crews wanting to recreate old Liverpool — the ways of the media were beyond Arnold. In front of them, in the canal basin were the masts of English, Malaysian and Indonesian craft, as well as a sardine boat from Portugal and a prahu from Bahrein.

They walked along the Quayside: the warehouses and cellars held fishing boats, coracles, a Venetian gondola dressed for a wedding. In the dusk, men were still working on a rowing boat in the open cellar of one of the warehouses.

'So where do we go from here?' Arnold asked. 'You've managed to trace the early years of Kenneth Andrew Orton and you're told he was a bad lot. We knew that already. But the trail is cold now: how can we find out what happened to him between the time he left Exeter and appeared in Durham . . . or at least, in the Green Howards?'

'I wouldn't say the trail is cold,' Jane disagreed. 'We know he had two cousins — one in Manchester and one in Bristol. If we want to find out more about Orton, let's trace his cousins. They may have kept in touch.'

'I'm still not certain of the point of this,' Arnold demurred.

She hesitated. 'I have to admit this man Orton is a sort of shadowy figure to me. I mean, it's wrong that the police are charging Fernlea, and in the first flush of anger I suppose I overreacted, trying to do an amateur detective job. On the other hand, now I'm started I'm reluctant to give up. It's like all research, isn't it? You get on a trail, and you want to continue to the end.'

'Except there never is an end,' Arnold replied. 'And that means you have to know when to stop.'

'I don't want to stop. Not yet.'

Arnold wasn't sure as far as he was concerned. He did not feel as committed as Jane Wilson — though he was beginning to feel she was now beginning to see the wild goose nature of her quest. They walked on and stood to watch the ferryman hauling on his rope to pick up a couple on the far bank of the Exe. The young man and woman clambered aboard and were hauled back across to the museum side. They were excited and laughing and obviously in love: their voices were sharp and clear in the evening air.

'I'd like to pursue things just a bit further,' Jane said quietly. 'We could make our way back . . . but you could drop me in Bristol. If Sue Elland lived there and got married there in the early seventies I should be able to trace her. I could have a talk with her. The more we know about Orton, the more likely we are to discover who might have been his enemies . . . someone who would want to kill him.' She looked at Arnold. 'If you drop me there, I could make my own way back north by train.'

Arnold nodded. 'No problem.'

'And what about you?'

Arnold groaned mentally. 'I'm not sure—'

'It could be useful if you were to stop off at Manchester make some inquiries about Barry Elland. Annie Fellwood said he'd got into trouble there. The records . . .'

She was a determined woman. Arnold had the feeling that if he did not agree immediately, he would agree in the end. It was easier to capitulate at once.

'I'll give it two days, no more,' he said. 'And that'll be the end of it. I've other things on my mind.'

'Treat this as recreation,' she suggested. 'A little holiday from the other problem you have in Morpeth.'

She had a point. It could take his mind off Bryman and the Senior Planning Officer. And at the very least, it was better than worrying about his suspension and the threat of legal action based on falsified claim forms.

4

Detective Inspector Greybrook stood uneasily in the private members' room in County Hall in Durham. Chief Superintendent Redvers was standing near the broad windows that gave a view of the rolling Durham hills and the cathedral. It had rained heavily in the morning, but hot sunshine had followed, so that the crag on which the castle and cathedral stood was now mantled in a grey mist rising slowly from the river and veiling the banks of trees on the steep slopes below the crag. It was a spectacular sight, but one he was sure Redvers was hardly seeing: he would be preoccupied with this call to County Hall.

They had been waiting for twenty minutes. The call had come from the Leader of the Council; it was suggested that the officer in charge of the Andrews investigation, together with the Chief Superintendent, take the short drive to County Hall from Aykley Heads.

It had been the Chief Constable who had taken the call, and he had not been pleased. He had arraigned them in his office.

'What the hell is going on? I don't know why the Leader of the Council wants to see you, Greybrook, but it's *my* idea that Redvers goes with you, because for some reason unknown to me he chose to begin this damned investigation! As you know, I'm a reasonable man—'

Greybrook had never been aware of that.

'-but some things really get up my nose. Political interference is one of them. I can handle problems like demos down in the city and all that sort of crap, but political interference I don't like. Especially when I don't have the answers to the questions. But maybe you pair do! So that's why you're going to see the Leader — and I'm not covering your backs! Do I make myself clear?'

It was very clear. To be fair, Greybrook conceded mentally, the Chief Constable was normally very sensitive about his patch: he was well known for his arguments with the Watch Committee. But he was backing away from this one — possibly, Greybrook suspected, because Redvers had not kept him fully briefed. If that was the case, the Chief Constable was the kind of man who would let Redvers and by implication, Greybrook — swing by themselves. It was indeed very clear.

Redvers turned impatiently from the window. His face was mottled with an uncertain anger. He had said nothing in the car driving up from Aykley Heads, but his breathing had been short and impatient. He was clearly under some strain, and this summons to County Hall did nothing to ease the strain.

'Bloody politicians! Do they think we have no job to do?' As if in answer to his criticism the heavy leather covered doors with the gold — embossed arms of the city swung open, and Arthur Towers, the Leader of the Council, walked in. A short, stocky ex-miner of the old breed, he had a long political history which had started when he became secretary of the local Labour party. He was seventy now, bald, with fiery red-rimmed eyes and a temper to match. He came straight to the point.

'I've asked you to come in to this meeting — the Finance Committee meets in fifteen minutes — because things can move faster that way. I signed the necessary warrants in this case. And I'm bloody unhappy about it now!'

Redvers stood stiffly to attention as the Leader glowered at him like an officer of the day inspecting his troops. 'Unhappy, Leader?' Redvers gritted his teeth. 'Just what exactly is the problem, sir?'

Arthur Towers was a man given to gestures. He swept his arm in the direction of the windows. 'Out there, Redvers is the city. It has a voice. That voice elects people like me — and the party elects me leader.'

Or not, as the case may be, Greybrook thought to himself. 'The voice of the city,' Towers went on, 'is getting bloody loud. A murder was committed not a couple of miles from the city centre. A "suspect" was apprehended — with admirable promptness. And I was persuaded but no mind to that. The bloody fact is, Redvers, and . . .and . . .'

'Detective Inspector Greybrook, sir.'

'The fact is I've been hearing things. I was at the Labour Club in Birtley the other evening and who should walk in but a certain doctor . . . Evans by name. Known him a long time. Trust his judgement. And he tells me the case you'll be presenting to me at the magistrates' hearing doesn't stand a snowball's chance in hell!'

'Dr Evans has an opinion—'

'He also is the forensic expert in Durham, the police surgeon. For Christ's sake, man, if your own expert isn't going to support you, what the hell do you expect to achieve?'

'Greybrook, you're the investigating officer. I take it there is some sort of case against this man . . .'

'Fernlea, sir. Yes, we have a case.' Greybrook paused. 'But there are two sides to every argument and it's always possible—'

'The evidence isn't good enough,' Arthur Towers snapped. 'And I'm warning you pair, if Evans steps up and casts doubt on issues you raise, I'll throw the whole thing out. So if you think you've got your teeth into this Fernlea chap, make your bite count! Or drop the bloody charge.'

Greybrook could understand his excitement. The noise in the city was significant: ward elections were coming up, and Towers would want no harassment, no . . . blurring of issues. Murder cases tend to excite people. They normally had no impact on elections, but there was a lot of gossip about this one. The Leader's eyes had switched back to Chief Inspector Redvers. 'I gather you have a number of . . . friends among the Northumberland Tory group, Redvers.'

'I don't check on my friends' politics, Leader,' Redvers said stiffly.

'Admirable,' Towers sneered. 'It's just that I hear . . . Well, no matter. The thing is, have I made my position clear? I hope you get hold of a solution to the murder, and I've no intention of interfering in police business, but as a magistrate, I must be sure justice is done — and seen to be done. So make bloody sure your case against this vagrant sticks, won't you?'

'I wasn't aware there were votes in vagrants, Leader,' Redvers said sarcastically.

For a moment Greybrook thought Redvers had gone too far. Towers's mouth hardened and his eyes glittered with anger. Then he controlled himself. 'I've got to be pragmatic about politics. We have an overwhelming majority on the council. I don't give a damn that the university intellectuals take up the case of a vagrant . . . but I like to see justice done, even to the unfortunate among us.' Even he seemed suddenly aware of the insincerity of his words. He consulted his watch. 'I have to prepare for the Finance Committee.'

The room was silent. The gritty ex-miner was glaring at Redvers. 'But remember what I said. If Fernlea is guilty, prove it to me! If there's anything shaky in the evidence like Evans says — find out just who *did* kill that bastard Andrews!'

The door swung softly behind him.

Chief Inspector Redvers let loose a string of profanities.

* * *

Back in Redvers's office, Greybrook was ordered to close the door. Redvers opened his filing cabinet and extracted a bottle of whisky. Greybrook was surprised: it was against regulations.

Redvers poured a drink for himself and finished it in a gulp. He offered none to Greybrook. He replaced the bottle and locked the cabinet. His face was flushed with anger.

'Well, you heard the man. What are you going to do about it?'

'We always knew Dr Evans was going to be sparing in his support, sir.'

'Sparing is one thing. Bloody undermining us is another. Fancy the bastard talking to Towers in the Labour Club!'

'I think Towers is scared. He wouldn't want any problems in court at the preliminary hearing. He's already been carpeted a couple of times by the Lord Chancellor.'

'He ought to be dumped from the Bench,' Redvers snarled. 'And the Chief . . . why isn't he backing us?'

Greybrook made no answer. He was watching Redvers sweat, and he was enjoying it. He had just a week to go before he finished his police career, and the time was tumbling forward when he would he free of it all. But right now he could enjoy Redvers's anxiety.

'So, what are you going to do, Greybrook?'

Greybrook hesitated. He was taking a chance, but in view of Evans's likely evidence, he had little choice. 'I don't think we can make the charge against Fernlea stick, sir.'

Redvers glared at him as though it was all Greybrook's fault. 'All right. You're the bloody investigating officer. Where else are we going to look?'

Greybrook's hands were sweating and his mouth was dry. 'I . . . I have a feeling there might be some connection between Andrews's murder, and the book he was writing.'

'Book? Which one do you mean?' Redvers had lowered his voice, an edge of wariness creeping into his tone.

'The one on the Rosicrucians, sir.'

'And why would you think that?'

Greybrook took a deep breath. 'I've read the materials and notes prepared by Andrews. I have a feeling something's missing. The general notes are unexceptionable enough, but I suspect that Andrews was also preparing local material.'

'What exactly do you mean by local material?'

'I think he was preparing to undertake research into the activities of the Rosicrucians in the North-East.'

'What the hell for? A remote secret society—'

'He moved in certain . . . circles in Durham society. Maybe he got a whiff of something. Land deals. Price rigging.' Greybrook hesitated. 'Building contracts.' Redvers peered at Greybrook. The silence grew around them. The Chief Superintendent shook his ponderous head. 'You said something about missing papers.'

'I think some may have been extracted.'

Redvers paused. 'By whom?'

'I don't know, sir.'

'And you don't know what such mythical papers contain! Rubbish, Greybrook, you're snatching at straws.' But Greybrook could see beads of perspiration on Redvers's bull neck and some of the panic in his chest subsided. He waited.

At last Redvers said, 'I can't see where we could even start on that one. Forget it.'

'You don't want me to press it, sir? Assign no one to it?'

'I said, forget it. The line would be a waste of time, unproductive . . . When do you finish with us, Greybrook?'

'In a week, sir.'

'Your notes up to date?'

'Yes, sir.'

Redvers grunted. 'Mistake, keeping you on this case. Time we brought someone else in to take over. After all, once you're gone we'd have to start again anyway, wouldn't we?'

'Yes, sir.' Greybrook almost smiled. The man was so obvious. And so scared.

'All right. I think we'd better do that. Hand over the files to me. I'll hold them until we can assign another officer.'

'As you wish, sir. I'll get them together at once. But do we drop the case against Fernlea?'

Redvers was reluctant to do so, but he was clearly faced with no choice. He nodded. 'We'll have to order his release and withdraw the charges formally before Towers at the hearing. It'll cause a stink, but there's no help for it. Get the files in to me today.'

Greybrook hesitated. Redvers was scared and wanted no investigation into the Rosicrucian book: Greybrook was now almost certain that he knew what had happened to the Andrews papers, even if he didn't know why. But there was one further knife blade he could insert, to see what effect it would have on Redvers.

'I've been working on this case pretty steadily, of course, Sir. There is one other thought that occurs to me.'

'What's that?' Redvers asked suspiciously.

'We haven't paid much attention to Peter Aspen.'

'The publisher? Redvers knitted his brows. 'I don't get what you're driving at, Greybrook.'

'It's just a thought, sir. The sequence is interesting. Aspen and Andrews moved in the same social circle. Aspen commissions a book from Andrews. Andrews is murdered. Aspen decides to go on with the book — but then suddenly changes his mind. Was it because he saw something in the papers that worried him? Or was he merely seeking to allay suspicion — get the papers suppressed, kill Andrews . . . it's all supposition, of course, but maybe Andrews went too far, maybe there was something in the Rosicrucian papers that was dangerous for Aspen . . .'

'You keep on about the bloody Rosicrucians.' But Redvers was thinking, concentrating hard. 'Aspen . . . Aspen . . . We've got him on file, haven't we?'

'Inconclusive stuff, sir.'

'But he is on file!' Redvers stirred angrily. 'Stop beating about the bloody bush! What's the story?'

Greybrook licked his lips hesitantly. 'Rumours, a couple of complaints. We had a watch going for a while, but manpower problems . . . The file is still pending, but no action taken. I believe there was some suggestion that the Cleveland business a couple of years ago, and the Yorkshire arrests . . . well, we didn't really want to stir any hornets up in our own back yard unless we were absolutely sure.'

'That's right, I remember. I wasn't involved, but . . . Aspen. The bloody paedophile ring!'

'Alleged, sir, just alleged.'

'Was Andrews on the file?'

'No, sir. But again, rumours have flown around from time to time.' Greybrook paused. 'He wrote military histories and occult books. Maybe he had other kinds of links with Aspen — or maybe in his dealings with Aspen he discovered something damaging to Aspen. Who knows?'

'Aspen.' Redvers's eyes were glistening. He nodded. 'All right, thank you, Greybrook. It's a possibility, something we'd better pursue once you hand the files over.'

It was interesting.

Greybrook went back to his office and pulled the files together. He called in Detective Sergeant Eyre and told him he was being taken off the case.

'The charges against Fernlea are to be dropped and another officer will be assigned in a matter of a day or so.'

'Not the most satisfactory way to end your career in Durham, sir.'

'I suppose not.'

But it wasn't over yet. There was a week to go. Greybrook settled back in his chair with a cup of coffee.

He was trembling slightly; the coffee would calm his nerves. Interviews with Redvers always unnerved him somewhat, and with the knowledge that Redvers had something to conceal — for Greybrook was convinced of that now — his edginess had increased.

He had not told Redvers what Arnold Landon had told him: that Aspen had been prepared to continue with the books until he had been threatened — possibly with exposure. But what had the threatening party to fear from the Andrews research?

Greybrook smiled thinly, and sipped his coffee. Landon would tell him in due course, no doubt, just who the man was. And then Greybrook could find out whether the man had any Rosicrucian connections.

And then there was that other lead . . . the woman Landon had mentioned . . . Jane Wilson. It was always possible she might come up with something that would lead to the killer. Greybrook sipped at his coffee, calmer now.

Maybe things would yet be cleared up. In a few days.

Perhaps even before he resigned finally from the Durham police force.

CHAPTER FIVE

1

Arnold dropped Jane Wilson at the Dragonara Hotel in Bristol; it meant she would be near to Temple Meads Station when she decided to make her way back north. He himself was tempted to dawdle a while: the spire of St Mary Redcliffe beckoned just a hundred yards away, but he resisted the temptation, for it was a long drive to Manchester, he did not know the city, and he had not booked into a hotel.

He drove through a heavy storm once he was north of Gloucester. The long black cloud that had built up in the west, menacing the motorway, finally burst ahead of him and rain lashed down fiercely against the windscreen. The sky was dark.

It was in accord with his mood: while he might have been persuaded in Jane Wilson's presence that this work was worthwhile, when he was alone in his car he had further misgivings. He felt no real involvement or need to be involved with the affairs of Kenneth Andrew Orton or Foxy Fernlea; his life seemed to be disordered, the threat of legal proceedings was a dark cloud hanging over him, and he felt listless, unable to concentrate on anything for any length of time.

He thought of the Savoyards and Master James of St Georges, but could raise little enthusiasm and when he drew near to Birmingham and the rain increased he was forced to concentrate on his driving. The road glistened ahead of him, lorries threw up vast amounts of spray, and impatient, more reckless drivers flashed their lights at him. Arnold felt thoroughly miserable.

He decided, in the late afternoon, not to drive into the centre of Manchester. He followed the signs for the airport, reasoning that hotels tended to cluster at such points, and then he struck out for Wilmslow. There he was fortunate enough to find a quiet hotel some five or six miles from the centre of Wilmslow, where he could relax and stay the night. The staff assured him that he could park easily near the railway station and take a train into Manchester city centre the next morning.

Arnold went to bed early.

* * *

The following morning the sky had a washed out look, a stiff breeze freshening the air after the storm and pushing high cumulus across the horizon. He had been aware of jet planes taking off during the early morning hours, flying holidaymakers to the Spanish Costas probably, but he was normally an early riser so was not too disturbed by the noise. It was better than the shattering sound of some of the RAF jets practising low-level flying near Otterburn.

Arnold parked his car in Wilmslow and took an early train into Manchester. A few inquiries sent him in the direction of the library, and from there to the Registrar of Births and Deaths. It proved to be a quick operation: the staff were helpful, a couple of phone calls were made, and by mid-morning he had learned that Barry Elland was dead. The man he sought had been killed in 1981.

'Was it a natural death?' Arnold asked.

'I'm afraid not,' the registrar said carefully. 'We don't have the details here, but it looks as though it was a violent death.'

Further inquiries sent Arnold in the direction of one of the local newspapers with a long publishing history: he had been told they kept extensive files.

They did.

'We're very proud of them, in fact,' said the bright-faced young blonde girl at the counter. 'Some of our files go back to 1793. Most of the stuff is on microfilm now of course, but we still have some of the old newspapers intact.'

'I'm really seeking information about someone who was around more recently than that,' Arnold assured her. 'A man called Barry Elland died here in Manchester in 1981. It seems likely there would have been an inquest. I imagine it would have been reported in the newspapers of the time.'

'Violent death?'

'It seems so.'

'Then we'll probably have something about it,' she replied confidently. 'Would you mind filling in this form?'

Arnold took the form to a small booth and completed the details as far as he was able. He had the date of death as well as Elland's name, and he presumed the inquest would have been held fairly near the date.

'Not necessarily,' the girl suggested. 'A lot depends on the police, you know. If they were carrying out a protracted investigation into the death, it could be some time before they got around to holding the inquest.'

'I see. So you'll have to make a search.'

'That's right. A lot will depend also on whether this Barry Elland is indexed. That makes it easier, of course. And if we've actually done a piece on him it gets even faster. Now then, when would you like to call back?'

The hills of Northumberland beckoned. 'This afternoon?' Arnold suggested hopefully.

She laughed; it was a throaty, worldly sound. 'Dear me, no! It'll take us at least two days, with the backlog, to get around to dealing with your form. We get a lot of official requests, you see, and it all takes time. I could try to rush things through, but I'm afraid it can't be done in less than forty-eight hours. Where can I contact you . . . ?' She consulted his form. 'Oh, Northumberland! Well, you wouldn't want to be waiting around here, would you? I think the best bet would be for us to contact you as soon as we have the material—'

'Or I could ring you in a couple of days,' Arnold suggested, aware that matters could sometimes get shelved until the shelves became dusty.

'Either way,' she replied brightly. 'But give us at least two days . . . and better, three.'

At least it meant Arnold could go home.

* * *

There was bad news waiting for him when he entered his bungalow. The Senior Planning Officer had moved quickly. There was a letter there to say that after consultations with the Chief Executive it had been decided that the matter of Arnold's expenses claim forms should be resolved without recourse to the law courts, but that Arnold was to present himself on Friday at the Senior Planning Officer's boardroom in Morpeth where a disciplinary hearing would be held.

It sounded as though the case had already been prejudged.

Arnold made himself a meal and opened a bottle of wine.

This was one of those rare occasions when possibly he should get drunk. He took the precaution of eating first, nevertheless, then settled down in front of the television set, hardly aware of the inane game show that was being aired and paying little attention to the quality of the wine he was drinking.

There were times when life could be lonely, and this was one of them. Solitude was normally something to be appreciated, not worried about. On this occasion, his depression, and possibly the wine, made him maudlin and sorry for himself.

The telephone rang.

'Arnold? This is Jane Wilson.'

He was almost pleased to hear her voice. 'So how did you get on?' she asked.

'Slowly. Barry Elland died . . . violently, apparently. But I can't get details for at least two days. That's why I've come home: no point in hanging around in Manchester.'

'Yes, when you hadn't rung me I took a chance that you might have gone north. I have to admit I had a sneaking suspicion maybe you were playing hooky.'

'I've got to contact them in a couple of days,' Arnold replied, ignoring the teasing note in her voice. 'How did you get on with tracing the whereabouts of Sue Elland?'

'It doesn't seem we're going to strike lucky with our investigations,' she replied. 'I've had great difficulty tracking her down. I checked the local registry, and it seems, whatever Annie Fellwood told us or might have been told, Sue Elland didn't get married in Bristol. Indeed, there's no record of her marrying. It looks to me as though she might have got involved with someone and told people back in Exeter that she was married. Remember, social situations were different then — for some people it was important to pretend to be married. Anyway, I drew a blank there.'

'Did you try the local census returns?'

'I didn't need to, in the end. The information I needed was there in the registry.'

'How do you mean?'

Jane sighed. 'Rather like your experience, I'm afraid. We're not going to get very far with this at all, it seems to me. As far as I can make out, Sue Elland committed suicide . . . not that long after she went to Bristol.'

'Suicide? When would that be?'

'About 1973.'

'So the Elland children didn't last long after their mother died,' Arnold said. 'Barry Elland died in 1981; his sister even before that. At least Orton had a reasonable run for his money.'

'Well, Annie Fellwood did tell us that Sue Elland was very tied to her mother. Maybe she couldn't stand the loss, or couldn't settle in Bristol or something.'

'But she apparently had found someone to lean on. The man Annie Fellwood told us about. You'd have thought that would have helped.'

'Apparently it didn't. But then, who can tell? Maybe the relationship broke up . . . maybe it only caused further problems.' Jane was silent for a while. 'Anyway, I'm not giving up on it just yet. I've seen a brief account of her suicide — the report of the inquest.'

'You've been luckier than me. Manchester want two days' notice!'

'Well, it seems Sue Elland had been hospitalized prior to her killing herself. I don't know whether it was over a previous attempt, or whether she'd been there for psychiatric help. Whichever way it was, Sue Elland was placed in a hospital for a while, here in Bristol, and it may be I can get some more information there. I doubt it, because it's a long time ago, and exactly where it's going to take us I don't know but I can try, anyway. And it is rather odd, isn't it both Ellands dying, and then Orton.'

'People do die, Jane. And it was over an eighteen-year period.'

'I suppose so,' she said reluctantly. 'Meanwhile, you'll be hoping to get a line on Barry Elland in the next few days?'

'If the newspaper library get off their backsides.'

'You sound pretty down.'

Arnold hesitated. 'Well, you know how it is.'

'The office?'

'Disciplinary hearing on Friday.'

'I'm sorry about that. I'm sure it'll all come out fine, though — I can't imagine they've got any charges that they can make stick.'

'I'm grateful for the confidence you're showing in me. At this moment, nobody else seems to be of the same mind.'

'You're beginning to sound sorry for yourself.'

'I am sorry for myself!'

'Have you been drinking?' she asked sharply.

2

The countryside Arnold drove through was open and desolate, scattered with derelict cottages and tumbledown farms. Clumps of tough trees struggled for survival on the windswept slopes: oak, beech, sycamore and rowan, red with berries. He knew the area well, with its ancient, abandoned lead mines and views of the distant peaks of the Pennines.

He made his way through Stanhope until he reached the marketplace. He parked his car near the old church, which was reputed to hold a two-hundred-and-fifty-million-year-old fossilized stump in its grounds, and crossed the road to enter the Pack Horse Inn.

Detective Inspector Greybrook was already there, sitting just inside the door, half hidden from anyone entering but able to see who came in and out. As Arnold entered he rose, stepped forward and held out his hand.

'Hello, Mr Landon. I'm pleased you could make it. What'll you have to drink?'

'Just a half of lager, please.'

'A sandwich?'

'No, thanks.'

He sat down while Greybrook fetched the drinks from the bar. He was intrigued. When Greybrook had rung him there had been no explanation for the location of the lunch-time meeting in the wilds of Wear dale. Nor had there been any communication of the reason for the meeting. Arnold had readily agreed to meet Greybrook, nevertheless: he enjoyed the wild Durham moorland he would have to cross, and he was still on edge, awaiting the disciplinary meeting.

'I'm sorry about the cloak and dagger stuff,' Greybrook apologized as he sat down, placing the two half-pints of lager on the table in front of them. 'It's just that I had to come up into Weardale and I thought . . . well, I thought it best that our meeting wasn't exactly common knowledge.'

'I don't mind coming here,' Arnold replied, 'but what do you want to see me about?'

Greybrook sipped his lager and frowned thoughtfully. He appeared hesitant, uncertain of how much he should disclose to Arnold. 'I've been taken off the Andrews inquiry.'

'Really?' Arnold was taken aback. 'Why?'

Greybrook shrugged. 'To be fair, I couldn't expect to have stayed on it much longer since I'm leaving the force at the end of next week, and taking a job out of the area. But I hate the thought of leaving this inquiry with loose ends untied. And I needed your help to clear something up.'

'How can I help?'

Greybrook was silent for a little while. He appeared to be reluctant to speak; his hesitation gave Arnold time to inspect the man more closely. Something was bothering him: his skin had an unhealthy look about it, and his lips were pale. Arnold suspected he had not been sleeping well, perhaps because of the activity over the murder, possibly because of other pressures. When he finally spoke, his voice was gravelly with tension. 'The fact is, I'm left with the feeling my superior officer doesn't want certain lines of inquiry followed.'

'I don't understand.'

Greybrook shook his head. 'Neither do I, exactly. But I have to deal in facts. I shouldn't be talking to you like this . . . but it's why I asked that we meet well away from Aykley Heads. The situation is . . . abnormal, though. You see, I think Chief Superintendent Redvers may be suppressing some evidence regarding the Andrews murder.'

'What sort of evidence?' Arnold asked in surprise.

'I can't be certain. But I think it's to do with the book Andrews was commissioned to write. On the Rosicrucians.' He hesitated, his grey eyes serious as he stared at Arnold. 'Let me give you the whole picture, as it's been churning around in my mind. When the body was discovered, Redvers came storming in and took over control of the investigation from me. He insisted everything wait until he personally had visited the scene of the crime.'

'Is that unusual?'

'It's unusual,' Greybrook said grimly. 'Then he was in the room itself, alone, for a short while — before the room had been properly searched. The police photographers had been in, however, and when I was going through the photographs later I was struck by an oddity regarding one of the photographs. In one photograph, of the room itself, there's something white on top of the cabinet. When the room was searched, nothing like a sheet of paper — which was what this looked like — was found. I raised it with Redvers — he just said it was a trick of the light. Maybe it was. But he didn't appear to be interested in even considering the matter any further, and certainly not the possibility of it being a sheet of paper — a letter, maybe.'

'I'm afraid I don't see the significance of it.'

Greybrook was slow in replying. His mouth was stiff when he finally spoke. 'I thought about it a long time. I have to accept the possibility that Redvers wasn't interested because there was a letter on top of the cabinet and because it was he who took that paper from the cabinet when he was alone in the room.'

'But why—?'

Greybrook held up a warning hand. 'Let me give you a hypothesis. I've had long enough to worry at this particular bone, so let me test it out on someone. Suppose we have an individual who was angry with Andrews. Suppose that person wrote a threatening letter. And suppose, when Andrews was dead, the letter-writer panicked, asked a friend to get in there quickly and abstract that letter before it pointed a finger at the letter-writer.'

'Asked Redvers to get the letter? That's a bit far-fetched!' Arnold exclaimed.

Greybrook regarded him owlishly. 'I was inclined to dismiss it myself, really, though the possibility bothered me. Not least because the letter-writer would have had to know Andrews was dead almost as soon as the police did! But then there was the Rosicrucian book.'

'What about it?'

'I asked you to check with Aspen — was there anything local in the book. The reason I asked was that I have a strong suspicion some sheets were extracted from Andrews's notes. Sheets that related to local activities of the Rosicrucians in the North.'

'But what could such sheets disclose?'

'Corruption,' Greybrook said shortly.

'And Redvers is involved? I find that hard to credit.'

Greybrook stared sourly at his lager. 'There have been rumours. Not about corruption as such. But Redvers . . . you see, he's a soured man. He's always seen himself as a high-flyer, and he's done well, but not well enough according to his expectations. He has powerful friends among the politicians, but they have been cool to him over the years. No one quite knows why. But I've done some research into the Rosicrucians in the North, as a result of this killing. They tend to have few members in the Durham area and in Durham City itself. Freemasonry is very strong, even in the mining communities. But not Rosicrucians. They tend to be drawn from north of the Wear. And there is a thought among those who chatter in Durham circles that maybe Redvers has too many friends among the High Tories north of the river. The more left-wing politicians in County Durham have objected to the kind of friends he's made. It's cost him advancement in Durham. At least, that's the rumour.'

'But surely a man can choose his own friends!'

'Not if they happen to be prominent businessmen who corner contracts, and who belong to an exclusive club which the copper himself has joined.'

'But surely half the senior officers in the police forces in England are Freemasons! Where's the difference?'

'Don't ask me: I belong to neither secret society. And all I'm doing is relaying rumour. But let's go back to my hypothesis. Let's assume that the Rosicrucian businessmen north of the Wear believe Andrews is going to blow the whistle on them in some way. What's more natural, when they're panicked, that they should contact one of their own who's in a position to help Redvers — and ask him to grab the incriminating threatening letter, along with the Rosicrucian notes, before anyone else in the force can see them?'

Arnold shook his head doubtfully. He sipped at his lager. It seemed to him there were too many leaps in the dark in Greybrook's hypothesis: something about it did not ring true. And yet . . . 'By the way,' he said, 'you keep talking of Andrews, but that wasn't his real name.'

Greybrook went still. He raised his head, stared at Arnold.

His eyes were blank and expressionless. 'What do you mean?'

'Your police work has slipped up. His name was Kenneth Andrew Orton. He forged papers, changed his name, to get into the Army. How come you haven't picked that up?'

'But we assumed . . . Redvers *said*.' Greybrook's face was pale, his lips tight with anger. He seemed momentarily confused and disorientated. He lapsed into silence. Arnold realized he was thinking hard, his mind racing with possibilities. 'Orton . . . if he changed his name . . . did he have a criminal record?'

Arnold nodded. 'Eminently traceable. He was in Exeter Gaol. We're sure it's the same person.'

'We?'

'Jane Wilson. We've been sort of working on it together,' Arnold said somewhat sheepishly.

'Ah . . . yes. You mentioned her to me.' Greybrook shook his head in irritation. 'This sets up a whole new line . . . but I need to think it through . . .' He sat silently for several minutes, obviously shaken. He ran his hand over his eyes, as though brushing away persistent cobwebs. He shook his head again, as if to clear it. 'Let's get back to the reason why I wanted to see you. It's because of my hypothesis about Redvers. When you and I spoke about the Savoyard material you told me Aspen was ending the commission because he'd been threatened. I didn't ask you then. I'm asking you now. Who was it threatened Aspen?'

'Is it important?'

'It is,' Greybrook said, 'if the man in question happens to be a member of the Rosicrucian sect.'

Arnold was silent for several minutes. Greybrook waited patiently. His fingers were twitching slightly as though he was on edge, eager to get the information from Arnold but unwilling to push too hard. But Arnold owed no allegiance or loyalty to Councillor Bryman. After all, he had little doubt that Bryman was behind the suspension he was suffering from.

'I've no idea if he belongs to the Freemasons, the Rosicrucians or any other secret society,' Arnold said, 'but his name is Sandy Bryman, and he's the Chairman of the Planning Committee I work to. That's how I knew him when he was shouting at Peter Aspen. And that's how he knew me.'

'Bryman.' Greybrook wrinkled his brow. 'I don't know about him. Who is he?'

'A successful, pushy sort of businessman. He's not averse to cutting corners, or using unethical means to get hold of information to further his own ends.'

'Which are?'

'The construction and property development business.'

'Classic' Greybrook murmured, and sank back in his seat. 'Councillor Sandy Bryman. You don't like him, Mr Landon?'

‘I’ve no reason to,’ Arnold replied shortly.

Greybrook was watching him carefully, as though trying to dig out the reasons from Arnold’s expression. Then he shook his head. ‘I’ll have to look into this Bryman fellow.’

‘But you’re off the case.’

‘I told you, I don’t like loose ends, and I don’t like the way Redvers seems to be handling things. If my hypothesis is right . . . Besides, things are getting out of hand. This is confidential . . .’

‘I understand.’

‘. . . the fact is, Redvers and I were carpeted. The evidence against Foxy Fernlea isn’t strong enough. He’s not going to appear before the magistrates after all. Charges have been dropped. He’s free to go back to his hill. And that’s why Redvers is flailing around, keen to find another scapegoat.’

‘How do you mean?’ Arnold asked.

Greybrook’s face was grim. ‘If my hypothesis is right and Redvers is covering for someone, he pressed for Fernlea to be charged thinking he could put him away for the killing of Andrews — I mean, Orton — without any trouble. That’s blown up in his face. So I tested him out. And now I think he’s going to go for someone else.’

‘Who?’

‘Peter Aspen.’

‘But why on earth should be think Aspen would kill Orton?’

Greybrook shrugged. ‘I guess . . . You say Orton was put inside. What was the charge?’

‘He was convicted of sexual offences.’

Something unpleasant happened to Greybrook’s mouth. He found difficulty in coming out with the words. ‘Bastard! All my police career, I’ve never been able to stand men who fiddle with kids . . . the bastards ought to be castrated!’ He struggled to control himself. ‘Well, my guess is that will be the key once Redvers finds out about it . . . if he hasn’t already done so. Peter Aspen, you see, is on police investigatory files as a possible member of a paedophile ring in Durham: Once

Redvers finds out about the Orton jailing, it will give him the link and he'll pull Aspen in, I've no doubt. At the moment, he's thinking along those lines simply because the two men were friends . . . or acquaintances. Orton's jail sentence will confirm his thinking.'

'Could it be true? Do you think Aspen would have killed Orton?'

The detective inspector's grey eyes were blank. 'Who knows? If Andrews — Orton — was capable of writing exposes of the Rosicrucians, maybe with a view to blackmailing Redvers's powerful friends, he would certainly be capable of exposing Aspen, if it suited him. If that's so, fine. But if Redvers is just using Aspen as a cover to protect someone else . . .'

He finished his lager. 'I'd better get back to Aykley Heads. I'm off the case, but that doesn't stop me looking into our Mr Sandy Bloody Bryman, does it?' He rose, hesitated, and looked down at Arnold thoughtfully. 'This Jane Wilson . . . she's been pretty sharp, if what you say is true. Is she still working on Orton's background?'

Arnold nodded. 'She's in Bristol at the moment. Orton was looked after by his aunt after his parents died. Jane has been tracing Orton's cousin Sue Elland. She committed suicide, apparently, not long after she went to Bristol. Jane's trying to find out a bit more about her.'

Greybrook sighed and stuck his hands in his trouser pockets. He jingled some coins there, almost nervously. 'Mmm. Doesn't sound too promising. And probably irrelevant, anyway. Still, if she's still at it, keep me informed, hey? When is she due back?'

'Tomorrow or the day after, I would think.'

'Right. But if she finds out anything interesting,' Greybrook said decisively, 'get in touch with me. Let's put it like this. There are powerful interests involved in this business. And Redvers may have things to hide. To go to Aykley Heads could be dangerous . . . very dangerous. On the other hand, I may be off the case, but I'm damned if I'll see evidence disappear into Redvers's drawer the way I suspect some has already gone. You get in touch with me — personally, OK? And keep Redvers and his minions out of it.'

It made sense. It was unlikely Jane would turn up anything more, but what Arnold had now heard about Redvers, convinced him he would be the last person they should turn to in the investigation. But secretly he hoped he would have no further reason to be involved with Greybrook, Redvers or anyone else concerned with the killing of Kenneth Andrew Orton.

In the morning he would be attending his disciplinary hearing.

3

Arnold made his way back over the Durham moors to the upper Tyne, crossed the river and meandered north towards Morpeth . . . He stopped on a windswept hill and tried to re-order his thoughts. His life seemed to be disarranged — a skeleton where the bones had been scattered. He had never thought that his job was an important part of his life, yet his suspension was affecting him badly. He could not be sure whether it was the job itself, or the blow he had suffered to his pride and reputation.

At least, it should be all over, one way or the other, next morning.

The thought made him reluctant to return home. He made a detour as he resumed his drive north, through Holystone Forest. He stopped there to take one of his favourite walks — passing through farmland and an ancient oak coppice before he came out on the track that led past a series of small waterfalls to the bottom of a gorge. He had seen red squirrels in the tall beeches; he sat down on a rock now and was still and at peace among the whispering wildlife in the undergrowth bordering the stream.

Detective Inspector Greybrook had disturbed him. The information he had imparted to Arnold had been surprising but Arnold was bothered by the thought that it was information which should have gone through official police channels. Greybrook had said he and Redvers had been 'carpeted': why did Greybrook not take his complaints to the Chief Constable? It was as though he himself was uncertain of his ground, needed more proof . . . or was aware that his dislike for Redvers might be obscuring his judgement. The man was certainly under pressure and Arnold suspected it was more than the mere thought that, as a perfectionist, he disliked leaving loose ends in the investigation when he left the force.

On the other hand, it certainly made sense to keep in touch with him if Jane Wilson came up with anything. Greybrook might have been exaggerating when he said it could be dangerous to talk to the wrong people in Aykley Heads, but it was as well to be safe on such matters.

It was a moot point whether Jane would come up with anything, however: as far as Arnold could guess, she would now have reached a dead end. He gained no amusement for the pun in the thought: the suicide of an unhappy young woman who could not face life after the death of her mother was no cause for amusement. But he could not see how Jane could gain any further information that would be of relevance to the death of Kenneth Andrew Orton.

* * *

The room was cool and elegantly furnished in a discreet, inexpensive manner. Light curtains lifted in the breeze through the open window and there was the sound of children playing in the park outside the nursing home. The group of tall horse chestnut and sycamore trees at the entrance to the residential home cast long shadows over the drive but there was little traffic in the road beyond and the whole area gave the residents the kind of peace and quiet that they were deemed to need.

'I feel sometimes that I could scream here!' Miss Greer said.

'You don't like it?' Jane asked in surprise.

The old lady with the iron grey hair and the indomitable mouth wriggled in her chair. 'Oh, I suppose I'm too fractious in my old age — though I always say that when you get to my age you've earned the right to be difficult. Don't you agree?'

Jane smiled. 'I suppose so.'

'What I'm really kicking against is old age, of course. You see, young woman, I've been pretty clear about my likes and dislikes all my life, I've known what I wanted to do, and I've done it. No one to gainsay me. No husband, no commitments to push me where I didn't want to go. Now, in old age, I'm told what is good for me . . . and I don't like it. Even though I have to admit the advice is good. But you don't have to like the medicine you're given, do you, even if it's the right medicine?'

'Is that why you went into psychiatric nursing?' Jane asked. 'Doing your own thing, I mean?'

'That's right. It wasn't exactly the kind of thing nice young girls did in my time. But then, I wasn't a nice young girl. I was an awkward one. Scrawny, independent, and difficult. I took a certain pride in it.' She looked at Jane with a malicious twinkle in her eye. 'I still do, as a matter of fact.'

She stretched her legs and looked at her slippered feet with distaste, as though recalling days when she had marched the wards in more positive footwear.

'You worked in a private hospital?' Jane asked.

'Did both. NHS and private. And I was always a rebel. Is that what they told you?'

Jane laughed. 'They told me you held strong views and weren't afraid to state them.'

'Nor speak out when things went wrong.' The old lady looked at Jane warily. 'Which is why you've come to see me, I imagine. You're looking for something other people won't talk about. For ethical reasons. Let's send her to Mollie Greer, they said. Is that it?'

'I have been having difficulty,' Jane admitted. 'And it was suggested . . .'

'So what are you after?'

'Information, really. And background. About what seems to have been a sad case of suicide.'

'Humph.' Mollie Greer pursed her lips. 'One of the problems I had was trying to control my tongue, stop myself telling people to snap out of it. Bad thing for a psychiatric nurse, hey?' She screwed up her old eyes to peer thoughtfully at Jane. 'Just who are we talking about, anyway?'

'A woman called Susan Elland. She came from Exeter. She lived in Bristol only a short time before she committed suicide. Her mother had died two years or so previously, and her brother had gone to live in the North-West. I understand she was in your care before she died. I just wondered what more there might have been, why she committed suicide, that sort of thing.'

'That sort of thing.' The old lady put her head back on the chair. 'It's a tall order, young woman. Long time ago. And unethical . . .'

It was the kind of response Jane had received in checking with the hospital about records. It was not ethical to discuss cases, even if they had occurred twenty years ago. The doctors concerned had moved on; the records were difficult to locate; there were ethical reasons why the information should not be made available.

It was only when Jane was on the point of leaving, giving up any hope of assistance, that the sister had spoken quietly to her, in confidence. 'You might try Mollie Greer. She's in a home for the elderly now, out at Shirehampton. She was working here in those days, and she's . . . well . . . she's always held fairly strong views. An early feminist, and tough as old boots. She might help. But this isn't official, you understand.'

'Susan Elland . . .' The old lady's brows were creased.

She closed her eyes, and began to murmur softly, words and names that had been half-forgotten for years. It was as though she was reciting a litany, softly, as she dredged back through her memories. And then, as Jane watched, something in Mollie Greer's face changed. A darkness came over her, the lips tightened and she clenched her fingers against the chair arms. She sat more upright, slowly. 'Ahhh . . . yes . . . Sue Elland.' She opened her eyes and glared angrily at Jane. 'Yes, I remember now. A long time ago . . . but I remember my fury. But what was there to be done?'

'Can you tell me about it?' Jane asked.

There was a hint of pain in Mollie Greer's eyes as she remembered. She put her head back again, and her voice softened. 'She was a gentle woman. I remember her now as soft, and vulnerable — the kind of woman who would never quite find the strength to cope with the world. Not a bit like me, you can believe that!' She snorted, impatient with herself. 'Perhaps that's why I felt sorry for her. No, not sorry. It was more than that, if I admit it now. I liked her, felt angry for her, because of the way life had treated her.'

'Did you know she was suicidal?'

'She had already tried to slash her wrists. It was why she was in hospital. There was a man. In a way, he was partly responsible for what happened, yet I didn't have it in my heart to blame him, much as I liked her, for he was genuinely in love with her. Indeed, he was obsessed with her, infatuated. Maybe that was part of her trouble, too . . . she couldn't cope with the relationship.'

'Are you saying he dominated her?' Jane asked.

'No, it wasn't like that. She told me he worshipped her. But there was a problem, I think, in the end. It was one she couldn't handle. And she killed herself.'

'I don't understand.'

The old woman shuffled in her chair. Slowly she shook her head. 'In those days, I didn't understand either. You see, I'm different from many women. I have never felt the need for a man. Are you married?'

'No.'

'Perhaps you will understand . . . perhaps not. No matter. The reality is that Sue Elland couldn't cope because of what had happened to her.'

Jane Wilson frowned, puzzled, not sure where Mollie Greer was headed. 'You mean in Exeter? The death of her mother?'

'In Exeter, yes.' Some of the fierceness had returned to the old lady's voice. 'But it wasn't the death of her mother . . . it might even have contributed to her mother's death. No, it was what happened to Sue Elland herself. That was the problem.'

Something slow and unpleasant moved turgidly in Jane Wilson's mind. She had a premonition; she felt she knew what Mollie Greer was going to say. She had to force the question out, almost unwilling to hear the answer. 'What *did* happen to Sue Elland in Exeter?'

'Betrayal. Hurt. Humiliation. From those people who were closest to her.'

Jane hesitated, a leaden feeling in the pit of her stomach. 'You mean her cousin?'

Mollie Greer looked at her sharply. 'So you know about him! But no, not just her cousin. Her brother as well. At the hands of that evil pair, Sue Elland had been the subject of continuous sexual abuse for years!'

There was a long silence between them. The cries of the playing children in the park seemed sharper, to have attained a poignancy that edged into Jane's brain like a sharp knife. She didn't want Mollie Greer to go on because it would open up a box of horrors, yet she had come so far there was now no turning aside to hide her eyes from a situation that many must have ignored over the years. Until Sue Elland committed suicide; and perhaps even after that.

'It started, apparently, when the cousin came to live with them in Exeter,' Mollie Greer said grimly.

'His own parents had died,' Jane explained. 'Mrs Elland took him in.'

'She obtained an evil reward for her charity. I spoke to Sue for many hours. She unburdened herself to me. She told me how it happened — she was a withdrawn, shy child. She couldn't speak to her mother, tell her what was going on; instead, she clung to her, tried to obtain the protection she needed. But Mrs Elland must have been an overworked, harassed woman. And perhaps not too bright. The fact is, once the cousin—'

'Ken Orton.'

'—once he came to live with them, he corrupted her brother and abused Sue. He taught the boy evil ways, he led him along, and the subject of their abuse was the sister, quiet, afraid, not even knowing what was really happening to her.'

'How long did it go on? Was there no one to help?'

'It went on for years, and who could she turn to? She was a gentle girl, frightened. Anyway, there was some small respite when this Orton man was imprisoned, apparently. The brother—'

'He was called Barry Elland.'

'That's right, she told me once. He was scared when Orton was jailed, and he left her alone for a while. Then Orton was released, came home, and within weeks it all started again. That was when Mrs Elland found out.'

Jane nodded. 'We were told there was some sort of row some sort of scandal, but it was kept rather quiet, concealed within the family, the neighbours never knew exactly—'

'Would *you* have told the neighbours?' Mollie Creel asked scornfully. 'No, it was too shameful. You see, Mrs Elland caught them in Sue's bedroom one evening. She was horror-stricken, of course: Sue told me her mother never guessed, though why she didn't when Orton was first jailed God only knows! Still, she had it thrust before her on that occasion, and there was one hell of a row. The boys were thrown out, and went their separate ways. Sue . . .' Mollie Greer's voice softened. 'Poor Sue was still there shamed, humiliated, guilty. She was left to feel she had broken up the family, and there was her mother's incapacity to deal with the situation. The mother went into a decline: she died shortly afterwards. Sue was left alone with the guilt and shame. Leaving Exeter was the obvious answer. But she was ill equipped.'

'What happened in Bristol?'

The old lady sighed. 'She got a job in Shire Mills. She worked in a shop there for a while, then got something in the city. Then she got engaged.'

'She didn't marry.'

'No. I'm not sure why the marriage never actually took place, but it was probably the same basic problem that drove her to suicide.'

Jane could guess what was coming, but she was forced to ask. 'What was it?'

'Inevitable, really. She was in love, that was clear. But she found she could not get close to her lover. For her part she craved love, affection, warmth, a close relationship. But what she had experienced with her brother and cousin was different — she had been used, shamed. The bridge between was impossible to cross. She wanted love; she could not accept lovemaking. In other words, a normal sexual relationship was beyond her. It was destroying her relationship with the man she wanted to marry. In the end, it destroyed her.'

'But could he not help?'

'I believe he tried. But there was an intensity about him that frightened her. He knew about her experiences — they even went back to Exeter once, at his request. He questioned her, and there was anger in him. In the end, she couldn't cope. Suicide was the way out. It offered peace from all the shame, the guilt and the frustration she was suffering.'

The old lady's hands were quivering with pent-up emotion. 'You were angry about it,' Jane said quietly.

'I'm still angry about it,' Mollie Greer almost exploded. 'Not just the events that led up to her suicide. It was the fact that nothing was done afterwards! Those young thugs got away with all the pain and humiliation and death they'd caused! Nothing was exposed in Exeter. Sue Elland's death achieved nothing, except peace for her. I tried to get the police to take some part in it, to pursue the Elland boy and Orton. I was told there wasn't the evidence to justify it. They talked about chain of causation, for God's sake! There was nothing that could be done.'

Jane was silent for a while, concerned about the old lady's distress. 'It'll be no consolation,' she offered, 'but both Barry Elland and Ken Orton are dead now.'

The old lady's eyes glittered. 'But how long did they live after her? Death comes to us all, young woman — but why did it have to come to the innocent so soon, as it did with Sue Elland all those years ago?'

4

There was some consolation in the fact that a couple of people in the office at Morpeth took the trouble to come across to the waiting-room to have a word with Arnold. Quite clearly, the news was out on the grapevine and there were people prepared to offer support and encouragement.

He was pleased to note that each had the same viewpoint: it was a matter of complete bewilderment to them that the charge of fraud should be made against Arnold. On the other hand, he was also aware that there was a certain, possibly subconscious, distancing from him in physical terms — none of them shook hands, as though fearful that some form of contamination might take place. It made Arnold wonder whether the Senior Planning Officer was about to start some sort of expenses witch hunt among his staff. It was always a substitute for decision-making, Arnold thought sourly.

One of the secretaries popped her head around the door and smiled nervously. 'I'm sorry you've been kept waiting, Mr Landon. It's the Chief Executive. He's not turned up yet. Shouldn't be long, though.'

Arnold leaned back in his chair. He had nowhere to go. His world seemed to be spinning gyroscopically at the moment, concentrating on his own misfortune. The thought immediately made him feel ashamed.

Jane Wilson had rung him last evening with an account of her conversation with the elderly nurse who had looked after Sue Elland. Arnold had found the account disturbing. So, apparently, had Jane Wilson. She told him she thought there was nothing further to be done in Bristol. She had decided to come home.

'You'll be pleased to hear, anyway, that Foxy Fernlea has been released,' Arnold told her.

'How has that come about?'

'Basically because of lack of evidence. I understand the investigating officers have been hauled over the coals. They can't produce a convincing case so they've had to release him.'

'Well, I'm damned!' Jane said in an unladylike outburst of temper. 'So we've all been wasting our time with the petition! And my trip down here, too! They shouldn't be allowed to get away with it. Foxy Fernlea must be given some compensation. I'm sure the petition—'

'I think you'd better leave it as it is,' Arnold advised.

'But it's not right!'

'Maybe so, but I wouldn't start stirring up any more hornets. There's some pretty sore heads in Durham. And one other thing . . . I've been advised we shouldn't talk to Aykley Heads directly about anything you might have found out in Bristol.'

'Why not?'

Arnold hesitated. 'Let's just say they're looking for a scapegoat. But I've got a contact who will listen. I think it's as well to take his advice.'

The contact — Detective Inspector Greybrook — had in fact rung Arnold later that evening. He had asked whether Jane had turned up anything fresh in Bristol.

'Nothing that gives us anything new,' Arnold suggested, 'other than to confirm that Orton, and his cousin Barry Elland, were both bad lots who sexually abused Sue Elland.

They certainly contributed to her suicide. But I don't see that it makes much difference to your investigation.'

'Hmmm. I'm not certain. I need to think about it. When is Jane Wilson returning?'

'She's picking up a train in Bristol tomorrow morning. I understand she'll be getting in at Durham around four in the afternoon.'

'Did you intend meeting her?'

'Not really. She lives in Framwellgate—'

'I think I'll try to get there to see her, at the station. About four, you say? You sure you can't make it?'

'I could try. But I'm due at County Hall in Morpeth.'

'Try to get there. I have a feeling . . . the way things have been bubbling at Aykley Heads today . . . Redvers has had Peter Aspen in, and I think we're going to find writs flying around like crazy over the next few days. But, well, I can't discuss it over the phone, but I believe I've found the key to the whole thing. And it may be that the information Jane Wilson has will help. So make it for that train tomorrow I'll meet you both there at the station, and I think we'll find I'll have the satisfaction of cracking this case before I leave the force yet!'

* * *

The door opened. The secretary had returned. 'They're ready for you now, Mr Landon.'

She made it sound like a walk to the gallows.

The interview was scheduled for the boardroom in the Planning Department. At least they hadn't decided to use the council chamber, Arnold thought grimly. The Senior Planning Officer was in the chair, in front of the gleaming table. On his left sat Tom Ellsbury, sitting in, Arnold guessed, as a member observer. On the Senior Planning Officer's right sat the Chief Executive, Powell Frinton.

Arnold did not really know Frinton. He had the reputation of being a remote, distant figure, cool with his staff, sober in all his dealings, a Methodist by upbringing and inclination. Seeing him seated beside the Senior Planning Officer, Arnold was reminded of an old drawing he had seen of a Victorian *Punch* character: tall, lean, angular, with a sneering superiority that was emphasized by a languid disregard for the opinions of his fellows. He was dressed in a dark suit; his cold eyes were fixed indifferently on Arnold; he seemed to feel the whole proceedings were beneath his notice. Arnold guessed he would find no friend at court here.

'Sit down, Mr Landon,' the Senior Planning Officer said. 'We're sorry you've been kept waiting, but I hope the proceedings themselves won't take too long. We've had a consultation with Mr Powell Frinton, and we believe there is a case to answer. On the other hand, we would certainly wish to give you the opportunity to present a defence to the charges laid. I—'

He stopped as Powell Frinton leaned forward and whispered something to him. He turned his Barrymore profile to listen intently, and a slow flush stained his face. He caressed his paunch nervously, and looked at Arnold.

'I . . . ah . . . I am advised you should have been asked whether you wished to have a friend present. You . . . ah . . . you were asked, I trust?'

'I was not.' Arnold hesitated, wanting him to wriggle a little. 'In fact, I've no desire to have a "friend" sitting alongside me.'

'The point is noted,' Powell Frinton said in his lawyer's voice.

The Senior Planning Officer stroked the shaved nape of his neck in a nervous gesture. 'We can get on, then. I have here a list of the . . . ah . . . discrepancies in your expenses claims. Perhaps you'd like to go over them with us?'

Powell Frinton opened his mouth again, then closed it like a trap. Arnold could guess what he was about to say: the details should have been given to Arnold in advance of this hearing, to give him time to study them. It was unimportant: Arnold scanned the details quickly and knew that the Senior Planning Officer was on very shaky ground — whatever advice he might have received from the Chief Executive.

'Do you have any comment to make?' the Senior Planning Officer asked.

Arnold took a deep breath. 'First of all, there are three of these items I have already responded to. As for items thirteen and fifteen in the list, they were occasions when I was actually accompanied by another member of the staff. I believe that makes a difference?'

Tom Ellsbury looked up sharply and glowered at the Senior Planning Officer. 'Has this been checked?'

'Who was the other staff member?' the Senior Planning Officer snapped, flustered. 'It doesn't appear on the claim.'

'It doesn't have to, according to the rules,' Arnold replied. 'But the officer was Sam Terry; his diary will show he was with me, and the rules say that where an officer transports another a higher rate may be charged on car mileage.'

Powell Frinton folded his arms as though erecting a barrier against the incompetence of his fellow senior officers, and the Senior Planning Officer coughed nervously. 'We'll look into that. Is there anything else?'

'Items seven and nine were tasks specifically undertaken at your request — and special rates apply where I move out of the county. Your own diary — or your secretary — should confirm the instructions. They were given by memorandum, as usual.' The Senior Planning Officer hated meeting his staff face to face. He tended to issue instructions in writing.

'Ha. Well . . .'

'And the other items in the list are, I think you'll find, sir, all covered by regulations. The only irregularity, in fact, that I am able to admit to—'

'Yes?' said the Senior Planning Officer, his eyes glittering.

'The only irregularity is not submitting claims for all expenses, and submitting on time. Neither, I believe—' and Arnold looked at Powell Frinton — 'is an offence which would justify a disciplinary hearing.'

Powell Frinton flickered his tongue against dry, thin lips. His voice was gritty, his tone curt. 'The only such "offence" is detailed as Item three. It is the only reason for my presence.'

Arnold felt the anger growing in his chest. 'Yes. I understand. The Spittal visit . . . where it is claimed I was actually at Chesters Fort on my own private business. I have yet to see the deposition made.'

Powell Frinton bared his teeth in an unpleasant grimace. He swivelled his long head slowly, staring at the Senior Planning Officer. Arnold guessed hard words would be spoken in private after this meeting. The Senior Planning Officer faltered. 'I'm not sure—'

'Mr Landon has made no formal request,' Powell Frinton enunciated slowly. 'But natural justice would demand he sees the deposition.'

'Give it to him,' Tom Ellsbury snapped irritably.

The Senior Planning Officer was reluctant to comply, but after a few seconds' hesitation he extracted the single sheet of paper and handed it to Arnold. It was a simple enough statement. It made out that Arnold had been seen on the site of Chesters Fort in Northumberland at four in the afternoon of a working day. The date was specified. It was the day on which he had worked at Spittal.

There were two signatures. One, as Arnold had suspected, was Sandy Bryman. 'The second signature,' Arnold said, 'is someone called Perry. Who is he?'

Powell Frinton glanced at the Senior Planning Officer. He clearly did not know. Tom Ellsbury did. 'Jack Perry is a quantity surveyor. He works for a company called Stradey Investments Ltd.'

'Isn't that a subsidiary of Mr Bryman's organization?'

Ellsbury nodded, without speaking.

'So there is a connection — a business connection — between the two signatories. Yes?'

'Yes.'

Powell Frinton leaned forward. 'That is of no consequence. They say they saw you when you should have been elsewhere, at Spittal on authority business. You claimed expenses for your travel, and the claim wasn't true. That's the essence here.'

'You speak of essence,' Arnold replied calmly, controlling the anger that was hot in his chest. 'Let me speak of another essence. The Senior Planning Officer will no doubt recall an interview with Mr Bryman recently. It concerned the Orion application.'

'Orion?' Powell Frinton questioned.

'A planning application for a restaurant and filling station. Mr Bryman questioned me about it . . . wanted to know what I'd be recommending.'

'Why?' growled Powell Frinton.

'Because he has an interest in the same site.'

'We don't know that!' the Senior Planning Officer expostulated.

'Why else would he ask for the information?' demanded Arnold in exasperation. 'And why did he then press me to disclose what the Government Working Party would be deciding with regard to distance yardsticks on major road developments?'

'A working party?' Powell Frinton asked silkily.

'One to which I am seconded, and with salary paid by the government, for the time I spend on it.'

'Dear me,' Powell Frinton breathed, and looked at his hands. Arnold had the feeling the Chief Executive was beginning to wish he had not come to the hearing.

'I don't know what that has to do with anything,' the Senior Planning Officer blustered. 'You still haven't answered the charge to my satisfaction—'

'Just why are you bringing up this matter, Mr Landon?' Powell Frinton asked coldly.

'To show bias,' Arnold replied. 'Councillor Bryman was not pleased when I refused to give him the answers he wanted. I believe he has a great deal of money tied up in—'

'I'm not sure whether that sort of bias is enough for you to conclude his deposition is made maliciously.'

'Standing alone, perhaps not. But there is also the matter of the threats issued . . . shortly before these charges were made.'

The Senior Planning Officer gaped at Arnold. 'Threats? You must be joking! I heard no threats!'

'You weren't there,' Arnold replied. He paused. 'The words, as I recall them, were to the effect that I was unco-operative, and that if I didn't stay out of his way he would "have my job". More specifically, Councillor Bryman stated he would break me — as he had broken others in the past. Very shortly afterwards, these charges were laid.'

There was a long silence. Tom Ellsbury's breathing was harsh; the Senior Planning Officer's face was now brick red. Powell Frinton leaned forward, like a predatory shark. 'You can prove this, Landon? You have a witness to this statement?'

'There was a third party present,' Arnold replied shortly.

Whether Peter Aspen would ever be man enough to stand up in Arnold's defence was another matter. Powell Frinton was still staring at him, eyes narrowed. 'What was the occasion for this outburst, Mr Landon?'

Arnold kept them waiting for several seconds. His anger was dissipating; he felt cool, and almost dispassionate about the whole proceedings now. It was all so contemptible. 'The statements were made in Newcastle, in front of a witness. Mr Bryman, mistakenly, thought I was interfering in his personal affairs. I was not. I was concerned with investigating Savoyard influences in Welsh castle building.'

Powell Frinton's mouth sagged in surprise. 'Savoyards . . . What's that got to do with Councillor Bryman?'

'I've told you. Nothing. But he thought I was investigating something else.'

'What?'

Arnold paused. He was on uncertain ground, but it was ground worth testing. 'Councillor Bryman,' he said slowly, 'thought I was looking into the possibility of corrupt influence being brought to bear on the awarding of construction contracts through membership of the Rosicrucian secret society.'

The room was still. The three men facing him presented a frozen tableau. Tom Ellsbury's eyes were open wide with undisguised shock; the blood was slowly draining from the Senior Planning Officer's face. Powell Frinton sat stiffly, as though carved in granite. Arnold let the silence hang heavy until, finally, he asked, 'Is Councillor Bryman a Rosicrucian?'

Ellsbury almost shuddered. He leaned back, saying nothing. The Senior Planning Officer stared at Arnold like a fascinated rabbit caught in the headlights of a car. It was Powell Frinton who was the first to regain control. 'Councillor Bryman's private activities are not the concern of this meeting.' There was a lack of conviction in his tone that he attempted to overcome. He took a deep breath. 'And even an accusation of personal bias against you, Mr Landon . . . it still doesn't overcome the argument arising out of the deposition.'

Sharply, Arnold said, 'The statement by Bryman and Perry is a fiction. And it's easily shown to be so.'

'How?'

'I did not go to Spittal in my own car: it was in the local garage having a new gasket fitted. I hired a car for that occasion, since there were no pool cars available. The hire company will have a record of the mileage undertaken. Check with them. Their records will show I did not drive to Chesters Fort on that date. They will show I drove to Spittal, not least because I used a petrol facility they own near Berwick.'

The Senior Planning Officer found his voice. 'Why didn't you tell us this before?'

Arnold looked at him coldly. 'Because you hadn't given me sight of the deposition. Because my desk diary has been taken from my office. And because there's clearly an intention here to get rid of me from the Planning Department — without good cause. You've never tried to look for the truth here: you haven't checked departmental records, or double-checked with staff with whom I work. When Councillor Bryman, out of malice, placed a complaint you just saw a chance to get rid of me. I'm afraid you'll have to make out a better case than this. Sir.'

The Senior Planning Officer's lips were white: he was almost beside himself with panicked rage. He opened his mouth to reprimand Arnold but was forestalled by Powell Frinton. 'A stolen desk diary? I've heard nothing about this. And the Government Working Party and this Rosicrucian thing. I consider, gentlemen, this hearing had better come to an end. There are matters to be investigated.'

In the heavy silence that followed the lawyer glanced at Arnold cautiously and cleared his throat. 'I imagine, Mr Landon, you have been put to some . . . inconvenience. I think, in the circumstances, you should be reinstated, and the suspension lifted while further inquiries are being made. The Senior Planning Officer, I am sure, will agree that you should now return to work.'

'As far as I'm concerned at this moment,' Arnold said, 'you can simply stuff your job!'

* * *

Arnold felt hungry.

Once he had walked out of County Hall he felt at a loss. His outburst had been heartfelt, and he knew he had left them with a problem. The way he now felt, bruised, hurt by the unfounded accusations, he had no desire to return to work in the Planning Department, continuing to cover up for the incompetence of his senior officer.

He felt shaky, nevertheless, and peculiarly hungry.

He walked along the street to the White Hart. It was not a hotel he visited often, and they did not know him there. He ordered a half bottle of wine and two pork pies. He drank a glass of wine before he ate. After he had finished the pies he continued to drink morosely, staring at the oak beams in the ceiling and ignoring the midday visitors.

When he finished the wine he felt depressed. Any bitterness and belligerence had been dissipated; he wanted to go home, to hide his face, creep into a corner where no one could see him. He was distressed, disorientated and feeling very sorry for himself.

He went back to his car and drove home.

He had difficulty opening the door. A postal packet had been pushed through the letter box and had fallen just inside the door catching under the lintel as he pushed. Arnold kicked the packet to one side and walked into the sitting room. He turned on the television set: the programme was concerned with racing from Newmarket. He had no interest in horse racing. He put his head back on the settee and drifted into a semi-conscious state.

He dreamed. The dreams were confused. He saw an image of Master James of St Georges and it was superimposed on the head of his father. He caught a glimpse of the Yorkshire Dales where his father had taught him of the wonders of wood and stone, and he saw again the tumbling waters of High Force crashing against the black rock. The rock was transformed into the dominating crag of Harlech, and he could hear a young girl crying, weeping for assistance but there was no one to help. There was blood on the floor and on the walls, and Arnold woke with a start.

The racing had finished. He turned off the television set.

He glanced at his watch. It was two thirty. There was something he had to do. He rose and wandered back into the hallway. He picked up the parcel: it had a Manchester postmark. He opened it, puzzled.

It contained some photocopies of newspaper cuttings.

There was a scribbled note attached: '*We managed it quicker than expected. Invoice enclosed.*'

The headlines leapt out at him: *PICCADILLY MURDER*.

Arnold read the first photocopied sheet slowly.

In the early hours of yesterday morning a young couple stumbled on the body of a half-clothed man in a street at the back of Piccadilly station in Manchester. It appeared he had been beaten about the head, and stabbed. There is no identification of the body at this stage. No police statement has been issued, but it is understood this is being treated as a possible gangland killing.

Arnold turned to the other cuttings. He read them more quickly. The investigation was spread over six weeks. The murdered man had a petty criminal record and was suspected of having been involved in drug distribution in the city. He was named as Barry Elland.

He remembered now what he was supposed to do. He glanced at his watch again. He hurried to the phone. He rang Aykley Heads and asked to speak to Detective Inspector Greybrook.

He was put through quickly.

'This is Arnold Landon. I . . . my business in Morpeth is finished. I should be able to get to Durham to meet you and Jane, but I might be a little late.'

'Good.' Greybrook's tone was guarded, as though he was wary of being overheard. 'We'll wait, if you're not there on time. But I'll not be parked at the station itself. I'll be about two hundred yards up the hill. You'll understand why.' The station was not far from Aykley Heads. Arnold nodded to himself. 'I've got some papers from Manchester here. About the killing of Barry Elland.'

There was a short silence. 'Barry Elland?'

'You know. I told you — I was looking into his death, while Jane was checking on Sue Elland.'

'Yes, of course. What have you got?'

'Newspaper cuttings. I haven't read them yet. Not properly.'

'Bring them with you.' Greybrook's tone was sharp and edgy. 'Things are really starting to blow here. I can't speak over the phone for obvious reasons, but I think I can see how everything fits now. Aspen is being held . . . helping with inquiries, Redvers says.'

'Did he kill Orton?'

'I don't know.' Greybrook sounded impatient, unwilling to continue talking over the phone. 'But I've been doing some checking, and I'm able to confirm that Councillor Bryman is a member of the Rosicrucians all right. And that there've been some odd goings-on in the building contracts world. Some of your own officers in Northumberland might be involved, at the periphery.' He cleared his throat nervously. 'Things are beginning to settle into place: the murk is clearing. I think we can find out pretty quickly now just what happened at Bodicote Barn House and who killed Orton. I'm pretty sure I know where the key lies.' He paused. 'You'll be driving?'

'Of course.'

'You pick up Jane Wilson. I don't even know what she looks like. Then drive up the hill and collect me once she's off the train. Then we're driving up on to the fell.'

'Where will we be going?'

'We'll be going to talk to the man who can put it all together for us. The one who holds the key to the whole thing. The only one we know of who was at Bodicote Barn House both before and after Orton was murdered.'

'Who's that?'

'The vagrant, Foxy Fernlea,' Greybrook said shortly. 'Get down here as quickly as you can.'

CHAPTER SIX

1

Arnold left Morpeth in a hurry, taking the Al south, aware he was short of time if he was to reach Durham before Jane Wilson's train got in. The road was fast; traffic in Newcastle had not built up for the rush hour period and he was quickly over the Tyne Bridge, past Gateshead and on to Chester-le-Street where he picked up the motorway. Thereafter it was a smooth run to the Durham slip road and he came over the rise past the College of St Bede and St Hild to see cathedral and castle shadowed in the afternoon sun.

At the junction he hesitated, checking his watch: he could see the railway bridge ahead of him, it was gone four, and he could not tell whether the train had arrived or not. He took the winding road up to the station, parked and got out.

The train was late. It was due to arrive in five minutes' time. He had made it.

He stood hesitantly on the platform for a few minutes, wondering whether Greybrook would be aware the train was late. The detective inspector was clearly anxious not to be seen in Arnold's company: Arnold could appreciate his wariness, since he was clearly behaving in a way that would cause him problems if Redvers were to find out he was carrying on the investigation behind his back. Even so,

Greybrook was over-reacting to a certain extent, Arnold considered — after all, the man was finishing his service with the Durham Constabulary in a matter of days. He had very little to lose.

Unless he feared something more serious than a reprimand if his activities were discovered at Aykley Heads. One man had already died. And Greybrook was convinced that Redvers was involved in some kind of cover-up.

The thought of Orton's death gave Arnold pause for a moment.

He checked his watch: three minutes before the train was due. In his rush he had not looked other than cursorily at the material sent to him from Manchester. He could wait in the car until Jane's train arrived. He left the platform, unlocked the car, sat inside. He picked up the cuttings again and read more about the death of Barry Elland.

GANGLAND SLAYING

Manchester police are now convinced that the murder of the man at Piccadilly was the result of a gangland dispute. The murdered man, identified as Barry Elland, was a petty criminal who was known to frequent clubs where 'smack' was freely available. The police are working on the theory that his attempt to set up a private deal outside the system resulted in a beating which went too far. It is unlikely that he was actually murdered at Piccadilly. The body was probably dumped there, police believe, after he was killed elsewhere . . .

The rest of the page was devoted to a commentary on drug abuse in Manchester among teenage groups. Arnold turned to the next sheet.

SUSPECT ARRESTED IN PICCADILLY KILLING

A man was taken to Oxford Road today in connection with the Piccadilly killing last week. It is understood he has connections with the drug-smuggling syndicate which is known to run its operations out of Teesside and Manchester airports. Police spokesmen declined to comment, or to reveal the identity of the arrested man.

There was a photograph attached to the brief account, showing three men emerging from a police station, pushing their way through a small crowd. The caption was uninformative, merely stating that 'Chief Inspector Daventry waved aside questions regarding the suspect held in custody.' The next sheet was the last, and it gave no help to Arnold at all.

POLICE BAFFLED BY PICCADILLY KILLING

Manchester police today called for assistance from the public in their attempt to apprehend the Piccadilly killer. The suspect arrested last week was released on bail after an appearance at the magistrates court on Monday, but he had been charged only with petty theft. It is now admitted that he had no connection with the murder of Barry Elland. Investigations among the drug syndicate have drawn a blank and the police are calling on anyone who might have information, or who might have been in the vicinity of Piccadilly on June 7th, to get in touch with them . . .

It was the last of the news clippings. The murder must have been pushed off the pages by other events. It would seem the killer of Barry Elland had never been found. Arnold frowned. It had been a pointless exercise. Both he and Jane had been wasting their time, travelling to Bristol and to Manchester . . .

He riffled back through the news cuttings. He paused over the photograph of Chief Inspector Daventry, angrily thrusting his way through a small group of people, and then he threw the papers on to the back seat of the car.

As he did so, he checked himself and turned to retrieve the papers. An image passed through his mind, a faded photograph, a man's face staring blankly at the camera.

Then he heard the train entering the station. He opened the door, got out and hurried to the platform.

A few minutes later he saw Jane Wilson walking towards him from the train. She caught sight of him and her surprise was obvious.

'Well, well, isn't this nice! How kind of you to meet me, Arnold! And how gallant!'

Arnold reddened and reached forward to take her case. 'The car's over here.'

He stowed her case in the back of the car and unlocked the door to allow her to slide into the passenger seat. There must have been something about the way he looked at her, for his tension was communicated to her. She stared at him as he got in.

'What's the matter? What's happened?'

He frowned. 'Did you learn any more about Sue Elland?'

'No. Nothing beyond what I told you.'

'I got the newspaper cuttings from Manchester. About Barry Elland's death.'

'Yes?'

'They weren't much use. He was beaten to death. The murder was never solved, it seems. It may have been a gang-land killing, possibly drugs related. But who knows?' Jane Wilson was puzzled. 'So why have you come to meet me?'

'The detective inspector — Greybrook — who was in charge of the Andrews-Orton murder has been taken off it. But he's carried on without official permission — and he wants to hear what you've learned. Apart from that, he thinks he's near to the solution. He thinks he knows who killed Orton. I can't explain now, but it involves a man called Bryman, and possibly the Chief Superintendent Redvers — who's been interfering with the investigation.'

'So where are we going now?' Jane asked as Arnold started the car and swung out of the car park and down the hill. 'We're going to meet Greybrook. And then we're going to find Foxy Fernlea.'

'What on earth for?'

‘Greybrook says he’s the key to the whole thing. He knows something, I imagine, or can confirm something, that has escaped us so far. But . . .’ Arnold hesitated, swung right into the road running up towards County Hall, and drove up the hill. ‘But before you meet Greybrook have a look at those cuttings on the back seat.’

Jane reached back and picked up the cuttings. She leafed quickly through them. Arnold reached the top of the hill and saw the blue Ford Fiesta parked on the grass verge. Greybrook was in the driving seat. ‘What am I looking for?’ Jane asked.

‘Look at the photograph.’

‘So?’

‘Leave it for now.’

Arnold pulled in to the side of the road. Greybrook got out of his car and walked forward. He was wearing a dark suit and, surprisingly, a light raincoat. No rain had been forecast. Arnold wound down the window. ‘The train was late.’

‘I guessed as much. Miss Wilson? My name’s Greybrook, Detective Inspector. Has Mr Landon filled you in?’

‘He’s told me you’d like to learn what I discovered in Bristol.’

‘That’s right.’ Greybrook looked about him nervously. ‘But that can wait for the moment. We need to move away from here.’

‘He says you want us all to go up to see Foxy Fernlea.’

‘That’s right. If you’ll just hang on a few minutes, I’ll move my car to a safer position, and then perhaps you can drive us, Mr Landon.’

‘Fine.’

Greybrook turned and walked back to his car. Arnold watched him drive off, to park in the pub car park some three hundred yards down the hill. While he was there a police car coming down from Aykley Heads drove past Arnold, slowing as the driver glanced at Arnold and Jane in the car. It moved on, down the hill and out of sight.

Arnold sat quietly while Greybrook walked back to them.

He glanced at Jane. 'His legs will be longer than yours. Do you mind getting in the back of the car?'

'No, of course not.'

She scrambled out and took the rear seat. She pushed the newspaper cuttings aside, and then picked them up again, glancing through them half-heartedly. Detective Inspector Greybrook reached the car and got in. 'Right,' he said heavily. 'We need to head for Neville's Cross now, and then up over the hill.'

Arnold knew the road vaguely and drove past County Hall, doubled back south and swung right out of Neville's Cross, scene of a famous defeat of the Scots by an English army, and headed up the hill. After half a mile Greybrook asked him to pull in.

'That's the Country Manor Hotel over there. It's easier to walk from here. And Bodicote Barn House — where Orton was killed — is just over the rise, just there.'

Arnold pulled the car into a narrow lane and parked on the grass verge. He looked in the mirror at Jane Wilson. She still had the cuttings in her hand, but she was staring at the back of Greybrook's head, a frown on her face. Arnold got out, and opened the rear door for her as Greybrook emerged from the passenger seat. The policeman looked tense and nervous as he stared up towards the hill.

'Fernlea has a hide up there,' he said. 'That's where we're going.'

Arnold glanced at Jane. She was staring at Greybrook, puzzlement still etched on her brow. It was confirmation for Arnold. She had seen what he had, in the newspaper photograph. 'Before we do go up there,' Arnold said slowly, 'I think we'd better have an explanation.'

'Explanation?' Greybrook turned, puzzled. 'About what?'

'This.' Arnold reached back into the rear of the car and brought out the Manchester cuttings. 'This photograph, here. That's Daventry, the investigating officer. But there are two policemen coming out of the station behind him.

That one there — it's you, isn't it? There's no name, but it's you, I'm certain.'

Greybrook took the newspaper from him and looked at the photograph. He was silent for a little while. A nervous tic had appeared in his cheek, but his hands were still. At last he raised his head and looked at Arnold. 'Not a very good likeness,' he said grimly. 'I've not worn well since that was taken.'

'You were in the Manchester police?'

'For several years.'

'And you investigated the murder of Barry Elland?'

'I was a detective constable then. Daventry was in charge.'

'You said nothing about it when I told you we were looking into the Ellands!'

Greybrook shrugged. 'What was there to tell? We never found out who killed Barry Elland, or why. And anyway, a few months after the file on Elland was closed I came north to the Durham force, and I've been here ever since.'

'It's an odd coincidence, you being involved in the investigation of the death of Barry Elland . . . and then investigating the murder of his cousin, nine years later!'

Greybrook half turned so he was facing Arnold and Jane squarely. A light breeze whipped around them, lifting Greybrook's raincoat and he pulled it around him more securely, as though he needed its protection. He looked tired and edgy and strained. 'I could say life was full of coincidences, Mr Landon. But I won't be so contemptuous of your intelligence. You and Miss Wilson here, you started digging into the background of Kenneth Andrew Orton because you thought there might be something in his past that gave a reason for his killing. Well, I think you were right. It's probably true of most violent crime. You can't just consider the present, there will be roots going back, deeply, into the past. That's where explanations, and reasons, and motivations lie.' He grimaced unpleasantly. 'Orton had a history — Elland too. We have to look to Orton's past . . . and that of Barry Elland. I learned a lot about Elland when we were investigating his killing. And I'm certain his death is linked to that of Orton by more than the mere fact they were cousins.' He looked back over his shoulder, nodded towards the hill. 'The answer lies up there. With the vagrant.'

'But I don't understand—' Jane began.

'You will,' Greybrook said grimly, 'once we talk to Foxy Fernlea.'

He turned away and began to climb the hill. Arnold looked at Jane. She shrugged, pulled a face, and began to walk after Greybrook.

Arnold followed on behind. They had received no explanation from Greybrook, but perhaps the answer did lie with Foxy Fernlea, on the hill. And he remembered Jane's phrase, at an early meeting, how death could hang in the air like a wisp of smoke.

The grass was springy under their feet. When he looked back, Arnold could see the towers of the cathedral, splendid on its crag above the river. The afternoon sun was hazy now, but it was warm on their backs as they climbed, and grasshoppers sawed away in the undergrowth. At the top of the hill Arnold saw the gully, thick with birch and sycamore and alder. It would be an ancient place, little touched by man over the centuries. No sheep would have grazed down there for the undergrowth and tangle of fern, bramble and bracken would deter them when richer grazing was available on the hill. There would be broadleaved trees deeper in the gully, trees that would have seen generations of children play on the slopes.

'I used to come up here as a kid,' Jane said, as though reading his thoughts. 'It was a place to escape to.' She laughed briefly. 'It was also a place to spy on lovers. Down below there, at the lower end where the water falls steeply down to the Wear we used to have hides. It's years since I've been there.'

Greybrook was descending the slope ahead of them. He paid no attention as they scrambled behind him, struggling to follow the steep, slippery path. He would have been up here before, Arnold guessed, when Fernlea had been arrested.

They crossed the badger tracks in the wild garlic and Arnold could hear the stream below them. Decayed tree stumps lay to their left, trees thrown to the ground by the winter winds that would surge up through the gully, but now there was no breeze, and the little valley was silent, wildlife holding its breath as it watched the invaders struggle down the path that only Foxy Fernlea normally trod.

They reached the bottom of the gully and the trees formed a canopy above their heads. Greybrook stopped, and turned to look at them. His eyes seemed deep-hollowed in the shaded light under the trees. 'Fernlea's hide is about fifty yards further up the gully. It's likely he'll be there, sleeping off whatever he had to drink at lunchtime. He tends to wander abroad mornings and evenings. I understand it's a habit of his.'

'He's harmless enough, you know,' Jane said stubbornly. 'I don't see how he can help us.'

Greybrook looked at her stonily and gestured for them to follow him. His back was stiff. He moved stealthily, almost catlike in the care with which he placed his feet, but the tension Arnold had noted in the man was still there. It was as though Greybrook was coming to the end of a long quest, and Arnold puzzled again at the nature of that quest — the relationship between the investigation in Manchester and that here in Durham.

Greybrook paused and held up a warning hand.

He pointed. 'The hide's just up there, ahead of us, against that bank.'

He beckoned, and led the way into the tiny clearing.

Foxy Fernlea lay in a foetal position, snoring gently. He had not removed the torn old overcoat he customarily wore, and a piece of old sacking covered his lower body while the fingers of his left hand still grasped the empty bottle that had seen him to sleep. A cloud of flies buzzed about his head, crawling in his beard, and Greybrook stood above him, lip curling in distaste. He glanced back to Arnold and Jane, standing just behind him.

'He's well away.'

Greybrook put out his foot and nudged the vagrant in the ribs. There was no response. Greybrook tried again, harder this time, and Foxy Fernlea grunted, champed noisily, exposing his blackened teeth, and then slipped into torpor again. Greybrook leaned over and, with some reluctance, twitched away the sacking and grabbed hold of Fernlea's filthy coat. He pulled at it, dragging the vagrant almost into a sitting position before releasing his grip, allowing Fernlea to fall back to the dank earth and rotting fern on which he lay. The empty bottle fell from Fernlea's grip and rolled into a dark corner of the hide.

'Wassmarrer?'

Fernlea was dragging himself out of his liquor-induced fog. He blinked and yawned, not certain what was happening. His rheumy eyes began to focus and as he realized he was not alone he cowered, drawing himself deeper into his hide, screwing his eyes against the light. 'Whassat?' he gasped.

'Come on out, Foxy,' Greybrook said quietly.

'I done nothing,' Fernlea whimpered.

'Come on out. It's the police. I want to talk to you,' Greybrook insisted.

'I seen the police. They let me go. I done nothing.'

'Just a few questions, Foxy. Come on, out you come.'

Greybrook reached in and grabbed Fernlea by the coat again. The vagrant squealed, wriggled for a moment, then gave up and allowed himself to be half dragged out of the hide. He was on his knees, glaring fearfully at the three intruders and Arnold felt Jane shiver beside him, as though she was sorry for the old man and wanted to intervene.

'Now then, Foxy,' Greybrook said softly. 'We must have a talk.'

'Talk about what?' Foxy asked, but there was a cunning look in his eyes, as though he thought he had something to trade in return for peace and quiet.

'You remember me? You've seen me before?' Greybrook asked.

'Police.' Fernlea screwed up his eyes again. 'Was you down at the station with the others? I dunno.'

'How good is your memory, Foxy? You too fuddled to remember anything?'

'I can remember,' the old man said stubbornly. 'I can remember the station. I had tea there, but they wouldn't give me nothin' to drink. I found some last night though, and—'

'Like you found some up at Bodicote Barn House is that right?'

The vagrant stared at Greybrook for several seconds and then he lowered his head anxiously. 'I talked about that. Don't want to talk any more.'

'Did you talk to the Chief Superintendent? Just what did you tell him, old man?'

'I dunno who I talked to. I don't remember.'

'But you remember Bodicote Barn House,' Greybrook insisted. 'And the blood. You were there, weren't you? Remember that?'

Sullenly Fernlea muttered, 'I remember.'

'And you went up there twice, is that right? Talk to me about that first time. That was good, wasn't it? The first time, you pinched a bottle of brandy. There was a case of wines and spirits at the back of the house. You took one of the bottles, didn't you?'

Dim memories of half-forgotten rights stirred in Foxy Fernlea's memory. 'I don't have to answer questions,' he muttered.

'If *I* ask them, you do,' Greybrook said sternly. 'Or else it's back down to a cell at Aykley Heads. You hear me? Now tell me, you stole a bottle there, didn't you?'

'Not exactly stole,' the old man said cunningly. 'I mean, it was there, like . . .'

'What did you do then?'

'Came home.'

Greybrook was silent for a while. Fernlea was half crouched at his feet, head down, but as the silence grew the vagrant seemed to regain some confidence. He looked up at Greybrook and slowly rose to his feet. He tried to smile shyly at Arnold and Jane, an ingratiating gesture, the pathetic attempt of a frightened man to convince himself that all was well.

'Let's think about it again,' Greybrook said quietly. Arnold could not see his face: the man had his back to him, hands placed on his hips, with the raincoat thrust back behind him. 'Let's start with when you went to the house. You found the case of spirits. You took a bottle. What did you do then?'

'I came home.'

'I don't think so.'

Fernlea scratched his wispy beard. 'Well, no, I guess I didn't. I was . . . there was cars . . .'

'Some cars came? What did you do?'

'I hid.'

'You had the bottle,' Greybrook said patiently, 'the house was empty, you'd stolen the bottle, you heard cars and you hid. Where?'

'It was in the orchard.'

Greybrook leaned forward slightly. 'How long were you there, Foxy, hiding?'

'Dunno.'

'Did you hear a car leave?'

'I . . . I think so.'

'What else did you hear?'

'Ahh . . .' It was an effort for him. He shook his befuddled head, and glanced at Greybrook fearfully. 'Before the car left, you mean? I think there was voices . . . shouting.

'A quarrel?'

'Thass right. A quarrel.'

'Then the car left. What did you do then?'

Fernlea rocked from side to side, struggling to remember a drink-hazed past. 'Came home. That's it, I waited, after the car had gone . . . I waited . . . then I came home.'

Greybrook was silent, staring at the old man. Softly he said, 'Didn't you see anyone else, on the way home?'

'I dunno . . . can't remember . . .' Fernlea dredged away in the thick mist of memory. 'Yeah . . . maybe I did. I had . . . I had to hide again. There was someone walkin' up the drive. I could hear his feet crunchin' on the gravel.'

'You hid?'

'Thass right. In the shrubbery. And after he'd gone I waited a bit and then I came home. Went to sleep.'

'With your bottle.' Greybrook glanced back at Arnold and Jane, frowning slightly. Then he turned back to Fernlea. 'There you are,' he said gently. 'It's wrong to say you can't remember. You're doing very well.'

Foxy Fernlea grinned at the compliment. 'I remembered, didn't I?'

'You've done well. But have you remembered everything yet?' Greybrook asked. 'Have you told us everything you remember?'

Fernlea grinned more widely. 'Dunno what you mean.'

'You heard a car come; you heard shouting; you saw the car leave; you saw a man walk up the drive. Is that all you remember?'

'Thassit.' Fernlea still grinned. 'Good innit?'

'There's one thing you haven't told us.'

'Yeah?'

'What did the man look like? The man walking up the lane.'

'Hooo . . .' Fernlea shook his head.

'You must be able to describe him.' Greybrook's tone was persuasive. Come on, Foxy, you remember so much. 'What did this man look like? Could you recognize him again?'

Arnold felt Jane grip his sleeve. She was tense, aware of the importance of the question. Arnold felt cold. There was something odd, an electricity in the clearing. Greybrook shifted his stance. 'Come on, Foxy, you'd recognize him again, wouldn't you?'

'No.' The grin faded, willing to please, but incapable. No, don't remember. Didn't really see him.'

'I don't think you're telling us the truth,' Greybrook said.

'Honest.' Fernlea spread his hands in supplication. Didn't see the man. I hid. Don't remember.'

'I think you're telling us lies,' Greybrook said grimly. 'You've told us so much, and yet you say you can't remember this. I think there's more you could tell us, Foxy.'

'Maybe I could and maybe I couldn't,' the vagrant said, twitching his nose cunningly, a child playing games, suddenly aware of the importance he was gaining. Thass for me to know and you to guess, innit?'

'Tell us, Foxy, what did the man look like?'

'Aha,' Foxy replied and grinned. Greybrook moved, blocking Arnold's view.

There was a moment's silence.

Then the bullet took the vagrant in the throat, knocking him backwards, and Jane Wilson screamed. The sound shattered the silence, slicing through the gully and losing itself among the broadleaved trees.

2

The old man lay on his back, fingers curling, a gurgling sound emanating from his torn throat as the blood pulsed out in a black rhythm, slapping on the leaves and fern underneath him.

Arnold was rigid with shock. Jane was leaning against him, shivering, hands over her mouth as Greybrook turned to face them. He was calm, his mouth quivering slightly, but his eyes were still and watchful.

The gun which had torn out Foxy Fernlea's life was pointing at Arnold's chest. Arnold now understood the reason for the light raincoat: the gun would have been obvious in Greybrook's dark suit.

'Why?' Jane gasped. 'For God's sake, why?'

Greybrook stared at her almost blankly. He shrugged. 'I couldn't trust him. Maybe he *was* telling the truth. Maybe he would never remember who came up the lane. But I couldn't rely on it. His drink-fuddled brain could clear. I couldn't leave it to chance.'

'You were the man he saw in the lane,' Arnold said.

Greybrook nodded. He fixed his eyes on Arnold, watching and waiting, as though expecting Arnold to say more. Arnold stared at him, puzzled, and then began to understand the obsession this man must have laboured under. He had killed Kenneth Andrew Orton . . . when he was working for the Durham Constabulary. And he had been in the investigating team looking into the killing of Barry Elland. Arnold's eyes widened.

'At Manchester . . . it wasn't a gangland killing.'

'It wasn't.'

'*You* murdered Barry Elland.'

Greybrook's thin smile was mirthless. He nodded. 'It was why I moved north, to join the Manchester police. It gave me the chance to get close to him, to find out about him. And to kill him. It took me eight years . . . but when it was done, I was clear. Free to come to Durham.'

'Looking for Ken Orton,' Arnold said grimly.

'That's right,' Greybrook said, and the muzzle of the gun lifted slightly, unwavering.

'But why?' Jane gasped, still shaking as she held on to Arnold's sleeve.

'Because Orton and Elland deserved to die. Because they were obscene animals. And because they were getting away with it. They had corrupted and killed . . . yet the law couldn't touch them, the police could do nothing. But *I* could.'

'But why did you take on the responsibility?' Jane asked, fascinated by the clinical coldness of the man.

'Haven't you guessed yet?' Greybrook replied with a twisted, unpleasant smile. 'You went to Exeter . . . you went to Bristol. Can't you guess where I fit in, who I am?'

Arnold felt Jane's shaking increase. He put his hand on hers, squeezed it, belying the thunder in his own chest. He stared at Greybrook, beginning to understand. 'It was Sue Elland,' he said slowly. 'You knew Sue Elland.'

'Knew her? We were engaged to be married,' Greybrook replied, with a slow surge of anger. 'Haven't you pieced together the picture yet? I thought you would . . . and if you hadn't now, you would eventually. I met Sue in Bristol, when I was a young copper. I loved her. We became engaged. But then I realized there were problems. She couldn't face up to the physical side of our relationship. I thought I could handle that, thought she would overcome the aversion in time. But then she told me why. And I couldn't get it out of my mind. But for her, too, telling me didn't help. It crawled back into her mind, all the self-loathing and the guilt. We went back to Exeter to try to exorcize it, but nothing helped. I watched her get worse. I was helpless. And in the end, she killed herself.' He was shaking slightly; slowly, bitterly, he brought himself under control. 'I couldn't help her. I told her nurse — that Greer woman — that the police couldn't help her. I knew it. But *I* could revenge her. And I swore I would revenge her, even if it took the rest of my life!'

'You've wasted all this time . . .' Jane whispered.

'Wasted? No, it's not been a waste.' Greybrook bared his teeth in an unpleasant, twisted grimace. 'It's given me a reason to live. When Sue died my world fell apart. But then I knew what I had to do. Remove that scum from the face of the earth. First, the brother who had betrayed her. He was a piece of dirt. It was easy. I beat him before I killed him. It was cathartic. It made up for the long, waiting years. It gave me strength to wait again.'

'You joined the Durham police deliberately, to get close to Ken Orton, to do to him what you'd done to Elland?'

'Exactly. Manchester gave me cover; Durham gave me the same cover. Didn't you know that murderers tend to repeat themselves?' he asked sarcastically. 'Don't get me wrong — I know I'm a murderer. But my motives were right. And I would do it again. She's been revenged now — and two obscenities have been removed. They can corrupt no one else. They're dead.'

Arnold shook his head slowly, fascinated. The man's logic was deeply held, his obsession clear, his commitment fatal. 'The Manchester killing was ascribed to drug gangs. But up here, you tried to pin the blame on someone else.'

Greybrook was silent for a little while as he stared at Arnold. Then he snorted. 'Redvers brought it on himself.

The Orton killing could have remained a mystery. I took the shotgun two years ago. The loss was never noticed, the gun was untraceable. But you heard Fernlea say there was shouting at the house. My guess is it was your Councillor Bryman, threatening Orton that if he published his Rosicrucian book there'd be trouble. I think he must have written to Orton in the same vein. I didn't know about that. I went up there and killed Orton because the time was right.'

'Because you would soon be leaving the force.'

'That's right. I'd planned, waited, made sure the time was right.' He paused. 'I'd hoped Orton's death would be seen as suicide. But I was puzzled when Redvers was so keen to get it shown as suicide and when that failed, so quick to pull in Fernlea. It did me no harm, and I teased it along. But I didn't know at the beginning — Redvers is a Rosicrucian. When he was told of Orton's death I think he phoned Bryman and as a result of the call he barged in to rescue that letter and to grab the incriminating material from Orton's notes. I didn't know that then, but I pieced it together. They wanted to silence Orton rather than be exposed. They were as corrupt as Orton, in a different way. Why shouldn't they take the responsibility for his death? I would be away from Durham shortly—'

'And with suspicion falling on them, no one would look for the Exeter and Bristol link.'

'Except you two. And you'd already started down that road.'

The muzzle was unwavering.

'You've justified to yourself the killing of two men,' Jane muttered, raising her courage. 'And you justify raising suspicion against Redvers and this Bryman person. But what about Foxy Fernlea? He did no one any harm.'

Greybrook licked his dry lips. He glanced inadvertently towards the body of the man at his feet. 'He was expendable. Flotsam. Of no use to anyone. But he was dangerous to me. I . . . I couldn't rely on the fact that he didn't recognize me walking up the lane that day.'

'And *us?'* Arnold asked.

There was a long silence. Arnold was aware the man was seized with doubt. For twenty years he had been pursuing an obsession. It had ended with what he saw as the justifiable killing of two people, men who had deserved to die. Now he was faced with the death of three more individuals one at his feet, two facing him. He was an intelligent man: he would be aware of the corruption that had silently crept into his own soul. He had killed for Sue Elland. That had been based on a reasoning that demanded the removal of the men who had corrupted and indirectly killed her. Now the situation would be different. What had been selfless in his own eyes, the destruction of his own peace of mind to fulfil a promise to a dead woman, all that was over.

Now he would be killing for himself.

Arnold watched him, saw the doubt grow in the man's eyes, and saw that doubt fade and die. He had gone too far now to turn back.

'You?' Greybrook said quietly, almost sadly. 'You're just unfortunate.'

The gun was pointed straight at Arnold's chest.

Foxy Fernlea sighed.

* * *

It was the last, bubbling sound from the ravaged throat, the final rush of life from the dying man, but it shivered through the clearing like a cold breeze. Inadvertently, Greybrook half turned, shocked by the sound, swinging the gun aside as though fearful of attack from the man at his feet. Arnold's reaction was almost instinctive. He threw himself across the three feet that separated him from Greybrook's grip as he staggered, grabbing at Arnold.

Jane screamed as both men stood, pulling at each other, neither obtaining an advantage, scrabbling wildly for purchase on each other's clothes. They staggered sideways, crashing into the bushes, feet stamping on broken bottles and tin cans, smashing into the undergrowth and colliding breathlessly with the trees. Arnold felt Greybrook's hands at his throat, tearing manically with biting fingernails, and he pulled backwards, trying to drag himself free. His feet slipped on the narrow path that the vagrant had beaten over the years to the water and he felt the soft earth giving way. He lurched, off balance, and then fell backwards, colliding with the craggy rock, Greybrook on top of him, to splash violently into the wide, dark pool that had served Foxy Fernlea for his ablutions over the years.

He heard Greybrook groan, and felt the grip on his throat weaken. He pulled free, thrusting Greybrook away from him with his feet and then he was scrambling to his knees on the rough stony bed of the pool. Greybrook was sliding past him, towards the white rush of the waterfall and a drop of fifteen feet. He seemed to be having difficulty keeping his balance, and his left arm was held at an awkward angle. Arnold realized he must have struck it against the dark rock, possibly breaking it.

Arnold took no time to think. He scrambled to his feet, his breathing ragged and panicked in his chest, his heart thundering with fear and excitement and the exertion of their struggle. He splashed out of the pool, scrabbling up the bank and Jane was there, pulling him out, gasping for him to hurry.

He looked back. Greybrook was on the top of the waterfall, braced against a rock. He was rising to his feet. His eyes were wild and glaring.

'Arnold, come on!'

Jane was pulling him to his feet. He stumbled, hearing Greybrook splashing back towards them, and then Jane was tugging him along, pulling at him as she thrust her way into the trees, following the line of the stream as it rushed down the gully on its way to the Wear and the distant sea.

'Jane,' he gasped. 'The gun . . . did you get the gun?'

She hardly heard him in her panic. She dragged him along, and bushes whipped at his face, briars and brambles tearing at his arms and hands. The breath was sharp in his chest, he was wheezing from the sudden exertion but she seemed to be endowed with an almost superhuman strength as she half dragged him along, fear pumping adrenalin through her veins.

The sky darkened above them as the broadleaved canopy grew thick above their heads. Arnold was forced to stoop as she pushed her way along, still holding his hand. He remembered she had said she used to play up here as a child: clearly, panicked though she was, she was running for some sort of cover.

A crashing in the undergrowth ahead of them brought her up short. Suddenly her commitment had deserted her and she stopped, pressing against Arnold. The crashing stopped for a few seconds, and was then renewed, a light, thrusting sound ahead of them, fading up the hill. 'Deer,' Arnold said, almost whispering. But their halt gave them the opportunity to pause and listen for pursuit.

For a moment all was silent. Then, fifty yards behind them they heard him: Greybrook was following them, his progress slower, more deliberate. But he had not given up. He was coming.

He had to come.

Arnold cursed under his breath. They should have searched for the gun. He turned Jane to face him. 'Can we get up the slope . . . make for the hill?'

'It's open up there. I . . . I should have grabbed the gun. I didn't think. But if he's got it again, and catches us in the fields on the hill, we wouldn't stand a chance.'

'Why did you run down into the valley? We *might* have made it up above.'

'It was automatic. I know the gully. The hides . . .'

He remembered; she had told him of playing up here, children's hides. He glanced at his watch. It was five o'clock. If they could stay hidden until dusk . . . 'Go on,' Arnold said. 'Show me.'

She resumed the track through the trees, more slowly now, but still aware of the methodical progress of the man behind them.

The burn became noisier as the gully cut more deeply into the rock, dropping in a series of small cascading waterfalls overhung by rowan and alder while above them oak and beech towered, hiding the sky. The rocky sides of the gully were scarred with landslips from heavy winter rains, and long horizontal strata of black and grey stone were exposed. Their feet slithered on loose scree while below them deep pools glistened blackly where the river bed flattened out. They scrambled downwards, and Jane led the way across the plate-like limestone basins to reach the other side of the burn.

The going became more difficult: the stream was dropping below them but the narrow, ancient track that Jane followed began to climb, straggling under the trees, crossing bare patches of earth and stretches of deep leaf mould, scuffing up under their feet as they hurried on.

Somewhere high to their right was the top of the hill they had climbed to come to Fernlea's refuge, but the open field would be dangerous. They were better where they were: Greybrook was behind them, following their trail but he was no countryman — he would not find it easy to track them.

The hurrying burn became noisier, and as they came to a level area, a small plateau of bare rock, Arnold was aware of a fine drifting spray thrown up by the water hurtling over a cascade ahead of them. To their left, the stream was reinforced by another beck, tumbling down in a fifty-foot drop to crash with the mingling waters below.

'Down here,' Jane said, gesturing towards the edge of the plateau. Arnold looked over. The rock was broken and striated, its crumbling face eroded by water and storm. It glistened wetly, black in the dim light, but it was climbable — and it would seem children had played here often enough. He took a grip on the crag and eased himself over. Jane followed him, and they made a slow descent into the narrow gorge. Fern gave them cover and soaked their heads and shoulders; the slippery rock made their progress dangerous, but at last Arnold realized why Jane had led them here. Twenty feet below the plateau the rock spread out in a long overhang; underneath was a cleft, wet, spray-dashed, but hidden from the crag itself.

'Push in further,' Jane Wilson gasped. 'It'll be dry there.'

It was. The cave was narrow and shallow, but protected from the spray. The grass was dank and sparse on the hard rock but they both sank down thankfully. Jane was shivering violently, not least as a reaction to the panic of their flight. Arnold's own heartbeat slowed now as he realized they were safe for the moment.

'If we wait,' he said quietly, 'we should be all right. He's unlikely to find us here. And as it gets dusk he won't want to take the chance that we might have escaped from the gully. He wouldn't want Aykley Heads to be out in force to meet him as he comes out himself.'

She seemed reassured. Arnold was not as confident as he sounded, however. Greybrook had made a commitment. If they managed to get out of the gully his future was inevitable: they would tell their story, and wherever he went, he would be a hunted man. He had to kill them. He had no choice.

Arnold understood the precautions at the railway station now. Greybrook had not wanted to be seen with them at the station. It was Arnold's car that had been used to drive up to the gully. Greybrook was due to leave the North within the week. It could have been months before the bodies of his three victims might be found: no doubt he had intended to hide them deep in the gully, and when they were found who would have been likely to connect him with their killing?

Nor, Arnold thought grimly, would there have been much of a hue and cry over their disappearance. There was only Ben Gibson to question Jane's whereabouts . . . and his own friends were few. There would have been few tears shed at the Planning Department, at least by the Senior Planning Officer, if Arnold Landon disappeared.

But he kept his thoughts to himself. Jane huddled close to him, still shivering. He sat still, listening, waiting, and scared.

The thunder of the falls was soothing, dulling the senses, and the light grew dimmer as the sun faded, slanting long shadows across the north side of the gully. A long half-hour passed, and Arnold's pulse had slowed, his senses lulled by the sound of the rushing water.

He was jerked back to reality by the shower of small, tumbling stones.

He grabbed Jane's hand and squeezed it. She pushed closer against him, as though for protection. The shower of stones increased for a few moments, and then stopped. Above the noise of the falls Arnold heard a scraping sound, shoes scuffing against the soft rock above their heads. His stomach contracted in the grip of fear: Greybrook had not given up the chase, he was directly above their heads, standing on the plateau, looking down into the falls.

Jane turned her face up to him, was about to say something, but Arnold put his finger on her lips.

Above their heads there were sounds of movement, an impatient scraping sound. Greybrook was up there, casting about to make the descent. If he came down five feet he would see the overhang; a little lower, the mouth of the cave. Arnold rose, crouching in the small space. There was still a chance. The man had an injured arm. Greybrook had the gun, probably stolen as the shotgun had been, but Arnold would have the advantage of surprise. He looked nervously towards the rocky falls. He would have to be careful. If they both went over that edge . . .

He stood crouched at the entrance to the cave, hidden by the overhang. His nerves were taut, his breathing ragged. He waited for the man to come down, to end it all.

The shower of stones had ceased. The scraping noises had stopped. Arnold listened, his heart pounding. There was no sound.

Arnold waited for what seemed an eternity. He looked at his watch. Ten minutes had passed. He waited. When fifteen more minutes had passed he turned back to Jane. 'I don't think he's coming down.'

'Do you think he's waiting up there?' she whispered back.

'I doubt it. He'll have thought there's no way down . . . and with his arm it would be chancy, anyway. He might have tracked us here, but he'll be worried, afraid we'll have found a way out. I think he'll be making his way back through the trees. But we'll wait, just to make sure.'

The evening wore on.

The light in the overhang faded quickly, and the spray outside the cave became a silvery mist in which strange, iridescent colours flickered palely. Dark shapes flashed past the overhang, bats flickering through the twilit gorge, and above the regular rushing of the water Arnold thought he heard an owl call, prowling early under the trees. He was stiff and sore, and his back ached from the collision with the rock when Greybrook had hurt his arm, and Jane was still shivering violently. It could have been coldness and the wetness of her clothes. It could have been shock.

He peered at his watch. They had waited long enough. 'Stay here,' Arnold said. 'I'll go outside and check.'

He moved out cautiously from the overhang. The light had faded now, though through the canopy he could see stray beams of sunlight. In another hour or so dusk would fall, and they would find some difficulty in making their way out of the gully. He stepped out away from the protecting overhang and peered up towards the climb above.

There was no one there. Greybrook had gone.

Arnold's stomach lifted with relief. He crept back into the small cave. 'Come on. It's clear.'

He took Jane's hand and pulled her to her feet. He led the way out of the cave. He stepped up to the shelf of rock above them, leaned back and gave her a hand. Slowly they climbed back up to the plateau. Jane slipped a couple of times, and Arnold himself felt immensely tired, drained of strength by the strain they had been under, and now losing adrenalin as the relief of their escape washed over them. They scrambled upwards until Arnold reached the plateau. He slid his buttocks on to the flat rock, braced a hand to stand upright, and pulled Jane up behind him. From here on it would be easier. They could make their way slowly through the dark trees.

He caught a movement in the dimness some twenty yards ahead of them, and he went cold, freezing in his tracks.

Greybrook had not gone away.

He was still there, a dim, menacing figure, waiting, braced with his back against the crag, in front of a dark old oak that seemed to spring from the rock, spreading its wide, heavy branches above his head. He stood there, unmoving. His left arm was dangling awkwardly.

In his right hand he held the gun.

They stood there on the crag, the sound of rushing water behind them, the last stray shafts of sunlight fading above their heads. Jane stood close to Arnold, half shielded by his body. Greybrook was motionless, the gun half lifted, as he leaned there, exhausted, staring at them. They could not make out his features in the dimness, but it was as though he was carved from the rock itself, silent, hard, unyielding.

A light breeze lifted, soughing through the branches above their heads, and at the sound Greybrook shifted slightly, looking upwards. He stayed like that for several seconds and then lowered his head again. He said nothing; he made no movement.

Arnold's mouth was dry. When he spoke, the words came out croakily. 'You'll never get away with this. You'll end up a hunted man . . . the way Orton and Elland were hunted.'

Greybrook stared at him, but Arnold felt that the man hardly saw him.

'They'll find us, in the end. There's the car to get rid of. Chances are someone will have seen you with us. The trail will lead to you. This . . . this was unplanned, unlike the Elland killing, and Orton. Don't you see, Greybrook? It's all so pointless . . .'

Greybrook made no reply. Arnold watched him, was about to speak again, and then remained silent. There was no tension in the man facing him. He had been up here, waiting, for more than an hour, among the silence of the trees, with the rushing, soothing sounds of the falls ahead of him. He would have had time to calm, to think, to weigh up what he was doing.

Arnold could guess what would be going through his mind. He would have been thinking of the people he was hunting, but he would have been thinking too of the past. Sue Elland had killed herself, and he had sought violent revenge. He had sought out two men, holding out to them the prospect of death, the murderous wisp of smoke hanging about them while he awaited opportunity.

When he had reached the end of his long obsessive hunt and the achievement was complete, what was left? Only a muddying of the waters. Only unnecessary, selfish violence.

Violence with no justifiable purpose. Except his own survival.

And perhaps, as he stood there in the cathedral quiet beyond the rushing of the waters, perhaps he no longer wanted to survive. Sue Elland was gone; his own obsession was over. Arnold wondered, and guessed, and in the end, knew.

He gripped Jane's hand tightly. 'Come on,' he said quietly. 'Let's move.'

They stepped delicately, as though fearful he would hear them. Greybrook watched them edge past him, but he made no move. His shoulders were slumped, his face drawn with pain from his left arm. But when Arnold drew close, he could see the man's eyes. They were empty of expression, the eyes of an automaton, a man who had lost any reason for living.

He made no move to stop them as they went past.

They climbed the crag, and Arnold looked back. He could see the dim, despairing figure of the man only vaguely, fading against the darkening trees. At the top of the crag they heard a sharp, cracking sound. Jane jerked around to stare at Arnold.

He shook his head wearily. 'It's all right. It's over, now.'

3

The office of the Chief Executive was surprisingly spartan. Arnold had thought the man's position would have dictated some opulence at least — a good quality carpet, a large leather-topped desk, some florid paintings on the wall. Instead, the room matched the man: remote, clinically functional in its furniture, lacking in warmth or welcome.

Powell Frinton was standing at the window, his hands locked behind his pinstriped back. He did not offer Arnold a seat.

Nor did he waste time on preliminaries.

'You have stirred up a hornets' nest in Durham, Mr Landon. A Chief Superintendent suspended. An investigation into a . . . ah . . . paedophile ring commenced, with a Mr Aspen under arrest. A murder and a suicide in the Durham hills. And a hell of a mess here in Morpeth.'

'No, sir. Someone else took the first step.'

Powell Frinton snorted. 'Perhaps so. But in Morpeth, I have to do the cleaning up!' The Chief Executive turned around to face Arnold. He glared at him, his eyes cold and accusing. 'As I understand it, you had no real grounds for some of the statements you made at the disciplinary hearing.'

'I had been given information—'

'By the man whose body they recovered up at the falls, I understand.' Powell Frinton sniffed. 'Well, it's not important. Greybrook — that was his name, wasn't it — Greybrook's information has some basis in fact. I'm afraid we've had to institute an inquiry here in Northumberland. It would seem there is some evidence that there have been some . . . ah . . . doubtful contractual dealings, involving members of this Rosicrucian secret society. And Councillor Bryman is a Rosicrucian.'

'Is Chief Superintendent Redvers really involved?'

Powell Frinton clucked his tongue. 'Ah, so you're aware of that connection with Bryman, too. Let's just say the matter is under investigation. It need no longer concern you. Bryman, Redvers, certain other members of the Planning Committee . . . I'm afraid, also, that the Senior Planning Officer has been rather . . . ah . . . indiscreet. He seems to have been a little too eager to go along with some suggestions from Bryman, and others. He's on . . . ah . . . extended leave at the moment. We're looking at the running of his department.' Powell Frinton raised his aristocratic nostrils, giving the appearance of an elderly horse sniffing at the breeze, remembering battle days of old. 'But that brings us to you.'

'The charges of false accounting are dropped?'

'They are dropped. But it seems to me that it would not be a good idea for you to return to the department. I am aware you . . . ah . . . told us what to do with the job.'

'That's right. And I haven't changed my mind.'

Carefully, Powell Frinton said, 'I wouldn't wish you to feel . . . penalized. I am forced to agree the charges were brought against you out of malice, a fact the Senior Planning Officer failed to consider. But—' he pursed his lips, considering — 'it could lead to a bad press. And one must be fair about such things.'

There would be enough on his plate already, Arnold thought, if he had to fight off the newspapers over the scandal of fixed building contracts in which councillors and perhaps senior officers were involved.

'So, rather than rush to judgement on this issue, Mr Landon, perhaps you should take time to reconsider. I thought, perhaps, you might be interested in a . . . er . . . change of environment.'

'Sir?'

'Something more in line with your interests and your talents,' Powell Frinton said silkily. 'And where your head would appear less, shall we say, above the parapet. A job, perhaps, in the Museums and Antiquities Department?'

* * *

'So what was your reaction to that?' Jane asked as she sipped her tea.

'Latrines.'

'What?' She looked around the cafe, grinning. 'You mean you turned him down?'

Arnold laughed. 'No, it wasn't that. It was just that when he mentioned Museums and Antiquities my mind went spinning elsewhere. It was like a veil lifting. I've had at the back of my mind for weeks something about your Harlech photographs, and when he offered me the job in Museums and Antiquities it sort of sent me along a track I've been unable to go for ages. I knew there was something I was missing in those photographs. And there and then it came to me.'

'Latrines?' she repeated, wrinkling her nose.

'Exactly that! One of the shots you took at Harlech was of the abutment of the curtain wall and the corner tower. If you look closely at that shot you'll see that just at the abutment there's a latrine chute. Now although one could argue there are certain similarities between the windows of Harlech, with their shallow curved heads, and the windows at the castle of St Georges d'Espéranche, that isn't conclusive evidence of the involvement of Master James of St Georges at Harlech castle. But the latrine chute now that's a different matter.'

'How do you mean?'

‘It’s an unusual construction. Built to quite interesting specifications. And I’m prepared to bet that in its form and measurement it is a precise copy of the latrine chutes at the castle of St Georges d’Espéranche. I’m now prepared to argue Ken Andrews had a point: the Savoyard Master James was certainly involved in the building of Harlech.’

‘And you work that out from a latrine chute.’

‘You once told me — look to the detail. You were right.’

Jane Wilson stared at Arnold thoughtfully, as he sat back, beaming, pleased that he had solved the puzzle that had lain at the back of his mind ever since he had been approached by Peter Aspen. She shook her head in mock despair, and smiled.

‘Have you never thought of getting married?’ she asked.

THE END

ALSO BY ROY LEWIS

ERIC WARD MYSTERIES

Book 1: THE SEDLEIGH HALL MURDER
Book 2: THE FARMING MURDER
Book 3: THE QUAYSIDE MURDER
Book 4: THE DIAMOND MURDER
Book 5: THE GEORDIE MURDER
Book 6: THE SHIPPING MURDER
Book 7: THE CITY OF LONDON MURDER
Book 8: THE APARTMENT MURDER
Book 9: THE SPANISH VILLA MURDER
Book 10: THE MARRIAGE MURDER
Book 11: THE WASTEFUL MURDER
Book 12: THE PHANTOM MURDER
Book 13: THE SLAUGHTERHOUSE MURDER
Book 14: THE TATTOO MURDER
Book 15: THE FOOTBALL MURDER
Book 16: THE TUTANKHAMUN MURDER
Book 17: THE ZODIAC MURDER

INSPECTOR JOHN CROW

Book 1: A LOVER TOO MANY
Book 2: ERROR OF JUDGMENT
Book 3: THE WOODS MURDER
Book 4: MURDER FOR MONEY
Book 5: MURDER IN THE MINE
Book 6: A COTSWOLDS MURDER
Book 7: A FOX HUNTING MURDER
Book 8: A DARTMOOR MURDER

ARNOLD LANDON MYSTERIES

Book 1: MURDER IN THE BARN
Book 2: MURDER IN THE MANOR
Book 3: MURDER IN THE FARMHOUSE
Book 4: MURDER IN THE STABLE YARD
Book 5: MURDER IN THE CHURCH
Book 6: MURDER IN THE HOUSE

Thank you for reading this book.

If you enjoyed it please leave feedback on Amazon or Goodreads, and if there is anything we missed or you have a question about, then please get in touch. We appreciate you choosing our book.

Founded in 2014 in Shoreditch, London, we at Joffe Books pride ourselves on our history of innovative publishing. We were thrilled to be shortlisted for Independent Publisher of the Year at the British Book Awards.

www.joffebooks.com

We're very grateful to eagle-eyed readers who take the time to contact us. Please send any errors you find to corrections@joffebooks.com. We'll get them fixed ASAP.

Printed in Great Britain
by Amazon

65289713R00137